ALSO BY VALERIE BOWMAN

The Unlikely Lady
The Accidental Countess
The Unexpected Duchess
Secrets of a Scandalous Marriage
Secrets of a Runaway Bride
Secrets of a Wedding Night

NOVELLAS
A Secret Affair
A Secret Proposal
It Happened Under the Mistletoe

ANTHOLOGY
Christmas Brides

The Irresistible Rogue

VALERIE BOWMAN

St. Martin's Paperbacks

This is a work of fiction. All of the characters, organizations, and events portrayed in this novel are either products of the author's imagination or are used fictitiously.

THE IRRESISTIBLE ROGUE

Copyright © 2015 by June Third Enterprises LLC.

All rights reserved.

For information address St. Martin's Press, 175 Fifth Avenue, New York, NY 10010.

ISBN: 978-1-250-07257-3

Printed in the United States of America

St. Martin's Paperbacks edition / November 2015

St. Martin's Paperbacks are published by St. Martin's Press, 175 Fifth Avenue, New York, NY 10010.

10 9 8 7 6 5 4 3 2 1

For my BFF, Danielle Aguirre,
who I met at church in 1980
where our parents had to tell us to stop trading
Hello Kitty stickers and pay attention.
We've been inseparable ever since.
Henry and Ethel 4 EVER!
I love you.

CHAPTER ONE
London, June 1816
The Earl of Swifdon's town house, Hanover Square

Daphne Swift eyed the mysterious present that rested atop her writing desk. It was wrapped in soft pink paper and tied with a wide white ribbon. Someone obviously knew her favorite color. But the gift did little to stop the dread that had been steadily rising in her throat all morning.

"I think it's an engagement gift," her young cousin Delilah said. "For your party tomorrow." Moments ago, Delilah had flounced into the room carrying the wrapped box in both hands, an impish smile on her face. "I simply cannot wait until I'm old enough to receive an engagement present." Drama dripped from Delilah's voice, and she clasped her hands together near her hip. She blinked rapidly. "*J'adore* presents."

"Delilah, you're barely twelve." Daphne nudged the gift with her fingertip. "And this is *not* an engagement gift. I am not engaged."

Delilah lifted both dark brows. "Not yet. But your mama says you're sure to receive an offer from Lord Fitzwell after the ball tomorrow night. He's been courting you for weeks." Delilah sighed again. "I cannot wait until I am old enough to receive marriage offers. I should like enough to have a choice. But not so many as to be vulgar."

Daphne shook her head. "Don't be so quick to want to grow up. Believe me, maturity includes far more trouble than you realize."

"What sort of trouble, Cousin Daphne?" Delilah's voice was filled with her ubiquitous curiosity.

"Like . . ." Daphne snapped shut her mouth. Trouble? A handsome face filled her mind. Laughing sky-blue eyes, a firm chin with an intriguing dimple, sun-streaked short blond hair, and the most devastatingly charming smile that ever graced the lips of a man. And oh, what a man he was, if infuriating. "Like . . . trouble."

"I don't care. *J'adore les cadeaux.* Who sent that one?" Delilah pointed at the box and twirled a long, dark curl around the tip of her finger. She hopped from the bed and skipped over to the desk where she plucked the calling card from the top of the box.

She held the card in front of her elfish face. Her dark eyes grew as big as if she'd seen the vicar sneaking gin. "Captain Rafferty Cavendish?"

Daphne's heart tripped in her chest. And the blue eyes reappeared in her mind. *Rafe?* That rogue. That liar. She swallowed hard and concentrated on keeping the anger from her face and the dread from suffocating her. She tugged on the finger that would have worn a ring, twisting her right fist round and round. She took a deep breath. She must open the present or give Delilah a sufficient reason why she wouldn't. She might as well get it over with. It was only a gift.

So why was her stomach pulling into knots?

Perhaps it was because of the note she'd received three days ago. The note she'd read and hidden in the back of her wardrobe. The note in which Rafe had insisted they meet immediately.

The note she had decidedly ignored.

"Does the card say anything else?" Daphne ventured, wincing.

Delilah flipped it over. "Upon the occasion of your imminent engagement. Many happy returns," she read. "Oh, I was right. It *is* an engagement present, Cousin Daphne."

Daphne snatched the card from Delilah's hand. She scoured the vellum but there was nothing else. Nothing save Rafe's bold, scrawling handwriting and the implied sarcasm that suffused those words. Sarcasm only Daphne could decipher.

"What did he send you?" Delilah nodded toward the gift.

"I've no idea. You open it," Daphne replied, swallowing hard.

Delilah didn't need to be asked twice. She promptly seized the package and ripped off the ribbon and the pretty pink paper to reveal a small white box.

The cousins exchanged a curious glance.

Delilah snatched off the lid and stared into the box. Her face crumpled into a scowl that looked as if she'd just drunk curdled milk.

"What? What is it?" Daphne's hands turned clammy. She clenched and unclenched her fists to keep the feeling in her fingers, which were quickly going numb with worry.

"It's a . . . little wooden ship," Delilah replied. "I cannot say *j'adore* it."

"Well, that would be a first," Daphne replied with a laugh. "But a ship?" She took the box from Delilah and stared down into it. There, nestled in white tissue paper, was a replica of a ship the size of Daphne's palm.

She carefully lifted it out of the box. There was something familiar . . .

Delilah waggled her brows. "Why would the dashing, *handsome* Captain Cavendish send you an engagement present, Cousin Daphne? Besides, I thought he was a captain in the army, not a captain of a ship."

"He is." Daphne turned the replica around in her hand. She caught her breath. The name was painted in bold black letters across the stern . . . just the way they were on the real vessel.

The *True Love*.

Daphne pressed her palm to the desktop, her knees buckling beneath her. She tried to drag air in and out of her lungs. She did *not* need this reminder, today of all days.

Delilah peered at her sideways. "What is it, Cousin Daphne?"

Daphne quickly dropped the small ship back into the tissue paper, ensuring that Delilah didn't see its name.

Knock. Knock. Knock.

Someone at the door had saved her. Thank heavens. Daphne quickly turned toward the sound. "Who is it?"

"It's Mama, dear."

"Just a moment, Mama." Daphne waved a hand at Delilah. She gave the girl a stern stare. "Not a word about this," she whispered fiercely. "You may borrow my diamond ear bobs for a fortnight."

Delilah gave her a conspiratorial wink and a firm nod. "I promise."

"Thank you," Daphne whispered, moving over to the window. Her cousin could always be counted upon to be bribed. "Now help me with this chair. I must hide this thing." She lifted the box.

"Why?" Delilah asked, springing into motion to assist Daphne with pushing the tufted chair near the window over to the wardrobe.

Daphne whispered while she pushed. "There's no time to explain now."

The chair scraped across the wooden floor.

"What's that noise, dear?" Mama called from the corridor.

"Nothing. I'm coming." Daphne mashed the lid back on the box, climbed up on the seat of the chair, and quickly shoved the gift onto the highest shelf of the wardrobe. She hopped down and smoothed her hands over her coiffure and skirts before hastily making her way to the door. She swung it open and stood facing her mother.

Her mother brushed past her into the room. "Delilah, there you are." Mama's gaze swept the room. "Why is the chair near the wardrobe?"

Daphne concentrated on keeping her face blank. "Because I was . . . looking for something."

Her mother's confused gaze met hers.

"A . . . fichu. The one Aunt Willie gave me last Christmas." She took a deep breath. At least that much was true. She had been searching her room for the little lace collar all morning. "Don't you remember it, Mama? It was a hideous thing. I think I put it in the top of the wardrobe and I'm too short to find it without the chair." She gave Delilah a pleading look.

"Yes, and I've been helping her," Delilah added in an overly loud voice.

Daphne let out a loud, long sigh. "It's ever so inconvenient being the opposite of tall."

"The opposite of tall, Cousin Daphne?" Delilah asked.

"I don't care much for the word 'short'," Daphne replied with another sigh.

Mama's brow wrinkled. "If the fichu is so hideous, why are you searching for it?"

Daphne made her way over to her dressing table. She sat and began rubbing cream onto her hands. "Because Aunt Willie would be disappointed if she arrives this weekend and doesn't see me wearing it at least once. I'd rather see a smile on her face and suffer through a few hours of wearing a hideous fichu."

Her mother's face was wreathed with a smile. "You're kind to your auntie, dear." Aunt Willie was her mother's and Delilah's mother's sister. The three women had grown up together, the daughters of the sixth Earl of Galverston.

Delilah absently patted the bow on the top of her head. "I agree. That's quite nice of you, Cousin Daphne. I will endeavor to do the same when you are elderly and present me with a hideous fichu."

Daphne let out a short bark of laughter. "Thank you, Delilah. I appreciate that, even though I am only seven years older than you. Not to mention I don't care for hideous fichus. Though I suppose, in my old age, I may endeavor to create a few of them, as Aunt Willie has done."

"You may be only seven years older than me, Cousin Daphne. But they are seven crucial years. You are about to become engaged and I am not even close to my come out. Alas." Delilah put the back of her hand to her forehead and let out an overly dramatic sigh.

"What's this, dear?" Mama asked, her eyes trained on Daphne's writing desk.

Daphne's mother stood near the desk looking beautiful

with her honey-blond hair now laced with white and her gray eyes that Daphne had inherited.

"What?" Daphne asked.

"This book." Mama slid a volume from the top of the desk.

"Oh, that." Daphne nearly sighed in relief. "It's just my copy of *The Adventures of Miss Calliope Cauldwell*. I found it in the back of my desk drawer earlier while I was looking for the fichu."

"I remember it now. This used to be your favorite book, dear," her mother murmured.

Daphne made her way over to stand next to her mother and stared down at the old, worn cover. She swallowed the lump in her throat. Mama was right. It had been her favorite book. Back when she dreamed of things like adventures and spying and—

Fiddle. None of that mattered now. She'd been on an adventure—thank you very much—and it had been positively dreadful. She opened her desk drawer and slid the book inside. Then she shook her head. "I know it's been exceedingly busy downstairs today, what with preparing for the party," Daphne said. "Why, I must have heard the knocker at least a half-dozen times. I promise to come down right away to assist you."

"That's not necessary, dear. Pengree and I have been seeing to all the callers, except—"

"I know, Mama, but I insist upon helping."

Her mother's smile was cheerful. "Nothing to worry about, my dear. I'm in my element. Notes are coming from all corners of London and the countryside. The party tomorrow night is sure to be a smashing success. All of our relatives, friends, and acquaintances are eager to wish you well on your potential engagement to Lord Fitzwell."

Daphne swallowed. Why did it still sound so foreign to her ears? *Engagement to Lord Fitzwell.* This is what she'd been planning for weeks. She'd been spending time with Lord Fitzwell, allowing him to escort her to events about town, riding with him in the park. It was time. It was past time. She was soon to begin her third Season out. But now, now that it was finally about to happen, the knots in her belly were forming an army. "The engagement has not been announced formally, Mama."

"Of course not, dear. Not yet, but everyone knows that the ball may very well turn into your engagement ball."

Daphne put the back of her hand to her forehead. "Is it hot in here?"

"Oh, dear. I do hope you're not coming down with something."

Daphne shook her head. "Oh, no, no, no. I'll be fine. I can count on one hand the number of times I've taken to bed ill. Besides, I have a myriad of duties I should be attending to, like helping you with the party preparations, Mama." Daphne bit her lip. The lovely, thoughtful, expensive party that would no doubt be difficult to call off. *Not* that she wanted to call it off. No, she did not. She was going to have this party and accept Lord Fitzwell's suit, if he proposed, of course, and nothing was going to stop it. Nothing save— There went the dread rising in her throat again. She gulped.

"The reason I came up is because you have a visitor, dear," Mama said quietly.

"Mama, you needn't have troubled yourself. You should have sent Pengree or one of the footmen."

Her mother pressed her lips together. "I wasn't certain you'd want to see this particular visitor."

Daphne whipped her head around, her brow wrinkled. "Who?"

"Who?" Delilah echoed.

Mama's kind eyes searched Daphne's face. "It's Captain Cavendish, dear."

Delilah's eyes rounded and her mouth formed a wide O. Daphne sucked in her breath but quickly shook her head and concentrated on keeping her face still. She mustn't allow her mother to see how greatly the name affected her. But she'd just named the one person who stood to ruin the entire party, indeed, the entire engagement. And her mother didn't even know why.

Captain Rafferty Cavendish.

Daphne's husband.

CHAPTER TWO

Daphne turned to Delilah who still sat on the bed, now with a catlike smile pinned to her gamine little face. "Why didn't you tell your mother that Captain Cavendish sent you that gift?" Delilah asked as soon as Mama had left the room. "Why did you hide it?"

"It's quite a long story and one I don't have time to explain, now—"

"Oh, pleeease tell me, Cousin Daphne. I do so *j'adore* a good mystery."

"If you enjoy a mystery, then my telling you will rob you of the pleasure of solving it. And I hate to mention it, but I don't think you're using *j'adore* correctly in all instances."

Delilah tapped her cheek. "I am still learning French, cousin. And you are right about the mystery. Very well. I shall settle for a hint. A good one, if you please."

Daphne couldn't help but shake her head and smile.

"No, Delilah, not now. It's something complicated that only adults should discuss."

"I cannot wait to be an adult. You get to hear all the best gossip."

Daphne stared at her reflection in the looking glass. "As I said, Delilah, don't be too quick to want to grow up."

"But I want to grow up. I want to have adventures like Calliope Cauldwell. I want to have handsome gentlemen send me gifts even if they are odd ones like tiny wooden ships. Though I am certain I would prefer jewelry." Delilah fell back onto the bed with her hand on her forehead again. "Oh, I wish something would happen. Nothing ever possibly in the least ever happens around here."

Daphne turned to her cousin and put both fists to her hips. "Don't be so dramatic, Delilah. Adventures can be quite dangerous. In more ways than one. And as for something happening around here, you don't find an engagement party to be exciting?"

Delilah sat back up and braced both hands behind her on the quilt. "I suppose an engagement party is a start, but I'd like there to be something *truly* exciting."

"Like what?"

"Like a plot, or a *mésalliance,* or a scandal!"

"Fiddle. Think what you're saying. We don't live in the middle of *The Adventures of Miss Calliope Cauldwell.* True life is much less exciting, I assure you. I am going to marry Lord Fitzwell and that is far from a *mésalliance.*"

Another sigh from Delilah. "More's the pity."

"Delilah Montbank, think about yourself."

"I shall endeavor to, Cousin Daphne. But I don't hold out much hope for reforming myself. I believe I'm quite a lost cause." The gamine smile popped back to Delilah's lips. "Now, are you going to go downstairs and see Captain Cavendish? Thank him for his gift?" The girl's dark eyebrows waggled.

Daphne twisted her finger and pointedly ignored the eyebrow waggling. "I suppose I must."

"I suggest you take your time making your way down to the green drawing room," Delilah said.

"Why?" Daphne furrowed her brow.

"You should keep a man waiting. They positively *j'adore* it. Though they'd never admit it."

"Delilah Montbank! Who told you that nonsense?"

Delilah fluttered a small hand in the air with practiced nonchalance. "Oh, Cousin Daphne, everyone knows you should keep a man waiting."

"Everyone, you say?" Daphne eyed the girl warily. Just how much did her scamp of a cousin know about Daphne's love life?

Delilah cleared her throat. "Next, you should peer into the looking glass and ensure you have color in your cheeks."

Daphne narrowed her eyes on her cousin. "I don't even want to know how you know about such things."

"Do it," Delilah ordered, pointing toward the looking glass.

Daphne reluctantly turned toward the glass and did as she was told. Her cheeks pinkened immediately.

"I'm told a stiff bit of liquor helps if you can't manage enough pink with the pinching. But it looks as if you've succeeded." Delilah clapped her hands.

"Good heavens, Delilah. How do you know anything about drinking?"

Delilah shrugged. "I heard the vicar talking about it."

"Why, the very idea . . ."

"It's quite all right," Delilah said with a sigh. "Just the pinching will do."

Daphne took a deep breath and looked in the mirror, studying her reflection. "Captain Cavendish told me I was beautiful once."

Delilah's smile widened. Daphne could see the girl's face behind her in the mirror. "What I wouldn't give for someone as handsome as Captain Cavendish to tell me I am beautiful."

"You are lovely, Delilah. You'll have a string of suitors after you when you come of age. I have never thought of myself that way, though. I suppose I am passably pretty."

"You *are*, Cousin Daphne, so pretty. Why, quite one of the prettiest young ladies in town, I should say."

Daphne frowned at her reflection. "No doubt that scoundrel Cavendish only said it as part of the other pack of lies he fed me."

"He could feed me an entire plateful of lies, as long as he did it with that roguish smile of his on his face." Delilah sighed. "What sort of lies did he tell you, Cousin Daphne?"

"Consider that more of the mystery, Delilah. And I needn't tell you that Mother's not to hear a word about any of this."

"I may be young, but I can keep a secret. Besides, you're not likely to tell me more if I go spouting off about what I already know, are you?"

"You make a good point." Daphne continued to stare into the looking glass. "I wonder if Lord Fitzwell thinks I'm pretty. He's never said so."

Delilah wrinkled her nose. "Lord Fitzwell doesn't say much that isn't about Lord Fitzwell."

"Oh, Delilah. Lord Fitzwell is perfectly respectable. He's handsome, eligible, and titled."

"And more interested in your family lineage than your beauty, Cousin Daphne. Not to mention a dead bore."

Daphne turned to face the girl and waved a finger at her. "He is far from boring. And as for him being interested in my lineage, gentlemen like Lord Fitzwell take a wife to secure a better place in Society and gain riches through her dowry. I'm interested in *his* lineage, too, you know."

Delilah's nose remained wrinkled. "Sounds entirely un-romantic. I could not *j'adore* a man who was only inter-ested in my family's ranking in *DeBrett's Peerage*."

Daphne shook her head. "Just wait until you're my age."

"I cannot wait. That's what I've been telling you. It's going to be a sheer lifetime before I'm old enough to go to balls and dance with handsome gentlemen. And I don't care what you say about Lord Fitzwell. I much prefer Cap-tain Cavendish."

Daphne pressed her palm to her belly. She needed to get downstairs and confront Rafe. She'd been using this discussion with Delilah to calm her nerves and afford her time. But the reckoning would be upon her soon. "Captain Cavendish couldn't be more unlike Lord Fitzwell if he tried. He's not a bit interested in lineage or money or anything of the sort. He's a mere captain in His Majesty's army."

And a spy. But she wasn't about to admit that to Delilah. The girl already knew far too much.

No, Rafe hadn't wanted her for lineage or money.

"He may have no title to speak of, but he couldn't be more handsome," Delilah replied.

Daphne gritted her teeth. She couldn't argue with Delilah there, but she'd learned her lesson when it came to Rafe Cavendish. Daphne had married him last year. A grievous mistake and one that needed to be rectified post-haste. At the time, she'd been under the mistaken impression that he had some feeling for her. She'd thought their marriage could be more than a business arrangement set up for the Crown. Rafe had insisted on the marriage, hadn't he? Fine. The mission may have been a part of his assignment for the War Office. But Rafe had been the one to insist that he would not allow her to accompany him unless they were man and wife. And Daphne had seen her chance. Not just her chance to marry the man she'd longed for for years, but also a chance to prove herself a benefit to the war cause. Both her brothers, Donald and Julian, had served. Julian had nearly died fighting Napoleon at Waterloo and Donald had given the ultimate sacrifice when he'd left for an assignment in France, accompanied by Rafe. Daphne wanted to prove that though she might be a female, she, too, could be of service to her country. Like all the Swifts before her.

Daphne shook her head. She was not one to dwell on the past. She'd made her mistakes and she had a plan to fix them. Mama must never find out, nor Lord Fitzwell, of course. She'd thought she'd made that clear to Rafe. God knew why he was paying her a call on the eve of her engagement party. She took a deep breath. There was only one way to find out.

By the time Daphne strolled into the drawing room, she just so happened to be wearing her favorite pink gown. She just so happened to have her hair pulled up in her favorite fetching chignon, and she just so happened to have a bit of pink in her cheeks caused by more of Delilah's recommended pinching.

Feeling quite confident, she pushed open the doors to the room and sashayed her way inside. Rafe immediately stood.

Seeing him was like a punch to the stomach. Not that she'd ever been punched in the stomach, but this was no time for mental quibbling. The man was too handsome by half. No, *more* than half. Twenty-seven years old and fit as a fox. He had bright blue eyes, shortly cropped, dark blond hair, a strong brow, and a cleft in his chin that had always driven her mad. She concentrated on making her way toward him and taking a seat in front of the fireplace in a rosewood chair that sat at right angles to the one in which Rafe had sat.

"Captain Cavendish," she intoned in her most affected, haughty voice. She stared at the mantelpiece above his head so she wouldn't be distracted by his face.

He bowed to her. "Lady Daphne."

"You're calling me Lady Daphne now?" she replied with a tight smile.

"It's only proper when I've come to call at your town house, is it not? Would you rather I call you Grey?" His voice was strong, sure, always tinged with the smallest bit of charming arrogance. Blast him.

"No! No." Blast. Her voice had been too high. She made herself count three. "Lady Daphne is quite preferable, thank you."

Besides, what did it matter if he called her Lady Daphne? The formality was fitting, actually. She shrugged one shoulder and then cursed herself for the unladylike gesture. Not that Rafe had ever cared how ladylike she was. Quite the contrary, he'd seemed to revel in the fact that she'd been game enough to wear breeches and pretend she was a boy last year when they'd worked together. There went her wayward thoughts again. Must concentrate on the matter at hand. Namely, making Captain Rafferty Cavendish rue the day he'd informed her their marriage would be annulled.

She took a deep breath. "I do hope you weren't planning to stay long, Captain. I'm quite busy today. Planning for my *engagement*, you know. The party is this weekend and it's quite large." She said the word "engagement" as if she was chewing glass between her teeth. And what did it matter if she was telling a white lie? Rafe had obviously heard the rumors that her engagement was imminent, or he wouldn't have sent her that confounded ship.

Rafe arched a brow at her. "That's why I've come."

"For my party? I don't recall sending you an invitation." More glass between her teeth.

"Your brother invited me, actually, but that's not why I'm here. I'm here specifically to speak with you."

"About?" She feigned interest in the crystal vase that stood atop the small rosewood table next to her chair, drawing her fingertip along its base.

"You really don't know?" His voice dripped with skepticism.

She directed her gaze back at him and gave him a you-can't-affect-me smile. "Know what?"

"That you shouldn't be planning an engagement given the fact that you are married to me."

CHAPTER THREE

"But Julian, you promised me a favor." Daphne paced back and forth in front of the windows in her brother's large study that overlooked the square. After what Rafe had just told her moments ago, she'd hurried from the drawing room, telling him she'd return shortly and refusing to listen to his entreaties that she hear the rest of it.

"Yes," Julian replied. "And I delivered on that favor when I resisted the urge to thrash you or throttle you when you told me a few weeks ago that you're secretly married to Cavendish. Your favor is all used up."

"But you *must* help me," she pleaded, wringing her hands.

"No, I mustn't. I'm still incensed over the fact that you did something so reckless without consulting me and that you—"

Daphne reached out her hands to him in supplication. "But everything is about to be ruined. Lord Fitzwell is coming and I'm to be engaged and Captain Cavendish is here and I can barely breathe and—"

"Good heavens, dear. Calm down. I'm quite worried for you." Cassandra, Julian's new wife, came floating into the study just then with the tea tray she'd gone to fetch so that Pengree wouldn't overhear their private conversation. A bit of news like a lady of the house already being married during her supposed engagement party was bound to be a popular bit of gossip even among the most steadfast servants. "Julian, darling, hear her out."

Julian let out a deep breath, but smiled at his wife as she laid the tray on the desktop and poured a cup of tea, adding two lumps of sugar before handing it to Daphne.

"Yes, see, Cass knows. She wants you to help," Daphne said.

"I didn't say that, dear," Cass replied. "I merely think it best for Julian to hear all of the facts before he makes a decision. Not to mention I'm quite curious to learn exactly what happened between you and Captain Cavendish that resulted in a wedding and your desire to get an annulment as soon as possible."

"Very well," Julian said, pouring his own drink. Brandy, not tea. "I'll hear you out, Daphne, but you'd best make it quick. I've little patience for this."

Cass finished pouring her own cup of tea and hurried over to the settee where she curled up and sipped while she listened.

Setting her teacup aside, Daphne resumed pacing in front of her brother's desk, her hands folded in front of her. "You remember last year when Donald and Mama wrote to you and told you that I'd run off for a fortnight?"

Julian's eyes nearly bugged from his skull. "Lower your voice."

"I remember!" Cass piped up.

"I do, too. You never did explain what that escapade was about," Julian said.

"Donald knew, part of it. But I never told Mama. I didn't want to worry her. I'd convinced Rafe that he needed me for help on a mission. For the War Office."

If Julian's eyes had seemed to bug from his skull a moment ago, now they were in imminent danger of actually popping out and rolling about on the fine rug. He lunged from his seat and braced his hands on the desktop in front of him, looming over Daphne. "You accompanied Cavendish on a mission for the War Office? Are you mad? Is Cavendish mad? I'm going to murder him!"

"Now, Julian, you promised to hear Daphne out," Cass quietly interjected.

Julian growled but slowly resumed his seat. "Go on," he said through clenched teeth.

Daphne swallowed once but her voice was steady when she continued her pacing. "Yes, well. I sort of convinced him to, ahem, agree to allow me to come."

Julian's dark gray eyes narrowed on her. "How did you—" He groaned again. "Perhaps I don't want to know."

Daphne plunked her hands on her hips. "It was nothing indecent, I'll have you know."

"Thank God for that," Julian retorted.

"I merely threatened him," Daphne continued.

"Merely? Threatened?" Julian's voice dripped with sarcasm.

Daphne bit her lip. "I told him that I'd tell Donald he'd compromised me if he didn't agree to take me with him."

Julian cursed under his breath and lurched out of his seat again. "Cavendish compromised you! By God, I'll—"

"No! No. No. No." Daphne waved her hands in the air frantically. "No. He did not." She cleared her throat and lowered her voice. "I only threatened to *tell* Donald that he'd compromised me if he didn't do as I asked."

Julian breathed deeply, both nostrils flaring. He glanced at his wife, who merely took another sip of tea and shrugged. "I suggest you allow her to finish before you go flying off into any more rages," Cass said.

Julian dropped back into his seat. "Very well. Go on, Daphne."

"He still said no." Daphne tapped a finger against her cheek.

"I don't see how you ended up going with him then," Julian replied.

"I was able to convince him."

Julian eyed her warily. "How?"

"Because I knew the secret of why Donald went to France."

Julian's intelligent gray eyes snapped to her face. "What did you know?"

Daphne straightened her shoulders and kept her gaze locked on her brother's face. "I know that the official reason Donald went to France was because he was an earl and he appeared to be on a diplomatic mission."

"And?" Julian drew out the word.

"And I know the *real* reason Donald went was because the men who worked for the French were Russians and Donald spoke Russian."

Julian braced a hand on the desk in front of him. "How did you know that?"

"I know that because I speak Russian, too."

Julian's eyes rounded bigger than she'd ever seen them. "Pardon?"

"Pardon?" Cass echoed, her teacup frozen halfway to her mouth.

"That's right. Donald learned when he was a youth, after the ambassador paid Papa a visit. Papa told Donald it would serve him well to know more than English and French. The ambassador arranged for a private tutor."

"I knew all of that, Daphne, but how did *you* learn it?" Julian asked.

Daphne tugged at the strand of pearls around her neck. "As you can guess, Papa didn't know about it. He never would have agreed to tutor a seven-year-old girl in the language. And I needn't tell you that Donald was the only one he ever thought worthy of anything special."

Julian nodded solemnly. "Go on."

"So I asked Donald. I told him how much I wanted to be of use one day, to help the country in any way I could."

"And Donald said yes?" Julian breathed.

"He never said no to me," Daphne replied with a sad smile. "He taught me himself and sometimes sneaked me into his lessons with the tutor, Mr. Baskov, when he could. Mr. Baskov said it was easier for me to learn than Donald because I was so much younger than he. He said I was a stellar student."

Julian stood and turned toward the window. He braced a shoulder against it and looked out. "Why didn't you ever tell me, Daphne?"

"I didn't know if you'd share Papa's feelings. Or if you'd tell him."

"Of course I wouldn't have."

"By the time I knew for sure, you'd gone off to war, and—"

"And?" Julian prompted.

"I didn't know if I'd ever see you again," Daphne finished.

Julian turned to her, his face solemn. "I'm proud of you, Daphne. You're clever and quick and a credit to this family."

Daphne's eyes filled with tears. "Thank you, Julian."

On the settee, Cass was dabbing her eyes with her handkerchief. "I just love this. Daphne's secretly known Russian all this time. It's absolutely famous. Go on, dear, tell us how you convinced Captain Cavendish."

Daphne nodded. "Rafe, that is, Captain Cavendish, had wanted Donald to accompany him down to the docks. To pretend that he was one of the crew members on his ship. He was pretending to be a smuggler, captain of a ship called the *True Love*."

"And?" Cass had abandoned her teacup and had moved to the edge of her seat.

"And I informed Captain Cavendish that I spoke Russian."

"But Donald did, too." Julian's brow furrowed.

"That's what Captain Cavendish said. But I pointed out that if I went, I could pretend to be his cabin boy. God knows I'm small enough. And I would have more reason to be around when the Russians came to the ship. It wouldn't seem odd for me to be in the captain's cabin, for instance. Or to accompany him about the docks."

"Wait," Cass interjected. "I don't understand. Why are Russians involved with the French?"

"These particular Russians are mercenaries," Daphne replied. "They sold their loyalty to the French for money."

Cass nodded while Julian's face turned white. "And Donald allowed you to pose as Cavendish's cabin boy?"

"Yes. Donald agreed that I was the better one to go. He knew I wouldn't be in any danger with Captain Cavendish. He knew it was just the sort of thing I'd been waiting for my whole life, to help the war cause. Donald was correct. I couldn't have been more ready or more willing," Daphne finished with a firm nod.

"So Cavendish agreed?" Julian said.

Daphne nodded slowly. "Eventually. Though Donald also insisted upon one condition."

Julian rubbed his hand across his forehead. "Do I want to know what that condition was?"

"You must know," Daphne replied.

Julian winced. "Fine."

"Donald insisted that we marry before we embarked on the mission. He did not want my reputation in danger in the event that we were caught."

"And that's how you came to be married?" Cass asked, biting the tip of one fingernail.

"Yes," Daphne replied. "Captain Cavendish had a friend in the War Office get a special license and—"

"It was *Donald*'s idea?" Incredulity filled Julian's words.

Daphne bit her lip again and winced.

"Yes. He refused to let me go without that condition being met. I begged him to allow me to do this for my country. He agreed as long as Rafe and I promised to get an annulment when we returned. He even spoke to the Prince Regent about it. The prince agreed to grant a special dispensation and . . ."

"And?" Julian asked.

Daphne glanced away, her face heating. "And Donald made Rafe promise not to—"

"Not to?" Julian prodded.

Daphne stared down at her slippers. She couldn't face her brother while these words came out of her mouth. "Donald made Rafe promise not to . . . consummate the marriage."

Julian gritted his teeth again. "Astute of him. And did Cavendish—" Julian tugged at his cravat and cleared his throat. "Keep his promise?"

Daphne could only nod. Yes, the blasted man had kept his promise, but not from any lack of trying to seduce him on her part.

"Good, or I'd be on my way to find him in the drawing room and beat him to a pulp right now," Julian replied.

"So bloodthirsty," Cass murmured from behind the tea-cup that she'd picked up again. She tsked at her husband.

Julian pressed a finger to his brow as if he had a head-ache and focused his attention back on Daphne. "I don't see the problem then. If you've both kept your end of the bargain, an annulment shouldn't be difficult. There are very few legal grounds for one, but if the Prince Regent is involved—"

"It *shouldn't* be difficult," Daphne replied, wringing her hands again.

"Is that why you've come for my help? I'll ask some discreet friends in Parliament about it. Remind the prince. We can get it done quickly, quietly without anyone knowing."

"It *should* be that simple," Daphne said, "except . . ."

Julian's forehead wrinkled into a frown. "Except what?"

Daphne sighed. "Except Captain Cavendish just told me that he refuses to grant me the annulment."

CHAPTER FOUR

Daphne rounded the corner toward the drawing room just as Rafe was coming out the door. She nearly collided with his broad chest. The man smelled like pine needles and soap and—oh, something else good that she didn't want to think about. She swallowed and shook her head. "I, er, Captain Cavendish, I mean—"

"There you are. I'd nearly given you up for dead." His grin was unrepentant.

She took a step back and stared straight into his cravat. No good could come from staring into that handsome face. And that dimple . . . "I've just come from Julian's study."

He crossed his arms over his chest. "And?"

Delilah's little face peered around the far corner. "Do you mind?" Daphne pointed toward the drawing room where they would have more privacy. She waved Delilah away and frowned at the girl.

"Not at all." Rafe pushed open the door again with one hand and gestured to her to precede him into the room.

Daphne straightened her shoulders and marched inside, trying her best to ignore his scent. This time she detected a bit of soap and leather and— Ooh, this was not helping. Not at all.

She made her way around the table in the center of the room, using it as a shield from his nearness.

Rafe eyed her with his arms crossed over his chest again. "I must say the way you ran out of here earlier, I wasn't certain you were coming back."

Daphne glanced down at her hands, staring at the naked ring finger. "I didn't run."

"Didn't you?" She didn't even need to look to know his brow was quirked.

She cleared her throat. No use quibbling with him. And very well, the truth was, she had run. A little. "You quite caught me by surprise."

"I'm sure I did, but you didn't allow me to finish what I was saying."

Daphne tossed her hands in the air. "Finish what? Finish telling me you refuse to grant me an annulment? I'd heard quite enough. You've clearly lost your mind."

"And you ran off to tell your brother on me before hearing the rest of it." He scrubbed a hand against the back of his head. "Though I can't say I'm surprised. You seem to enjoy looking to your family to fix everything. I daresay there hasn't been a problem in your entire life that the Swift name hasn't solved for you."

Daphne's eyes narrowed to slits. His words rankled. Perhaps because they contained a bit of the truth. She *had* run off to enlist Julian's help and she couldn't deny it now. Instead, she scrunched up her nose and drew in a deep breath. "Very well. I'm back. Tell me. What do you want?"

"Want?" Again with the eyebrow quirk.

She nodded, her heart beating like a rabbit's foot in her chest. Julian had informed her that unless the groom was willing, the annulment could not possibly be done quickly or quietly. If she didn't get Rafe to agree to this, her entire weekend, her entire engagement, let alone her entire future, the one she'd planned with Lord Fitzwell, would be ruined. She feigned nonchalance by folding her arms over her chest and pushing out her cheek with her tongue. "Yes. In exchange for the annulment. What do you want?"

"That's more like it." Rafe inclined his head toward her. He slowly crossed his arms over his chest. "I want you to come with me, back to the docks, on Sunday night."

Daphne's stomach dropped into her slippers. "Whaaat?"

"You heard me."

"Back to the docks? Why?"

"The spy ring. The Russians. They've returned. I have it on the best authority that they'll be there. And they're bringing something I need."

Daphne pressed her hand to her throat. She'd gone to the docks with Rafe last year and had spent nearly a fortnight there with him, posing as his cabin boy. She'd worn stockings and breeches and a loose shirt and cap and— oh, God—she'd thought that was all long over. It had been an age ago, and she'd been stupid and naïve and that had all been before . . . Donald was killed.

"Even if I wanted to, Julian would never allow it."

Rafe arched *both* brows this time. "As if Julian's wishes have ever stopped you before."

Daphne nearly growled. Rafe had a point. He always had a point. "I'm—I can't."

He casually crossed his booted feet at the ankles and regarded her down the length of his perfectly shaped nose. "Why can't you?"

She lifted her chin. "I'm a respectable young lady. I'm about to become engaged to Lord Fitzwell. I cannot go gallivanting off in boy's breeches and a cap."

Rafe snorted. "Not so long ago, boy's breeches and a cap didn't bother you much. Lost your passion for adventure, have you? Besides, you can hardly become engaged when you're *married* to me. Even Julian's title can't fix that little problem."

Daphne turned her head away, refusing to answer. He was right about the engagement but those weren't the words that had stung so badly, more than Daphne expected them to. A vision of Calliope Cauldwell spun through her brain. Calliope Cauldwell had spent time on a pirate ship of all places. She'd been forced to walk the plank. Had been rescued by a privateer. She'd worn boy's breeches. Though a tricorn had been her headwear, not a cap. And Calliope Cauldwell didn't even speak Russian. But still . . .

Fiddle. Why was Daphne thinking about Calliope Cauldwell? She was made-up. Purely imaginary. A heroine in a silly novel. This proposal of Rafe's was far from imaginary. It was real and it was dangerous. Donald was dead, wasn't he? Killed by the Frenchmen whom the Russians worked for. This was far from a game and she refused to be bullied into it. Hadn't she spent the last year trying to forget about it? To forget about Rafe? To come to terms with the fact that she needed to stop longing for adventures and to save her country and focus on settling down to marriage and a family? "I cannot go with you. That's all there is to it."

Rafe walked around her in a slow circle while Daphne tried to ignore his nearness and calm her pounding heart. "I'm sorry, love, but you're forcing me to play my trump."

"Don't call me love." She tugged at the pearls around

her throat and lifted her chin again. But she couldn't help her curiosity. "What exactly do you think is your trump?"

"Seeking out Lord Fitzwell, of course. He intends to propose to you, does he not? I doubt that will happen if he discovers you're dragging him into bigamy." Rafe sauntered back over to the other side of the table, putting a safe distance between them again.

Daphne's head snapped to the side to glare at him. Her temper had sparked. Anger welled in her chest. There was no stopping it now. She advanced, coming around the table toward him. "I am not dragging him into bigamy. I have every intention of seeing our marriage ended before I marry Lord Fitzwell, of course, and if you think I'm going to gallivant off with you down to the docks . . . I'm getting married and settling down. How dare you threaten me? How dare—"

Rafe backed up and splayed both hands in the air. "Whoa. Whoa. Whoa. Whoa. Whoa. Wait, you little spitfire."

She didn't stop. She continued to advance on him, her eyes boring holes into his chest. "Why should I wait?"

Rafe's eyes turned to blue ice. "What if I told you I intend to use the Russians to hunt down the men who killed your brother?"

CHAPTER FIVE

"And I need your help," Rafe finished.

He watched as Daphne's wide gray eyes grew even wider. Her pink mouth formed an O as well. Her chest was heaving with her effort to breathe and— No, no. Better not to think about things like Daphne Swift's heaving chest. Though the way she was tugging on that necklace kept drawing attention to her décolletage and that was hardly helping matters. Nevertheless, Rafe had told himself a hundred times on his way here this morning . . . he must treat Daphne like a sister. Sister. Sister. Sister.

Very well. A sister he was married to. Temporarily. But that was for a very good reason and—

"How?" Daphne's single word jolted him from his thoughts.

Yes. Very good. Concentrate upon the mission. That's exactly why he'd come. "They're bringing information I need. Letters. And I must be there to intercept them."

"And what do I have to do with it?" She was eyeing him

carefully but he could tell she was intrigued. Of course she was intrigued. She might pretend to be more interested in engagement parties and marriages, but Daphne Swift was the kind of female who wouldn't pass up a challenge. He'd learned that about her last spring during their mission. And this would be the greatest challenge of them all. It was like dangling a bit of salmon in front of a cat. That's why he'd come.

"For one reason, you must be there for consistency's sake. The last time they saw me, you were with me, as my cabin boy. They only know me as the captain of the *True Love*."

She crossed her arms over her chest. "You can't tell them your 'cabin boy' is gone? Fell overboard perhaps?"

"Of course I can, but these are the type of people who will be suspicious of anything out of the ordinary. Any change. I need to keep as many things the same as I possibly can."

She pressed her small pink lips together. Lips that he'd had indecent dreams about. "And the other reason?"

"I thought it would be obvious, but I need you. To interpret their language, of course."

Daphne cupped a hand behind her ear. "Say that part again, Captain. What was it? I find I quite enjoy hearing that you need me."

He grinned and stepped closer to her, allowing her to see the true plea in his eyes. "It's true, Grey. I need you."

She tapped an obviously impatient foot against the floor. "My name's not Grey."

"Not now it isn't."

She wrinkled her nose in her adorable fashion. "You need me?" she echoed.

Rafe had doffed his gloves and slapped them against his

thigh. "Blast it, Daphne. I wouldn't be here if I didn't. It's extremely dangerous. Trust me. I wouldn't put you at risk again if it wasn't the only choice. I know I'll have to convince Julian also, but leave that to me."

Daphne considered him down the length of her button nose. "Fine. Grant me my annulment, and I'll consider it."

The smile he flashed her was meant to inform her that there was no chance of that happening. Of course he gave her credit for trying. Some. She had pluck. He'd give her that. But then again, she'd always had pluck. For a Society lady.

"I'm afraid that won't work," he replied.

Her face began to turn red. "What? Why not?"

He knew she was considering stamping her foot but he guessed she didn't want to appear childish. Good choice.

"We must remain married for the same reason we married in the first place," he answered. "If we're caught, you'd be ruined."

"I'll take my chances," she shot back.

"Will you? Truly? Do you want to take that risk? Not to mention if we're captured and we're married, standing trial we will be unable to testify against each other."

"You know as well as I that if we're captured . . ." Her voice trailed off but she'd been about to say "we'll be hanged." He knew it. They both knew it. And that was much more dangerous than any risk to her reputation.

"We'll be on English soil the entire time. Going to France is not a risk I'm willing to take with you."

"Why, because I'm like a *sister* to you?" She nearly spat the words at him. He'd known those words had rankled when he'd said them to her last year. But it was the only thing he could think to say to make her believe, to make her understand. They could *not* be together. Ever. It wasn't possible. And if he'd thought for one blasted moment that charming, smiling, adventurous, off-limits *Lady* Daphne Swift would have gone and fallen for him, actually believed their pretend marriage was more than pretend, he never would have agreed to take her with him on the first mission. Even if she did try to extort him by threatening to tell her brother that he'd compromised her, the little minx.

There had been something about the way that she'd threatened him so casually, as if it were part of her normal, pampered daily routine. "Take me with you to the docks. I'll pose as your wife."

"Never."

"Never? Not even if I threaten to tell Donald that you . . . compromised me?" Her smile had been so alluring. And in the end, Rafe had agreed. Not because he couldn't explain the situation to Donald Swift convincingly. Hell, he'd been convincing people of whatever he wanted to convince them of since he was a lad of thirteen. No. He'd done it because Daphne herself had persuaded him. He'd been intrigued by her bravery, her desire to help the war effort.

"What's the matter, Captain?" she'd taunted. "Afraid that a *lady* might show you up? I may wear skirts, but I deserve to do my part for my country the same as any man, regardless of what's between my legs."

Those had been the words that had sealed her fate. Damned if she hadn't been right. Daphne Swift came from a family of patriots. Both of her brothers had done what they could for their country and if the little Society miss wanted to prove her own worth, who was Rafe to keep her from it? He'd known that feeling after all. Wanting to prove your worth. His father had told him often enough that he'd never amount to anything.

"Very well," he'd told her. "But you won't be wearing skirts on this particular mission."

Her eyes had gone wide then, too.

"What do you mean?" Her words had been a rushed whisper.

"You cannot pose as my wife. It would be suspicious and you are far too beautiful. I'd never take you to the docks and put you at risk of rape or worse."

"If I'm not to be a lady, then what—"

"I'm in need of a cabin boy. And you are just the right size, if not shape."

He'd tried not to allow his gaze to linger on her breasts. He was already going to hell for half a score of reasons as it was, agreeing to this. "But we can take care of that," he quickly added.

Daphne had pressed a hand to her breasts. "We can take care—"

"We'll work out the details later," he'd said, waving a hand in the air and flipping his tricorn over and placing it back on his head. "I must get back."

But last time had been quite a bit different. Last time, he'd needed an interpreter, yes, but he'd have been able to talk Donald into going if he'd truly wanted the earl's help instead of his sister's. Now, however, he had no choice. This time he was desperate. Daphne was already established as his cabin boy and she spoke Russian. Donald was dead. It was hardly a difficult decision.

"Yes," Rafe answered simply, dragging his thoughts back to the question she'd just asked him. She hated it when he compared her to a sister. And the fact was, he thought of her as anything but. But he didn't much care for the thought of having Julian Swift knock every single one of his teeth down his throat.

"I'm not your sister and you'd better have a more convincing argument than that or I still refuse to help you."

Rafe let out his breath, slapped his gloves against his thigh again, and considered his options. She'd really got her back up this time. "As soon as the mission is over, I'll grant you your annulment. I'll go to the Home Office myself and see to it immediately."

She narrowed her eyes on him. "How long will the mission take?"

"A sennight, give or take a day."

"One week?"

"That's right. That's all." He took a deep breath and played his *real* trump. He glanced at her and blinked. "I thought you'd want to help, Daphne. Don't you want to catch the bastards who killed Donald?"

The glimmer in her eye told him he'd won. If there was one thing Rafe knew, it was people. Their motivations and their weaknesses. It's what made him a good spy. Daphne would never be able to resist that challenge.

"I'll do it," she said. "On one condition."

CHAPTER SIX

Daphne eyed the handsome rogue who stood before her. Rafe scrubbed his hand through his blond hair, mussing it so the short ends stood up straight. He was so certain of himself. So confident, strolling in here with ultimatums and bargains. Two could play at that game, and Daphne was no longer the unsure little ninny she'd been last year. He'd appealed to her sense of justice. He knew she couldn't refuse that. And she couldn't. If she thought for one moment she could help catch the evil men responsible for Donald's death and Rafe's torture, she wouldn't say no to the opportunity, but she certainly wasn't about to allow Rafe Cavendish to be in charge and order her about.

She was going to help him avenge her brother's death. But she would do so on *her* terms, by God. Not Rafe's.

"What's the condition?" Rafe asked, squeezing his gloves so hard his hands turned red. Oh, he wasn't pleased with her today. Not at all. Good. She wasn't pleased with him. But Daphne turned away so she wouldn't have to look at his mussed hair. It was too alluring by half.

"I refuse to allow the party tomorrow to be affected by this. I want you to leave. Come back Sunday night and I'll go with you then."

She shouldn't have glanced at him for his answer. His sparkling eyes, the cleft in his chin, they were too much.

"Not a chance," he replied, his grin positively wicked.

She crossed her arms over her chest and tapped her foot on the rug. "I'm sorry. I think you have me confused with someone who doesn't have the upper hand."

He gave her a look that clearly indicated he was sure she'd taken leave of her senses. "Who says you have the upper hand?"

She narrowed her eyes on him. "You're attempting to convince me to agree to help you, are you not?"

"I'm offering you the opportunity to keep up this charade of a courtship with your suitor. But there's no way in hell I'm leaving this house. I'm staying right here. I won't cause trouble."

"Charade of a—" Ugh. There was no arguing with the confounded man. She crossed her arms over her chest. "Why?"

His grin widened. "Why won't I cause any trouble?"

She narrowed her eyes on him. "Why do you insist upon staying? Why would you even want to?"

"I can't leave, Grey. I couldn't do that. That wouldn't be fair to you. You need me too much."

"I need you too . . . ? You've completely lost your mind."

"Not yet. Not completely." He sauntered over to the sideboard and poured himself a glass of brandy.

She pushed her nose in the air. "Still drinking, I see?"

He didn't even bother to glance over his shoulder. "Still being far too judgmental about it, I see."

"You didn't answer me. Why do you want to stay?"

The bottle clinked against the glass. "You are my wife, aren't you?"

Blast him. His words sent a little thrill through her, despite her best efforts to quell it. "Legally only."

"Maybe so, but I need to make certain this Fitzwillow fellow acts like a gentleman toward my wife."

Daphne growled under her breath. "It's Fitzwell. And don't call me your wife."

"Fitzwhatever. And you *are* my wife."

Daphne continued her foot tapping. No one could make her more angry more quickly than Rafe Cavendish. She felt a scream rise in her throat. No doubt that would bring the entire house running and she definitely didn't need that. Instead, she took a deep breath and counted three. "I don't for one moment believe you want to stay to keep an eye on Lord Fitzwell."

His grin made her knees weak. "That transparent, am I?"

She wished.

"Very well, the truth is I want to keep an eye on you." Rafe brought the glass to his lips and for a brief moment, Daphne was jealous of the glass.

"Me?" She pointed at her own chest, blinking her eyes wide.

He inclined his head toward her. "That's right."

She plunked a hand to her hip. "Do you honestly think I intend to do anything outrageous during this party?"

He took another quick sip. "Not at all. I merely think you might leave before Sunday night. Slip off when I'm not looking."

She flung her hand in the air. "That's preposterous. Why, I would never do a thing like that."

Rafe splashed another bit of brandy into his glass. "Ludicrous, is it? You're telling me you haven't done it before? Like, say, last time we went on a mission?"

She turned her back on him and marched toward the door. "Fiddle. I wasn't hiding from you then. You were *with* me, for heaven's sake."

"I'm merely making the point that you've been known to slip away and do exactly as you like. I can't take any chances with this mission."

She turned back toward him, glaring at him. "I would never abandon this cause. It's for Donald," she said through clenched teeth.

Another sip of brandy. "Then you shouldn't mind if I stay."

Daphne rubbed her fingers against her forehead. There was no winning with him. The man was completely impossible to reason with. She shouldn't have bothered. "Fine. But I swear, if you do *anything* to ruin this engagement party . . ."

He grinned at her and swallowed the last of his drink. "You mean like informing the potential bridegroom that you're married?"

Another scream rose in her throat. She bit the inside of her cheek and ground her slipper against the floor. "Yes."

Rafe shrugged. "As long as he behaves himself, he has nothing to worry about it."

"It's not Lord Fitzwell's behavior I'm concerned about. It's yours."

"Ah, yes, the rich and titled are always so well behaved, aren't they?"

"I never said he was rich."

Rafe eyed her carefully, but she quickly changed the subject. "Stay if you must, I refuse to argue with you." She turned on her heel and made her way to the door. A small smile that Rafe couldn't see touched her lips. "By the way, Julian's in his study. He wants a word with you."

CHAPTER SEVEN

Rafe poured himself another finger of brandy and downed that, too. He needed to fortify himself before speaking to the Earl of Swifdon. The odds were good that Daphne's brother would take a swing at him and experience had taught Rafe well that punches were much less painful when one had a bit of liquor in one's belly. Most things hurt less when one had a bit of liquor in one's belly.

He downed the drink, blew out his breath, and straightened both his shoulders and his cravat. Then he marched out of the drawing room, down the corridor, around the corner, and stood in front of the imposing double wooden doors to Swifdon's study.

Jesus. The last time Rafe had been here, it had been to consult with the former earl, Donald, about their trip to France. That mission had been important to Rafe. All of his missions were. Rafe had grown up on the wrong side of town, to the wrong father, with the wrong . . . everything. But he'd used his cunning and skills with people to make a life for himself in the army, to make a name for himself in the War Office. And now, here he was, in a place he never belonged, in the corridors of the rich and titled in Mayfair. God, life was unpredictable. That last mission had been important, yes, but it was nothing compared to this mission. This mission wasn't for the War Office or the Crown though on the surface it might be. This mission was for him. This mission involved settling an old score.

Rafe shook his head and knocked once.

"Come in," came Swifdon's sure voice.

Rafe took a deep breath. In his experience, angry older brothers of angry, young, beautiful ladies were not easy to deal with. Best get this over with. He pushed open the door and strode inside.

A good spy was always aware of his surroundings. Escape routes, possible hiding spots, and exit strategies. Rafe scanned the room in an instant. Four walls, two doors, and a plethora of windows that lined the wall facing the street. A sofa, three chairs, a large desk, a potted palm, and rows of dark bookshelves.

"Swifdon," Rafe intoned, coming to stand in front of the earl's desk, his booted feet braced apart, his hands clasped behind his back. He nodded to the earl once.

"I see you made it here safely," Swifdon said.

Rafe inclined his head. "I did."

"No wounds from my sister?"

"Only to my confidence, my lord."

Swifdon laughed at that. "Allow me to cut to the chase, Cavendish."

"By all means."

"Why did you think it would be a good idea to *marry* Daphne? You must know that grounds for an annulment are extremely rare."

"I do, my lord. Insanity is one." Rafe cleared his throat. "And impotence. I beg you to claim I'm insane, because I doubt anyone would believe I'm impotent."

Julian shook his head. "Daphne told me that the prince has agreed to see to it himself. I'm not sure he has that authority, to be honest. Regardless, I have no idea what the hell you were thinking by marrying her and I frankly have no idea what the hell Donald was thinking to allow it, but I know my sister can be convincing and she somehow induced you to allow her to be part of an operation last spring."

"That's the gist of it."

"I must admit it was news to me that Daphne is fluent in Russian."

"I was equally surprised when she informed me of that in Donald's presence," Rafe answered.

"I can't say I'm particularly surprised, though," Swifdon added. "She's always been uncommonly intelligent and dedicated toward helping her country. If my father thought Russian would be useful for Donald, I can only imagine how she begged Donald to allow her to study it."

"Lady Daphne is quite convincing, my lord. I've experienced it firsthand."

Swifdon raised a brow. "And Daphne . . . convinced you to allow her to take Donald's place on the first mission?"

"That's the nice way of putting it." Rafe tugged at his cravat. It was hot in the earl's study. Exceedingly so.

"Extorted is more like it," Swifdon said with a smile.

Rafe cleared his throat. "She, uh, did mention that she'd tell Donald that we—"

Swifdon raised a hand to stop him. "I feel a bit sorry for you, Cavendish. When Daphne wants something, she gets it."

"Yes, my lord. I've learned as much."

"And now she wants an annulment."

"Yes."

"But you refuse to give it to her."

"Not at all. I need her help again and getting the annulment afterward makes more sense."

Swifdon narrowed his eyes on Rafe and pushed back in his large leather chair. "And ensures that she will agree to help you?"

"That, too," Rafe admitted.

"Does Daphne want to help you?" Swifdon asked.

"She says as much."

"That sounds like Daphne." Swifdon nodded. "Is she still angry with you?"

"She wouldn't hear me out earlier when I tried to explain why I wouldn't grant the annulment right away. And she's worried that I may ruin her potential engagement to Fitzwell."

Swifdon shook his head. "Fitzwell seems like a decent enough chap and Daphne appears to have made up her mind about him."

Rafe inclined his head toward the earl. "I hate to point it out, but given the circumstances, such a marriage would hardly be legal."

Swifdon grinned at him. "Ha. You're right, Cavendish. And I obviously cannot allow her to become engaged knowing she is legally bound to you, but if I know Daphne, she'll marry Fitzwell one way or another. Regardless, I'm willing to allow her to accompany you and see to the annulment immediately after."

Rafe shifted on his feet. "But?"

"But what?"

Rafe coughed lightly into his hand. "With all due

respect, my lord, what are the conditions? I know your family well enough to know there are always conditions."

Swifdon laughed aloud at that. "And so there are."

Rafe smiled. "I thought so."

Swifdon leaned back in his chair and steepled his fingers in front of his face. "The first condition is that not a hair on her head is harmed."

Rafe bowed slightly. "Rest assured. I will protect her with my own life."

"I know you will, Cavendish. If I didn't believe that, I'd never allow her to go with you."

Rafe kept his eyes trained on his boots. "I am amazed at your faith in me, my lord. After what happened with—"

"Donald's death was not your fault, Cavendish. No one believes it was but you."

"I intend to avenge him, Swifdon."

The earl's gray eyes took on a hard sheen. "You're just the man for the job. And if you must know the truth, I'm doing this for Donald, and for Daphne. Donald saw fit to allow Daphne to go with you last time, I cannot but imagine he would agree to it a second time, especially when this time is for his own sake." The side of his mouth tucked up in a half-smile. "Besides, since the marriage has already taken place, we may as well get more use out of it."

"I'm glad you find this amusing, my lord. I had entered this room not knowing if you would welcome me or call me out."

Swifdon leaned forward, and braced his arms on the desk. "I'm not unfamiliar with this case. I spoke with a friend at the War Office. You have a good chance at tracking down the men the Russians work for if you can trade for the letters."

"Yes. They believe me to be a ship's captain. And

Daphne is my, er, cabin boy. I believe they'll trust me again. Daphne will be completely safe."

"I have no doubts."

"My lord?" Rafe shifted again.

"Yes?"

"What is the second condition?"

Swifdon folded his hands together. "I hope it goes without saying, but the second condition is that you keep your hands to yourself. Regardless of the law, as far as I'm concerned, your annulment is contingent on your marriage remaining unconsummated. If you so much as lay a finger on her, I'll kill you myself."

CHAPTER EIGHT

Rafe watched from afar as the guests arrived one by one. He'd been taking brandy and cigars in the study with Swifdon but a seat in a corner of the drawing room provided a better view of the proceedings.

One by one Pengree ushered in the guests. This small group would be staying overnight and attending the ball the next evening. Derek Hunt, Duke of Claringdon, and his wife, Lucy. Garrett Upton, the future Earl of Upbridge, and his new wife, Jane. Upton's mother, Mary. Viscount Berkeley, Sir Roderick Montague, Adam and Collin Hunt, the duke's brothers, and finally, Lord Edmund Fitzwell.

Rafe disliked the man on sight. He narrowed his gaze on him. Rafe *supposed* he was handsome enough, if one liked men with short-cropped blond hair and light blue eyes and a bit of an arrogant attitude that was off-putting to say the least.

Minutes after the baron had strolled into the room as if he owned the entire town house, Rafe stood and made his way over to meet the man. Daphne scurried in between the two and looked as if she might jump from her skin with fright when she introduced them.

"Lord Fitzwell, Captain Rafferty Cavendish." Her gaze darted back and forth between both of them as if she expected Rafe to blurt out their secret in front of the room at large.

Rafe was accustomed to quickly sizing up a situation, watching for small clues. People always gave away cues. For instance, Daphne was twisting her ring finger so vigorously Rafe wondered if it might come off. It smacked of guilt. He smiled to himself. Conversely, Lord Fitzwell had swallowed, his Adam's apple working, which belied his seeming ease in the rest of the company.

Lord Fitzwell bowed. No doubt the tightness of his obviously expensive custom-made buckskin breeches made raising his back a bit difficult. But Rafe stuck out a hand the man was forced to take. The baron's clasp was firm. But his hand was smooth. Clearly the lord had never worked a day in his life. No doubt the most danger he'd ever encountered was seating himself in his carriage.

"Captain Cavendish," Fitzwell drawled, flashing a white-toothed grin at Daphne that made Rafe want to punch him in the gut. "How exactly are you acquainted with the Swift family?" The implication was clear. What was a mere army captain doing rubbing elbows with the *haute ton*?

Rafe arched a brow at Daphne.

Daphne's nostrils flared and she jerked her head in a shake. Rafe had been so preoccupied by Lord Fitzwell, he hadn't taken a good look at Daphne since she'd entered the room. Why was she wearing a marmish fichu? It gave the effect that she was being swallowed by a lace monstrosity.

Rafe forced his attention away from Daphne's insane fichu and back to the baron. "I'm a longtime friend of the Swifts," Rafe answered, squeezing his hand too hard. He let go but didn't fail to notice that Fitzwell flexed and rubbed his palm. Rafe grinned at him.

"Claringdon and I both served with Cavendish in the army, you know, Fitzwell," Swifdon offered. But Rafe couldn't help but think, of course he didn't know. Men like Fitzwell didn't know anything about the harsh realities of war. They preferred to read about it over snuff and lace cuffs in their gentlemen's clubs. They would never deign to get their soft hands mussed with blood and dirt on the battlefields.

"Well done." Fitzwell gave Rafe a throwaway smile before returning his attention to Daphne, or more precisely, her brother. "It's good to see you again Lord Swifdon." He glanced over Swifdon's shoulder. "I'd not realized the Duke of Claringdon would be here."

Swifdon turned to include the duke in the conversation while Rafe eyed the baron carefully. He blinked rapidly. Fitzwell was a liar and not a particularly adept one. Everyone knew Swifdon and Claringdon were thick as thieves, their wives close friends. Of course Claringdon would be at a party hosted by Swifdon. Claringdon turned toward them. Fitzwell leaned closer to the duke and opened his mouth to speak.

"Have . . . have you met his grace?" Daphne rushed to ask. She looked flustered. Her pale skin was turning a bit pink underneath her fichu. Rafe had never seen Daphne flustered. It was disarming to be sure. He watched her from behind his brandy glass with ill-concealed amusement.

"I have not." The baron's smile widened. The man had far too many teeth. He immediately bowed to Claringdon.

There was something irritating about that bow. A bit too practiced. A bit too obsequious.

Claringdon inclined his head.

"His grace, the Duke of Claringdon, please meet Lord Edmund Fitzwell," Daphne said.

"My pleasure, your grace." Fitzwell clicked his heels together and bowed again. There was something irritating about that, too.

"Nice to meet you," Claringdon said, eyeing the shorter man carefully.

Lucy, Claringdon's wife, was introduced next and the baron acted as if he'd never been in the presence of a duchess before. It was "your grace" this and "your grace" that.

"Makes one want to start a drinking game, don't it?"

Rafe turned to see Sir Roderick Montague at his elbow. Sir Roderick was a confirmed bachelor who was more interested in his clothing and carriages than ladies. He had an eye for detail, fashion, and a famous biting wit. He'd been a close friend of the Swifts for years and he and Daphne often attended many of London's amusements together with other friends.

"Eh?" Rafe turned to the knight.

"Let's take a drink every time Fitzwell here says 'your grace,'" Sir Roderick offered.

Rafe was forced to turn his head to hide his laugh. "I expect we'd both be beneath the table in a trice," he whispered back.

"You're probably right. The cut of his coat is fine, though, I'll give him that. Looks a bit like you, Cavendish." Sir Roderick sniffed before blending back into another group of guests.

Rafe eyed Lord Fitzwell again. That pompous oaf didn't look like him . . . did he? Rafe narrowed his eyes.

Regardless, Fitzwell was being far too effusive about telling Lucy Hunt how beautiful she was. Perhaps Rafe took these things for granted. He'd known Claringdon and Swifdon for years through the military. They didn't intimidate him. Quite the opposite, actually; he forgave both men their social status because of their connections to the military. Fitzwell, however, had no such connection.

"Tell me, your grace. How did you get such unusually colored eyes?" Lord Fitzwell asked Lucy.

Lucy, who had one blue eye and one hazel, turned to look directly at the baron. "Why, I ordered them from a shop, of course," she answered simply, with a completely straight face.

Lord Fitzwell blinked at her as if he had absolutely no idea what she was talking about.

"Oh, that is too much fun," Rafe heard Sir Roderick say under his breath.

Rafe scanned the baron from head to toe. His hair was too slick. His cravat too neat. His coat too lint-free. His boots too polished. His nose too straight. His eyes too blue. No. There was not much to like about Lord Fitzwell. Not much at all.

The duke and duchess soon extracted themselves from the baron's company, and Rafe watched as Fitzwell made his way around the room, ingratiating himself with the other guests. First Swifdon, and then each man of the next successive rank. He completely ignored the Hunt brothers, mere misters, and of course he didn't bother saying another word to Rafe.

Rafe returned to his seat in the corner. Being ignored by that pompous jackass didn't bother him. Rafe had dealt with people like Fitzwell his entire life. People who believed the measure of a man was taken by his title and lineage and little else. Rafe turned the brandy in his glass and stared into its amber depths. He'd long ago given up caring about the doings of the nobility. He wasn't a part of it and he never would be. He concentrated on his job. And at the moment, his job had brought him to Mayfair to the elegant party of the Earl of Swifdon. It was true he respected Swifdon and Claringdon, and Donald had been a fine fellow. But they were clearly the exceptions to the rule. Rafe wouldn't even be here tonight if it weren't for his needing Daphne. He took a deep breath. Daphne. The lady might be diminutive but she certainly knew what she wanted and how to get it. And apparently, at the moment, she wanted Lord Fitzwell. She remained at his side laughing at his jests and generally peeping up at him with those wide gray eyes above that questionable fichu.

Rafe let his gaze rake over the baron one last time. Fitzwell walked with a self-satisfied swagger, and after he was done greeting those whom he obviously felt were worth his attention, he posted himself to the right of the duke's elbow and proceeded to comment on every word out of Claringdon's mouth.

Rafe's eyes narrowed on Fitzwell. Everyone had a tell. If you looked long enough, you'd see it. Told you a great deal about a man. Yes, everyone had a tell. And he'd just witnessed Lord Fitzwell's. Rank and status were his gods.

The drawing room door opened just then and a heavy-set older woman wearing a purple turban came strolling slowly into the room thumping a well-worn cane in front of her.

"Aunt Willie!" Daphne exclaimed, turning and rushing toward the lady.

"Daphne, my dear, you look as fresh as a daisy." The woman took a moment to pull a quizzing glass from her ample bosom. "Is that the fichu I made for you last winter, dear? It looks just right on you."

Rafe struggled to keep a smile off his lips. Ah, that was why Daphne was wearing that thing.

Daphne's mother, the dowager countess, hurried over to greet her older sister as well, and the three of them returned to the group standing in the middle of the room. Daphne helped her aunt sit in a large chair that faced all the occupants. "This is my aunt, Lady Wilhelmina Harrington," Daphne announced to the room at large.

"And who is your rumored bridegroom, Daphne?" Aunt Willie asked, gazing about the room, her quizzing glass pinned to her cloudy grayish-blue eye.

Daphne winced. "Oh, Aunt, I—"

Aunt Willie pointed her quizzing glass directly at Rafe. "Because I certainly hope he's that delectable young man right there."

CHAPTER NINE

"*Bonsoir, Capitaine* Cavendish."

Rafe was standing near the door of the drawing room, waiting while the other guests gathered before they all went into dinner together. He glanced over to see a young girl dressed in some sort of pink concoction of tulle and satin that looked like something a carnival performer would wear on stage. She was busily batting her eyelashes at him and spoke with a decided French accent. He looked twice.

"Good evening, Miss . . . ?"

"Mademoiselle Montebanque. Mademoiselle Delilah Montebanque." The French accent did not dissipate. No doubt the name was actually a solid English Montbank, but the way the girl pronounced it, Rafe was certain she'd added a few unnecessary letters. "Do forgive me, I know we should not speak as we have not been formally introduced."

Rafe bowed over the hand she delicately offered. "I'm

happy to correct that error now, Miss Montbank. A pleasure to make your acquaintance."

"I simply *j'adore* parties, do not you? Although I am
not yet allowed to attend them. At present I am avoiding
my governess, who is no doubt desperately searching for
me." She plucked at the large pink bow that sat on the top
of her head.

Rafe couldn't help but smile. Her beginner's French was
charming and he admired the girl's pluck. "Forgive me for
being rude, but are you related to the Swifts?"

"Oh, *mon Dieu. Je suis désolée.* How remiss of me
not to explain. I am Lord Swifdon's cousin. My mother's
sister is his mother's sister. *Comprenez-vous*?"

"I think so," Rafe answered. "How did you know my
name?

"Oh, how could I not know your name, *Capitaine*?" the
girl answered vaguely. Her dark eyes grew wide. *"Vous ne
parlez pas français?"*

Rafe coughed lightly into his hand. "I speak it, Miss
Montbank. I merely don't prefer it to my native tongue. I
spent a bit of time in France, as you may know, and none
of it was pleasant."

"I'm so sorry, *Capitaine*." Miss Montbank's face fell.
She immediately began speaking in English again. "I did
forget. Please forgive me. *J'adore* my French studies but
I must remember that not everyone is as fond of the place
as I am."

"No apology necessary. Your French is quite good, by
the way. Have you been there?"

She beamed at him. "No, I have not. But I do so hope
to rectify that as soon as possible."

Rafe looked twice again. Had the girl just winked at
him? He glanced around the room. No one else seemed to

take notice of them. Daphne hadn't arrived yet and Lord Fitzwell was busy dividing his time between the duke and the earl. Poor chap's head just might swivel off given the amount of times he had to turn it to give them equal attention. Rafe turned back to his young companion.

"You know there is to be a dance here tomorrow night, *Capitaine*?" she asked, spinning around in what Rafe could only guess was some sort of pirouette.

"Yes. So I've heard," he answered, wishing his hostess would call them in to dinner where there would no doubt be wine. Lots of wine.

"I wish I was old enough for you to ask *me* to dance, *Capitaine*," Miss Montbank continued. "And then you could ask me to stroll with you in the gardens and I would slap your arm with my fan and say no, but then I might very well meet you there later."

Rafe nearly choked. He pounded his chest with his fist. He had to smile. The girl's honesty was downright refreshing if a bit overwhelming and slightly alarming. This was Daphne's cousin? "How old are you, Miss Montbank?"

"Alas, I am twelve and am not yet in possession of a fan. Though I ask for one every Christmas. Aunt Willie prefers to give fichus that are often quite hideous."

"I think I have seen her handiwork," Rafe mumbled. To Miss Montbank, he said, "Even if you were old enough to dance with me, there is no music at present."

The girl twirled again and then performed a perfect curtsy. "Oh, I wouldn't let that stop me. I hear music in my head most of the time."

Rafe smiled again. Daphne's young cousin was a peculiar little thing. "Are you enjoying yourself so far then, Miss Montbank?"

"The truth is it's unpleasant to be forced to elude my

governess so often." She smiled up at him. "But I had to meet you, *Capitaine*. I must ask you, why did you give Cousin Daphne a little ship?"

For the second time since he'd begun speaking with Delilah, Rafe nearly choked. "I, erm . . . She showed it to you?"

"*Oui*. She asked me to open the box, actually. She didn't tell me why you sent her a ship, though. She only said that being an adult is complicated."

Rafe nodded. "That's true."

"But why a ship?"

Rafe rubbed his chin. "I thought she would like it."

"I think there's something you're not telling me, *Capitaine*." Delilah sighed. "But I'm used to it. No one ever wants to tell a child very much. Daphne says there's a mystery here."

Rafe lifted both brows. "She said that?"

"*Oui*. I tried to guess why she refused to tell me why you would send her a gift and I declared it a mystery. She agreed. Well, at least she didn't disagree with me. *Comprenez-vous*?"

"I do, indeed."

"I don't mind, however," Delilah said, pointing her small nose in the air. "I've grown quite adept at finding out things that adults don't want me to know."

"I don't doubt it." Rafe grinned at her. "Now, may I ask you a question, Miss Montbank?"

"I should be delighted." She curtsied again.

Rafe scanned the room and found the baron still hanging on the duke's every word. "What do you think of Lord Fitzwell?"

Delilah's face crumpled into a scowl. "I don't think much of him. Not at all."

"You don't?"

"No."

"Why's that?"

"It's difficult to put it into words precisely, but I just feel as if the man never had a day's fun in his whole life. *Comprenez-vous, Capitaine?*" Delilah blushed beautifully. The pink in her cheeks matched the pink of her tulle skirt.

Rafe couldn't help his answering grin. "I do indeed know exactly what you mean, Miss Montbank."

"And it's unfortunate that Cousin Daphne seems to be enamored of him. Aunt Wilhelmina and I are quite agog at it."

Rafe lifted his brows. "Aunt Wilhelmina doesn't approve, either?"

"It's not that she doesn't approve, exactly. Lord Fitzwell is quite eligible, after all. It's just that he's not particularly . . ."

Rafe leaned forward. "Yes?"

Delilah glanced around the room. "This is our secret, is it not?"

"Of course." Rafe crossed his finger over his heart and leaned down to better hear her.

Delilah smiled at him. "He's not particularly dashing?"

Rafe leaned back against the door beam and crossed his arms over his chest. He stared across the room to where Lord Fitzwell was conversing with Daphne, who'd just made her appearance in a gown of sunny yellow. Daphne looked positively bored. "Dashing," Rafe answered. "What do you mean?"

Delilah giggled. "It's funny you should ask that, *Capitaine,* as I find that you are the most dashing gentleman in the room."

Rafe pointed at himself. "Me?"

"Of course. You are always off on an adventure, are you not? You see? Dashing."

Rafe blinked. He'd certainly never thought of himself that way but he couldn't help but smile at the girl's description.

"Cousin Daphne is quite dashing as well. She's so game and full of life. Why, she's always willing to play hide-and-seek with me and go for long rides in the country and race and run and laugh. While Lord Fitzwell is decidedly *un*-dashing. He's always asking who someone is related to. Or pointing out who he is related to. It's ever so dull. I simply cannot imagine Cousin Daphne living with that stuffy Lord Fitzwell."

Rafe rubbed a hand across his chin. "Neither can I."

Delilah sighed again. "I've been quite beside myself thinking of ways to stop the party."

Rafe nearly laughed aloud at that. "What do you mean?"

"Oh, you know. I might come down with a convenient case of plague or the like."

Rafe shook his head. "That doesn't sound particularly convenient to me. And it seems difficult to manage, given your circumstances."

"I agree," Delilah answered with a resolute if unhappy nod. "Plague is far too dramatic. I continue to think upon it. The trick, of course, would be to get sick enough to send everyone home but not so sick that I cannot recover."

"I see." Rafe continued to smother his laugh. "And how exactly would you contract such an illness?"

"It's not easy, obviously, or I would have done it by now. I am quite at my wit's end. I've decided it may be more prudent to pretend I am ill than to actually *be* ill. I was in the library earlier reading about cholera and scurvy."

"I doubt very much you could claim a case of scurvy."

"You're quite right. I've eaten at least three oranges today and Cousin Daphne's seen me with two of them. Cholera seems an unpleasant business altogether and anything involving pox requires far too much work with a rouge pot."

Rafe had to press his lips together hard to keep from laughing at the earnest young lady. "I beg your pardon."

Delilah fluttered a hand in the air. "I'd settled on a megrim but I somehow doubt that would stop the party. I believe they would merely send me to bed and all that would accomplish is my not being here to keep Lord Fitzwell from proposing to Daphne."

Rafe nodded sagely. "It does seem as if you're in quite the bind."

"Oh, don't worry, *Capitaine*. I have a trick up my sleeve. *Sacrebleu*, there's my governess. I must go." Delilah winked at him for certain this time and scurried from the room, just before the dowager countess announced that they would all go for dinner.

CHAPTER TEN

"Lady Daphne, may I escort you for a walk about the room?"

Daphne breathed a sigh of relief. She turned to see Lord Fitzwell holding out his arm clad in a fine dark blue velvet jacket. Dinner earlier had been lovely. The men had had their drinks in the dining room and now all of the guests were together again, milling about the large drawing room.

"I would be honored, my lord," she replied, stepping closer to him and sliding her gloved hand over his sleeve.

Lord Fitzwell led her toward the far end of the room. On the way, she endeavored to sniff at his jacket. Just a short sniff. Nothing too obvious. But her nose couldn't seem to detect a scent. Every time she was in that rogue Rafe Cavendish's presence, she smelled his alluring combination of soap and leather and pine and whatever else he smelled of that made her senses reel, blast him. But trying to find a scent on Lord Fitzwell was a lesson in frustration. It seemed she'd have to get even closer and that seemed unlikely. Why, she couldn't exactly stick her nose up to his collar and sniff. That would be entirely unseemly and most likely unwelcome and probably wholly impossible to explain. A bad combination to be sure.

She decided to give up for the time being and attempted to enjoy their stroll around the room, even though Lord Fitzwell hadn't yet said a word. Hmm. Things had got off to a bit of a precarious start this afternoon, what with Rafe skulking about and staring at her constantly. Didn't he know how difficult it was for one's future bridegroom to court a lady when one's husband was glaring down one's neck the entire time? The frustrating man. But now, at least she'd had dinner seated next to Lord Fitzwell, and even though the conversation had lagged a bit, she was quite encouraged by the fact that he'd asked her to take a turn about the room. Today, a turn about the room. Tomorrow, hopefully, a proposal.

And she was hopeful, wasn't she? Lord Fitzwell was handsome, he was well mannered, eligible, titled, and he ran in the right sorts of circles. He was not known to have any scandal attached to his name. He was not a drinker. Most importantly, according to all of the sources she was able to consult, he was loyal. Loyal with no hint of being a rake. None whatsoever. That had been exceedingly important to Daphne. Yes, all in all, he was exactly the sort of man she should *want* to marry. Mama agreed. Julian seemed to approve. Lord Fitzwell was steadfast and sure, not the sort of man who would be, say, gallivanting across the Continent putting his life in danger at a moment's notice. She was done with that sort of adventure, and with her childish attraction to that sort of an adventurer. So why couldn't she muster enthusiasm when it came to the thought of an engagement to Lord Fitzwell?

The baron inclined his head toward Rafe who stood near the far wall talking to Aunt Willie. "Your aunt seems to be particularly taken with Captain Cavendish."

Daphne turned her head to look. It was true. Aunt Willie appeared to be happily chatting with the rogue. Leave it to the old matron to be sidling up to the wrong gentleman. Had Aunt Willie's eyesight begun to fail her? Couldn't she see her niece over here with Lord Fitzwell? At any rate, her hearing seemed to be fine and she'd certainly heard that Rafe was an army captain and Lord Fitzwell, a baron. Daphne had nearly gasped when Aunt Willie had pointed out the wrong man in the drawing room earlier. It was so like Aunt Willie to say the wrong thing, loudly. Daphne hadn't had a chance to correct the older woman. She'd have to do so later.

"I can't imagine why," Daphne mumbled, turning her attention back to Lord Fitzwell.

"What's that?" Lord Fitzwell asked, stooping a bit to better hear her.

"Oh, nothing." Daphne turned up her face and gave Lord Fitzwell a bright smile. Enough talking about Rafe Cavendish. He'd come here today and insulted her, extorted her, threatened her, and finally got her to agree to his imperious commands. He'd also apparently talked Julian into going along with his scheme, but there was nothing at all in their agreement that said that she must pretend to like him. Or even had to be friendly with him. In fact, she would simply ignore him. Much more effective than arguing with him.

Daphne tipped back her head to glance up at the baron.

He might have been a bit stiff and he had the tendency to stare above her head, but perhaps he was only concentrating on walking and she was not tall, after all. Regardless, she needed to begin a decent conversation.

"Are you enjoying yourself, my lord?"

"Why, yes. I am. I had no idea his grace would be here, nor the future Earl of Upton. This is quite a party."

Daphne frowned. What if it had only been her, her brother and sister-in-law, and her mother? Were they enough to impress Lord Fitzwell? Oh, what did it matter? He was as close to perfect as she was going to get. He met all of her standards. And everyone in this town cared about rank and social status. Well, everyone, except . . . Rafe. Rafe didn't seem to care a fig about social standing. In fact, he seemed to consider it a detriment.

No! No more thinking about Rafe.

Lord Fitzwell turned just then and Daphne realized he'd been tapped on the shoulder. She swiveled to see Rafe standing behind them, his irascible grin on his face.

"Yes?" Lord Fitzwell said, obviously confused.

"May I?" Rafe asked.

"May you what?" Daphne glared at him.

"May I cut in?" Rafe asked.

Daphne clutched at Lord Fitzwell's arm. "We're not dancing, Captain Cavendish. We're merely taking a turn about the room. There is no precedent for cutting in on such a pastime."

"I'm willing to be the first." Rafe's grin didn't falter. He blinked at Lord Fitzwell, clearly awaiting the man's answer.

"Well, I—I never—" Lord Fitzwell glanced at Daphne.

"There's a first time for everything, my lord," Rafe said. "I expect you'll make a full recovery." He didn't wait for an official *yes*, just smoothly slid into place next to Daphne and pulled her hand onto his arm. They were off before Daphne had a chance to say a word, leaving Lord Fitzwell standing there with his mouth open.

They'd barely got to the opposite side of the room when Daphne turned her head sharply toward Rafe. "Are you proud of yourself?" she asked, resisting the urge to grind her short heel into his instep.

"A bit." Rafe's grin was unrepentantly wicked.

"Why would you do that?"

"What? Were you having such a good time with Lord Fitzbore?"

She clenched her teeth. "You know perfectly well his name is not Fitzbore."

Rafe didn't miss a step. "It might as well be. He didn't even look at you the entire time you were speaking. He can't have been good company."

Daphne clamped her mouth shut. Rafe's point hit home, but even more annoying, he was looking straight at her, despite his being head and shoulders taller than she.

"What do you know about it?" she shot back.

There went that arched brow. "Quite a lot, actually. I've been told I'm charming."

"Really? Who has told you you're charming?"

"Your aunt and your cousin for two and that's just within the last few hours."

"Aunt Willie and Delilah told you that?"

"Among other things."

"Like what?"

"Like Delilah told me she's considering faking a case of the plague to keep you from engaging yourself to Lord Fitzbore and your aunt informs me that I'm one of the best-looking young gentlemen she's ever seen."

Her mouth open, Daphne stopped walking and put a hand on her hip. "Aunt Willie said *that*?"

"Most assuredly. Would you like me to call her over and ask her to repeat her words to you?"

Daphne turned away from him and continued walking again. "Oh, shut up."

"I must admit, I'm a bit worried for my virtue around her. She mentioned that she'd like to pinch me."

"I find it exceedingly difficult to believe you're worried for your virtue given the fact that you're one of the biggest rakes in the land."

Rafe looked a bit chagrined. "Who told you that, Grey?"

"Stop calling me Grey." She glanced around. "And no one had to tell me, or are you forgetting the blond woman I found in your bed?"

Rafe scowled. "Now, listen—"

"No. I'm decidedly *not* listening to you any longer," Daphne replied with her nose in the air.

"Very well. Tell me, what did Fitzbore say that was so stimulating?"

"I never said it was stimulating. I—" She coolly lifted her chin. "Didn't I tell you to shut up?"

"But how can I be charming if I shut up?"

She covered her unwanted smile with a gloved hand. "There's hardly a need to be charming with me."

Rafe smirked. "That's right. You've already rejected me."

Daphne stopped abruptly. "I never—"

"Didn't you?" He leaned down to whisper in her ear. "Aren't you the one who is so hell-bent on an annulment?"

Daphne's heart lurched in her chest. She jerked her head from side to side and glanced about to ensure they would not be overheard. "I refuse to have this conversation with you here." She continued to walk again, mindful of the few sets of eyes that had turned their attention to the two of them.

"Come with me to the library then," he challenged, still whispering and staring into her eyes.

Daphne concentrated on putting one foot in front of the other. Her heart rose and fell in her chest. He wanted to meet her in the library? She was frightened, she realized. Anxious. But why?

"Fine," she answered through clenched teeth.

Rafe didn't wait for another word. He tugged her wrist and pulled her along behind him through the drawing room doors and into the corridor. Once they were alone, she ripped her hand from his grasp and spun away from him. "I cannot believe you did that. I thought you meant that we should meet there later. The entire room must have seen us leave together."

"I'm certain they did. Your aunt is probably smiling right now. But the damage is already done so you might as well come with me." He turned on his heel and strode off down the corridor toward the library, leaving Daphne no choice but to pick up her yellow taffeta skirts and follow him.

By the time Rafe pushed open the door to the library and strode inside, she was a bit winded keeping up with him. Her hands hadn't yet stopped shaking, either. What else could he possibly have to say to her? He'd already made clear his demands and the fact that he had no intention of leaving the party.

He strode into the middle of the room and then turned and crossed his arms over his chest, glaring down the length of his nose at her.

"Well?" she said, trying to calm the rapid beating of her heart.

"Well?" he echoed.

She clasped the back of the settee with both hands. "What did you want to say to me?"

"You said you refused to continue our conversation in the ballroom. I thought perhaps we should go somewhere more private."

"We don't *have* to have any conversation."

"I say we do."

"What else is left to say?" She put a hand up to her forehead to swipe away a curl. Her reticule dangled crazily from her wrist.

"Quite a lot, actually."

She put her hand to her hip. "Really, that's amusing. I thought I said it all when I found that blond doxy in your bed."

"Damn it, Daphne. I told you a dozen times, she wasn't—"

"She wasn't what? Blond? A doxy? In your bed? Which one of those things isn't true?"

Rafe gritted his teeth. "Individually, they are all true, but—"

"I don't want to hear any more of your excuses."

"Fine. At least I'm not attempting to engage myself to a bore."

Daphne gasped. "A bore! How dare you?"

"You heard me. The man is a bore. A social-climbing bore."

"He's not a bore."

Rafe pursed his lips. "But he is a social climber?"

Daphne tossed a hand in the air. "Some people in our Society find social status important."

"And some of us find it boring."

Daphne took a deep breath. "There's no need to argue. You have your blond. I have my baron."

"She's not my blond. I—"

Daphne raised her palm. "No. No. Please spare me. You were quite clear on the subject. We were married due to a business arrangement only. And our annulment will be yet another business arrangement. There's nothing more to say."

Rafe's eyes were flashing ice-blue fire when he stepped closer to her. "Perhaps, but what if there is more?"

She narrowed her eyes on him. "What do you mean? I told you I'd go with you on Sunday night."

"What if I tell you I want one more thing from you as part of the agreement?"

Daphne turned away and stared hard, yet unseeing, at the vast wall of books in front of her. Why was he making this so difficult for her? She knew she should have *insisted* he leave for the remainder of the party. She should have pleaded her case to Julian. She should have forced Rafe to leave. "What else? What else is there, Rafe? What else do you want?"

There was a pause. A pause in which she could hear and feel the beating of her own heart. A trickle of sweat ran down between her breasts.

Rafe's voice was low and clear. "A kiss."

CHAPTER ELEVEN

Rafe's eyes never left hers. He took a deep breath. He wasn't entirely certain why he'd said it, wasn't at all certain she wouldn't slap him for suggesting it, and was reasonably certain she was about to say no and stalk from the room.

There was something about her casual dismissal. The way she'd been talking with that fool Fitzwell, as if she gave a damn about him. Did a title matter so much to her? He'd tried to explain the blond in the bed more times than he wanted to remember. Daphne had refused to believe any of it, but in the end, it hadn't been the point. Daphne wasn't for him. She wasn't for him a year ago and she wasn't for him now. She was so far above him he couldn't even see her. But even had they been of the same social class, she was young, she was innocent, she was interested in settling down to a nice income and children and a Mayfair town house. That would never be for Rafe. Rafe couldn't come home each night from a useless gentleman's club. He couldn't even stay in London longer than a week or two,

let alone England. Daphne couldn't live a life where she
was constantly in upheaval, following him around from
mission to mission. He might be ordered to stay home for
the time being due to his injuries, which was driving him
slowly mad, but he'd healed and would soon be completely
reinstated and then be gone. That was who he was. The
mission starting Sunday night would be his first time back
on duty since he'd been hurt. Daphne Swift, sweet, beautiful, innocent Daphne Swift, did not belong there with
him. After she completed her part of the mission, she belonged safely back in this town house with her mother and
her aunt and her fichu and her funny little cousin. Not on
a ship to France to track down murderers. That was where
Rafe was going.

So why had he been so jealous—yes, jealous, damn it—
when he'd seen her walking in the drawing room with
Fitzbore? And why had Rafe asked her for a kiss? Blast it.
He didn't know why.

"A kiss?" she whispered a bit brokenly.

"Yes." His heart thumped in his chest.

"Why would you want a kiss from me?"

"I want to have it to remember you by."

Daphne turned slowly, and while he expected he might
see tears shimmering in her eyes or anger glowing there,
instead he saw a look he could only describe as . . . determined.

"And if I kiss you, what will you give me in return? Will
you leave?"

"Yes."

Her eyebrow arched at that bit of news. "Fine." She
stalked over to him, arms still crossed over her chest.
"Let's get this over with." She stopped a foot in front of
him, puckered her lips, and squeezed shut her eyes.

Rafe chuckled at her. He moved backward toward the settee and took a seat, spreading his legs wide and opening his arms across the back of the thing.

Daphne opened her bright gray eyes and glared at him. "What are you doing?" Her mouth was open, her eyes rounded.

"I'm not about to make this easy for you."

She scowled at him, her arms still tightly crossed over her chest. "What is that supposed to mean?"

"It means that you have to kiss me. A real kiss. A *memorable* one."

The look she shot him could have melted armor.

Daphne swallowed and walked in a tight line, pacing first away toward the door and then back to where she'd previously stood. She removed her gloves and poked them into her reticule. Then she tugged at her third finger, flicking the nail back and forth, then pausing to nibble at it.

Rafe was playing a game and she didn't understand the rules. She closed her eyes at the memory of the last time she'd tried to kiss him. Tried and failed. Didn't he remember that? Or had it just been another casual interlude with a female that was relegated to the back of his memory? Oh, God. The worst part was that it was *better* if he didn't remember it. Better for her at least. She'd be spared the humiliation of him reminding her that he'd rejected her.

And if he tried to lie to her about that confounded blond harlot one more time, Daphne wouldn't be responsible for her actions!

She supposed it didn't really matter whether she kissed him or not. As long as no one found out and as long as she got what she wanted. At present what she wanted was for

Rafe to leave this party and not come back until she was happily and officially engaged.

She opened her eyes again and met his gaze. He looked almost boyish in the softness of the candlelight. He was as handsome as she'd ever seen him and she couldn't lie to herself and say that it wasn't tempting to . . .

Kiss him. Kiss him. Kiss him? She took a deep breath. She wanted to go. She wanted to stay. She wanted to . . . kiss him.

She let the air settle silently in her tight lungs, but her mind had sprinted two steps ahead. She was going to kiss him.

CHAPTER TWELVE

A memorable kiss. Daphne straightened her shoulders. Very well. She could do this. The man was half lounging against the settee, his arm tossed casually across the back, his knees spread apart, his booted feet planted on the rug in front of him. He was watching her with a mixture of amusement and wariness. He looked as if he half expected her to bolt at any moment. What could he be about by asking her to kiss him?

It finally struck her. He didn't want her to kiss him. He merely wanted to call her bluff. But he was going to be quite surprised. She wasn't about to back down from this challenge, however harrowing it may be.

And there was another part of her, a part that had a thrill shooting through it right now. She'd imagined kissing this man a hundred different ways over the last year. Had lain in her bed fevered by the thought. And now, now, she was getting the chance. It didn't change the fact that he didn't care a fig for her and they were going to get an annulment.

But it severely tempted her to have at least one of her old dreams come true.

"Scared?" he taunted.

"Never." She lifted her chin.

"I thought you were too perfect and pure to do anything half as scandalous as kissing one man during your would-be engagement party to another."

"Is that why you're testing me?"

He shrugged a shoulder. "Perhaps. Partly."

She clamped her hand into a fist, itching to slap his handsome face with it. "Would someone so pristine and pure have paraded around as a cabin boy for a fortnight?"

"Ah, but you yourself told me that you've changed. You're no longer that adventurous young lady. Or do I have it wrong?"

A memorable kiss?

She'd make it memorable all right.

Closing her eyes until they were half hooded, she invoked the most sensual pose she could muster and sauntered toward him with swinging hips. She stared him straight in the eye, completely unwilling to let him see a moment's hesitation. The man had made a grievous mistake asking her if she was scared. She was a Swift. Swifts didn't back down from challenges. Swifts stood their ground.

The look in Rafe's blue eyes turned from amusement to surprise in a matter of seconds as she advanced on him. She wasn't about to demurely lean down and peck him on the lips. No. She was going to make this *memorable*. The fact that she'd neither been kissed nor kissed anyone before was hardly the point. She'd heard enough in snippets of conversations from the married ladies through the years to have a general, if vague, idea of how one should go about it. Once she'd accidentally interrupted one of the footmen kissing one of the housemaids in the kitchens. She hadn't told a soul, but it had certainly been an informative experience for her. They'd had their mouths open! So Daphne wasn't completely uneducated. The rest she would just make up as she went. It couldn't possibly be that difficult.

She made her way to the edge of the settee, then stopped. Hmm. Where should she sit? How would they go about this? She decided to truly shock him by sitting on her side directly next to him, facing toward him, her legs out to the right. She positioned her skirts to make it work and sidled up next to him.

Rafe arched both brows. Then she lifted up on both knees and placed her hands on either side of his shoulders. Her fingers trembled and she silently cursed herself for it. She pressed her fingertips into his shoulders to keep them from trembling. Oh, but touching him had been a mistake. The man's shoulders were pure muscle. Strong, and square, and . . . The scent of him so near made her mouth water. Perhaps that was why open mouths were involved in some forms of kissing.

He'd crossed his arms over his chest and regarded her with a bit of nonchalance. She mentally vowed to wipe that look from his handsome face.

He'd not make this easy for her, indeed. Well, she wouldn't make it easy for him.

Rising up higher on her knees, she towered above him. He lifted his chin to meet her eyes but his arms remained tight across his chest.

She slowly lowered herself, hooding her eyes more and more as she got closer to his mouth. And what a mouth it was. His lips were firm, but perfectly shaped. They were closed, but puckered slightly at the corners. As she moved closer, she heard the sharp intake of his breath. That was it. The one moment. The only moment she knew that she'd got to him, affected him.

Her mouth hovered a scant inch above his. "Memorable, you say?"

"If you can manage it." Blast. His voice had been strong, sure, slightly mocking.

"Oh, I can manage," she breathed, just before her lips met his.

His lips were warm and dry. But his mouth wasn't open. Nothing happened. No great passion. No insane lust like what she'd seen between the footman and the maid. She pulled back and stared at Rafe quizzically. He shrugged.

She nearly laughed aloud. All these months she'd fancied herself in love with him. Thought she wanted him. But there was no passion between them at all. None. That kiss was going to be memorable all right. Memorable for being *bad*.

"Is that the best you can do?" he mocked.

Daphne frowned at him. How dare he? Clearly, the man didn't understand that there were no inherent sparks between them. How did he expect her to make up for that? But the competitive side of her nature whispered in her ear and she scrunched up her nose. "No," she replied, merely to be contrary.

She might as well humor the poor man and give him one more sad little kiss just to say she tried.

She leaned back down and pressed her lips to his again. There was a bit of friction this time, a pop, a spark. Her eyes widened in surprise and she wrapped an arm around his neck to steady herself.

The moment she did, Rafe's mouth opened and slanted across hers. His hot, wet tongue plunged inside of her mouth and she whimpered. He growled. His lips were no longer warm and dry. They owned her. With another growl, he shifted her body in his lap with ease and she was lying across his thighs, her arms clutching his strong neck.

His hands moved up into her hair and loosened the pins holding up her chignon. His fingers rubbed along the back of her neck. Gooseflesh popped up along her bare arms.

What was that about there being no passion? Rubbish.

He kissed her eyelids, her cheeks, her temple, and when his hot tongue traced the seashell of her ear, Daphne's entire body bucked. One of his hands went to her hip to steady her. It burned through her skirts, scorching her. She suddenly had the urge to flip up her skirts and let his hands move along her thighs, up, up, until—

No. This was only supposed to be a kiss. But she couldn't think with him touching her like this.

His mouth was back on hers. Her fingers threaded through the short hair along the back of his neck. She was clutching his muscled shoulders for dear life. Afraid that if she let go, she'd fall, or cease to exist. It was like there was only him in the universe and nothing else mattered.

His teeth tugged at her bottom lip and she moaned. His mouth slanted over hers again. Again. Fiery hot slashes of lust roiled through her entire body, pooled at a spot between her legs where she desperately wanted his hand.

"Rafe, I—"

But her thought was forever lost to the sound of the door opening and someone's throat clearing.

CHAPTER THIRTEEN

Daphne snapped from her haze. Dear God. Who was it? She hastily pushed away from Rafe and slid onto the opposite corner of the settee. Rafe had apparently heard it, too. They both swung their guilty gazes toward the door to see Lucy Hunt standing there, her eyes politely averted.

Rafe stood, cleared his throat, and adjusted his breeches. "We're just . . . I'm—"

"Not to worry, Captain Cavendish. I didn't see a thing," Lucy said. "And had I seen a thing, rest assured that I most certainly would never repeat that news to a soul."

Rafe straightened to his full height. It seemed to Daphne that his shoulders bowed a bit in relief. Was he that pleased to know that the person who had caught them in a compromising position was someone who could be counted on to keep it to herself? Hrmph.

"I'll just get back to the ballroom. Good evening, Lady Daphne." Rafe bowed to Daphne, then to Lucy. "Your grace."

He strode past Lucy, who had a tiny smile on her face. "Good evening, Captain."

The door shut behind him and Lucy tilted her head to one side and arched a brow at Daphne.

Daphne's head was still reeling. How was it possible that something that had begun so, so, uninterestingly, had turned into *that*. The footman and the housemaid had seemed to be quite taken with each other, but even they couldn't have felt anything like *that*. Daphne was certain of it. If they had, there was no way they could have done so while standing. Even now her legs felt like water and she didn't dare stand. She could also barely look at Lucy.

Lucy whistled. "Well done."

Daphne put her hand to her forehead. What was wrong with her? She still felt too hot. Was it possible that she'd been struck by malaria? In London? She had been to the milliner's last week. And the fabric shop. Perhaps she'd caught malaria there. Yes. The fabric shop was the likely culprit.

"Well what?" She mustn't have heard the duchess correctly.

"I said well done. That man is gorgeous. Now, do you want to explain what *that* was about?" Lucy waved her hand toward the door.

"What?" Stalling was a tactic that had usually worked on her brothers.

Lucy moved closer to the settee. "You're beginning to echo, dear. Now out with it. Explain yourself."

"I don't think I can." Daphne winced.

Lucy stamped forward and slid onto the settee next to Daphne. "No you don't. You're going to cough up the details and now. And while you're at it, might I suggest you see about your hair."

Daphne's hand flew to her coiffure. The mess of pins had come loose.

"Here, lean forward. I'll help," Lucy offered.

Daphne nodded shakily. "Thank you, your grace."

"Now, none of that. I thought we established at Julian and Cass's wedding that you were to call me Lucy."

"Yes, Lucy. Though I must say it feels quite queer to have a duchess acting as my lady's maid."

"We must adapt to our circumstances, mustn't we? Now, stop trying to stall. I'm ever so familiar with that tactic. You're speaking to the lady who came up with the idea to hire a nonexistent chaperone for Jane Lowndes. In fact, I was explaining the concept to your cousin Delilah earlier. I like that girl. She reminds me of me when I was a child."

Daphne had to smile at that. "Very well, I'll explain. But promise me you won't tell Julian."

Lucy clucked her tongue. "Of course I won't tell Julian, but you're going to tell me. What exactly is going on between you and Captain Cavendish?"

Daphne expelled her breath. "I don't know."

"You don't know?"

"I haven't the faintest idea."

"You are still married to him, aren't you?"

Daphne groaned. Lucy and Derek had been there last spring when Daphne had announced to Julian and Cass that she was married to Rafe and she needed an annulment. At the time it had seemed logical to tell her brother and his friends all at once. Daphne knew for certain that Julian would tell Cass and Cass would tell Lucy and once Lucy knew, there was little hope of Jane Lowndes and Lucy's cousin Garrett Upton not finding out. The six of them were as thick as thieves, after all. And all of them could be trusted, but now Daphne wished she hadn't been quite so loose-lipped. "Yes." Daphne glanced around. "But please keep your voice down."

"No one is here." Lucy pushed a pin into Daphne's coiffure.

"Ouch." Daphne rubbed her head.

Lucy bit her lip. "I'm terribly sorry. I never claimed to be good at filling in as a lady's maid."

"Oh, Lucy. I have absolutely no idea what I'm doing."

Lucy stuck another pin back into Daphne's hair. "You might start by explaining how you came to be alone in here with Captain Cavendish and him kissing you."

"He wasn't kissing me. I was kissing him."

Lucy snorted. "It looked to me as if he was doing a fair amount of the kissing."

"He *asked* me to kiss him."

Lucy's fingers fell away from Daphne's head. "That's surprising."

Daphne slapped her hand to her forehead. "What am I going to do?"

Lucy reached over and squeezed Daphne's shoulder. "You just so happen to be sitting next to a person who is well versed in both awkward situations and surprising ones. Not to mention scandalous ones. Don't worry a bit. We'll figure it out. It's quite simple, really."

"How could it possibly be quite simple?"

"You merely have to ask yourself, what do you want?"

Daphne blinked. "What do I want?"

"Yes. What do you want?"

"I . . ." Daphne tugged at her third finger. "I don't know what I want."

"We always know what we want, dear. We usually just don't want to *know* that we know what we want."

Daphne furrowed her brow. "That's exceedingly confusing."

Lucy smiled at her and resumed her work on Daphne's chignon. "Allow me to present it another way. Do you want Captain Cavendish?"

"I want to kiss Captain Cavendish. Or at least I did while I was doing it. The whole thing has completely befuddled me."

"I don't blame you, dear. The man is positively delicious. And might I suggest you hire Mrs. Bunbury as your chaperone if you intend to go about kissing men who are not your betrothed at house parties."

Daphne shook her head. Mrs. Bunbury was Jane's fictitious chaperone, whom she'd used to fool her mother last spring when she'd attended Cass and Julian's wedding house party. "I have no intention of employing Mrs. Bunbury. I don't need her. It's not as if I could marry Rafe. He's completely unsuitable and—"

"I do believe you're forgetting that you're already married to him, dear."

Daphne sighed. "Yes, but we're not *married*, married. Not really. And Julian's already agreed to help me with the annulment as soon as we—"

"As soon as you what, dear?"

Daphne leaned her neck against the settee and blew out a long breath. "I'm so confused."

Lucy pushed another pin into place. "I know all about confusing kisses. Derek once punched a tree, climbed into my window, and kissed me. I had no idea what to do."

Daphne pressed a hand to her still-warm cheek. "What? That seems ever so much more complicated than my little kiss in the library tonight."

"It wasn't little, my dear. And I might further point out

that you kissed a man at your supposed engagement party. But you're missing the point. What about Lord Fitzwell? Do you want him?"

Daphne thought about it for a moment. "I can't say I've imagined kissing him. But I do want him to ask me to marry him. At least I think I do."

Lucy's hands fell away from Daphne's coiffure again and Lucy eyed her closely. "You're certain?"

"Yes."

"Entirely certain?"

"Yes."

"Well, then. Problem solved. Don't get yourself alone with Captain Cavendish again and don't kiss him again. Lord Fitzwell is sure to propose. He hasn't done so yet so there is absolutely no harm done. Think of it as a last moment of being unattached. And your hair is set to rights again, by the by."

For the first time since Lucy had entered the room, Daphne smiled. "Yes. Yes. That's just what I'll do. It meant nothing. It was completely harmless, really. Thank you, Lucy. Thank you!"

"It's my pleasure, dear."

Daphne tugged at her bottom lip. "I do think he only asked me to kiss him as a prank. It went too far, that is all. He didn't believe I had the courage to do it."

"I think he knows you well enough to know you have courage in spades, Daphne. But at any rate, clearer heads often prevail when one thinks things through rationally."

"Yes. I quite agree. The good news is that now that I've kissed him, he's agreed to leave."

"Really?" Lucy arched a dark brow over her blue eye.

Daphne nodded. "That's right."

"Well, then. It's all sorted." Lucy patted Daphne's hand again.

Sorted until Daphne was left alone with him on the *True Love* for a sennight. But that wasn't the point at the moment and she wasn't about to tell the Duchess of Claringdon about her scandalous mission. All of that could be sorted later. At the moment, Daphne was merely desperate for Rafe to leave so that she could progress with her engagement. It was true that she was normally not one to make plans or follow rules, but she had a plan at present, by God, and the man was disturbing it. Check one, get rid of pesky husband. Check two, ensure engagement to handsome, titled, eligible bachelor. Check three, help to exact revenge upon the men who killed Donald. Check four, secure annulment. Check five, return to Mayfair, marry said eligible bachelor, and live a long, happy life with a blue-eyed son and blond daughter. Both of whom would hopefully be considerably taller than their poor mother.

"Thank you, Lucy, for your help . . . and your discretion. I greatly appreciate it."

Lucy stood. "Don't mention it, dear." She glanced around. "Now, I came in here to fetch a book for Jane. She said she left it on the desk." She wandered over to the desk and picked up a tome. "Ah, here it is. *The Long History of Ancient Greece*. That's Jane for you. Always reading something that would surely put the rest of us to sleep immediately."

Daphne smiled at that. "I suppose I should be grateful that you found me instead of Jane."

"Don't be too certain about that. Before Jane and Garrett were married, they engaged in some antics in libraries that would make you blush."

And with that astonishing pronouncement, Lucy turned and sauntered from the room.

Daphne counted ten, stood, smoothed her skirts, patted the pins in her coiffure, then straightened her shoulders and made her way to the door. Surely the fact that she'd returned to the festivities so long after Rafe's reappearance would cause any suspicions about them leaving together to be overlooked.

She hoped.

The door closed behind Daphne and Delilah popped up from behind the settee and rested her chin on the back of the furniture. "Oh, this was all *très intéressant,*" she announced to the empty room. "Quite interesting, indeed."

CHAPTER FOURTEEN

The next morning, Daphne's maid had no sooner finished pulling up her hair and pinning it in a soft knot on the top of her head than Delilah came strolling into the room. Daphne had chosen a lavender gown with white ribbons at the top and silver cording along the hem. Delilah was wearing a pretty light green day dress with an emerald-green bow on the top of her head. The girl balanced a plate of teacakes in her dainty hand and wore an irrepressible smile on her face.

"*Bonjour,* Cousin Daphne."

"Good morning, Dee. Looks as if you've been downstairs already."

"Indeed I have. The breakfast display is particularly impressive. Though I must admit I had a bit of a tussle with Mrs. Upton to get these teacakes. They were the last on a platter. And *j'adore* teacakes."

Daphne turned in her seat to look at her cousin. "You *won* in a fight over teacakes with Jane?"

"I sniffed a little and allowed my upper lip to quiver. I believe she thought I intended to cry. No one likes to see a little girl cry."

Daphne shook her head, but couldn't suppress her smile. "You are an irrepressible scamp, Mademoiselle Montbank."

Still balancing the plate, Delilah took a bow. "Thank you. I consider that a great compliment. There is something much more interesting downstairs than the teacakes, however," Delilah added.

Daphne widened her eyes. "What's that?"

"*Capitaine* Cavendish."

The brush that had been in Daphne's hand clattered to the carpet. "Captain Cavendish is still here?"

"Yes," came Delilah's swift reply. She popped a bit of teacake into her mouth. "Isn't that interesting?"

Daphne dismissed her maid and quickly bent and retrieved the brush. There was something in her cousin's demeanor that told her she knew more than she was letting on. She eyed her cousin warily. "Delilah Montbank, what do you know?"

Daphne set her plate of cakes on the nearby writing desk and did a perfect pirouette in front of the looking glass. "Not much. Only that *Capitaine* Cavendish kissed you last night in the library and then her grace came in and—"

Daphne gasped. "You were hiding in the library, you little elf?"

Delilah sighed. "Hiding and wishing to Hades that I was you."

Daphne's mouth dropped open. "Delilah! I cannot believe you said that."

Delilah fell to her knees in front of the stool upon which

Daphne sat. "Oh, tell me, Cousin Daphne, tell me. What did it feel like? Did your legs turn to jam? Did your heart pitter-patter?" She put the back of her hand to her forehead. "Did you nearly swoon?"

Daphne struggled to keep the smile off her face. "I did nothing of the sort. You are being quite ridiculous." But Delilah had been right. About the legs turning to jam, and the heart pitter-pattering, too. And there *may* have been a moment where she'd considered swooning.

Delilah's brow furrowed. "Well, that is *très* disappointing."

"Tell me, you little urchin, what do you want in order to keep silent about this? I cannot allow anyone to find out."

Delilah's catlike smile returned to her face. "Don't worry, Cousin Daphne. I have no intention of telling anyone. Well, Aunt Willie suspects something but—"

"You mustn't tell Aunt Willie!"

"Aunt Willie is quite clever. She may not make an attractive fichu but she certainly knows more than she lets on." Delilah hopped to her feet and paced back and forth in front of the windows. "Now, I should think you might give me a bit of your pin money for the next month."

"Done."

"And allow me to dress up in your prettiest ball gowns at least once a month for the next year."

"Done."

"And let me come with you on Sunday night."

Daphne gasped again. "How do you know about that?"

"I know lots of things."

"You are a wicked little eavesdropper and if I didn't like you so well, I'd beat you."

"I doubt beating would work on me, Cousin Daphne. I'm far too stubborn."

"Isn't that true?"

Delilah's face lit up. "So, you'll let me come with you on Sunday?"

Daphne slapped the hairbrush to the tabletop. "Absolutely not. You cannot come with me on Sunday. It's far too dangerous. And you're not to mention that to anyone, either, do you hear me?"

Delilah shrugged. "Very well. I'll make do with the pin money and the ball gowns."

"That's quite big of you. Now, tell me. Did Captain Cavendish say when he intended to leave?" Surely, if he'd stayed for breakfast, he'd be gone by now.

"No. In fact, I'm certain I heard him tell Julian that he'd be up for a game of piquet with him in the study later."

"You cannot be serious."

"I am. Seems *Capitaine* Cavendish has no intention of leaving here today."

Daphne plunked her hands on her hips. "We'll just see about that."

Delilah picked up her plate of teacakes and made her way to the door. "Well, do come down and see him."

"I intend to do just that."

"And don't worry, Cousin Daphne," Delilah said as she danced out of the door. "I won't tell Auntie that you're married to him."

CHAPTER FIFTEEN

Daphne scurried down the stairs and into the front hall like a hare being chased by a hound. Instead of a hound, Delilah was close on her heels. Delilah had returned to the kitchens for more teacakes and then came back to find her cousin. After some additional negotiation on Daphne's part that involved offering Delilah an even larger portion of her pin money and one of her favorite silken fans, Delilah had agreed to keep her mouth shut about everything she knew.

"I wonder if they're still in the breakfast room?" Daphne peered into the corridor that led to that room.

"There's only one way to find out." Delilah nudged her shoulder.

Daphne straightened up and lifted her chin. Her cousin was right. If Rafe was still skulking about, she might as well confront him and get it over with. "Follow me."

Delilah's obvious look of delight was followed by a great deal of hand clapping.

"Stop that, you're making a racket."

Delilah sighed. "That is one of my specialties, Cousin Daphne."

Daphne shook her head and motioned for her cousin to stay behind her. The two made their way down the corridor and into the breakfast room. All of the men present stood as soon as they walked into the room. Daphne scanned their faces. Rafe was there. She glared at him.

"Good morning, Lady Daphne," Lord Fitzwell said with a bow. He was wearing a well-cut emerald-green coat and brown breeches and Hessians. Quite dapper.

She beamed at him. "Good morning, my lord."

He sat back down and returned his attention to his paper. Daphne turned to her mother, pointedly ignoring Rafe for the moment. He continued to stand.

"Good morning, darling," her mother said.

"Good morning, Aunt," Delilah shot back.

"Delilah, I've already seen you this morning. Where did you put that plate of teacakes you left with? I do hope they aren't under your bed like last time. We'll get another mouse."

Jane Upton looked up from her book, obviously interested in the fate of the teacakes.

"Oh no, Aunt," Delilah said. "This time I left them in Cousin Daphne's room. There would never be a mouse in Cousin Daphne's room."

"Lady Daphne wouldn't stand for it," Rafe said.

"What was that?" Daphne snapped her head to the side to look at him.

"Nothing." Rafe gave her a tight smile.

Daphne frowned at him. Why did he always have to look so handsome? He was wearing a dark gray topcoat, silver waistcoat, and tight black breeches with top boots. The man knew how to fill out a pair of breeches, she thought wistfully as she caught a glimpse of his backside when he turned. She glanced over to where Lord Fitzwell sat, his face nearly buried in the newspaper. What did Lord Fitzwell's backside look like? She'd never noted it.

"Come sit," Mother offered, pulling out a chair near Lord Fitzwell. Mother addressed her remarks to the rest of the room. "I was thinking everyone could take a rest after breakfast and then we'll meet in the drawing room for charades before lunch."

"Oh, goody. Charades," Sir Roderick Montague drawled from behind his newspaper across the table. He folded down one corner and rolled his eyes at Daphne. She gave him a warning glance.

"I quite enjoy charades," Lord Fitzwell offered, setting down his paper. "Don't you, Lady Daphne?"

But Daphne was staring at Rafe, who still had that godforsaken grin on his face. Daphne cleared her throat and answered Lord Fitzwell. "I'd very much like to discuss charades with you, my lord. But first I wondered if I might have a word with *you,* Captain." She leveled her gaze on Rafe.

Rafe's brow arched, but he flourished a hand in front of him as if allowing her to lead the way. "By all means."

A few of the diners looked up to see them leave the room together. Delilah made as if to follow them. "Not you, Delilah," Daphne said, pointing her cousin back toward the seating.

Delilah wrinkled her nose in a pout but flounced back over to the table where she grabbed another teacake from a new platter that had just been brought from the kitchens.

Keeping her head high, Daphne marched out of the

breakfast room, down the short corridor, and into the drawing room. Rafe followed her.

As soon as the door was closed behind them she turned to him, her arms crossed over her chest. "Please tell me you intend to leave immediately after breakfast."

"I do not," he said simply.

Daphne's face heated. She forced herself to count three. "What do you mean?"

He casually slid a hand into his pocket. "I mean I have no intention of leaving after breakfast or anytime today actually."

Counting three wasn't sufficient. She wanted to scream at him like a fishwife. She forced the words through her clenched teeth. "What about our agreement?"

"You mean the agreement in which you promised to give me a memorable kiss?"

More face heating. "Yes."

"I daresay that momentous occasion, although admittedly well on its way to being memorable, was unfortunately interrupted."

Daphne clenched her fists. "That was hardly my fault," she snapped, though she was somewhat mollified that he agreed it was memorable.

"I didn't say it was your fault. It's simply a fact."

"Are you mad? You're going to use *that* as an excuse as to why you refuse to leave?"

"It's not an excuse. I did leave. Last night. I'm back. I've also decided that the agreement was foolish. I need to keep an eye on you."

"Keep an eye on me?" She fought the urge to stamp her foot. "In a house where my mother, brother, and sister-in-law reside? Truly?"

"They all seem to like this Fitzhorton chap. I don't trust him."

"And you're the person to judge him? Not my family?" Daphne pressed a hand to her forehead. A headache was quickly forming behind her eyes. She was going mad. She could feel it. It was not possible that she was standing here having this absolutely infuriating conversation with this man. It defied logic.

"I've been trained, Daphne. I've seen quite a lot of human nature. Your brother is astute, no question, but he's been trained for war, not for assessing the details in human behavior. Spying is a very different line of work."

"Your arrogance astounds me. I cannot fathom how you think you're the best person to judge someone with whom I should keep company."

"I feel an obligation to your family." He paused. "And to you."

Daphne's heart wrenched. That's all she was to him. An obligation.

"So you refuse to leave?" she forced herself to ask.

"That's right."

She clenched her teeth and stomped past him. "Fine. But stay out of my way."

CHAPTER SIXTEEN

Rafe took a brandy glass from Swifdon, who had just finished handing another to Claringdon. The three men stood in Swifdon's study. Rafe had asked them to have a drink with him. Swifdon and Claringdon were both privy to the secrets of the War Office, having been high-ranking military officers as well as current members of Parliament.

"My thanks. I needed this." Rafe lifted the glass and tossed half its contents into the back of his throat.

"I thought you might. You look a bit worse for wear. A house party is not exactly your preferred venue, is it, Cavendish?" Swifdon took a seat behind his large cherry-wood desk and gestured to the other two men to sit in the dark leather chairs that rested in front of it.

"You're right," Rafe replied.

"I wondered why you stayed for the weekend," Claringdon added. "You're not *that* fond of free liquor."

"Lady Daphne would disagree with you," Rafe replied.

He glanced up to see Swifdon and Claringdon exchange a look.

"My sister's opinion matters to you so much?" Swifdon wanted to know.

Rafe shook his head. "Isn't it obvious she doesn't want me here?"

"That's an understatement." Swifdon laughed. "You told me she was angry with you, but until seeing her in the breakfast room this morning, I didn't realize how serious you were."

"You feel it's necessary to stay, though?" Claringdon asked.

Rafe took another sip. "I don't want Lady Daphne to change her mind about the mission, but there's something else."

The two other men exchanged another quick glance. "Yes?" Swifdon prompted.

"I don't particularly care for this Fitzwell chap."

"Can't say I know him well, myself," Claringdon said.

Swifdon pushed back in his chair and let out a long sigh. "Daphne's usually daring and free-spirited but in this case she made a list. A long list of eligible gentlemen. She rated them and ranked them. Apparently, Fitzwell had the highest score."

Rafe nearly spat his drink. "She scored them?" She actually gave them *scores*?" Rafe gaped. "I can't believe it."

"It's not particularly romantic but you must admit, it's efficient," Swifdon said with another laugh.

"Seems a sight better than how I went about finding a wife," Claringdon added.

Rafe sat up straight and set his glass on the desk in front of him. "Good God. If Fitzwell earned the highest marks, I shudder to think what I received."

Julian cleared his throat. "I can't say I saw the list myself but I don't think you were on it, Cavendish."

Rafe rolled his eyes. "Of course not."

"What's the matter, Cavendish? Don't think you'd stack up against Lord Fitz?" Claringdon laughed.

"If the point system is based on titles, then obviously not." Rafe swiped his drink off the desk and finished it in one swift gulp. "You cannot think he's the best suited for your sister."

Swifdon shrugged. "I don't, particularly. But I've learned the hard way that trying to talk Daphne out of something once her mind is made up is a losing proposition. Cass seems to think he's suitable. And so does Mother."

Rafe stood and crossed over to the sideboard to pour himself another drink. "Suitable and right are two different things."

"Careful, Cavendish, methinks you're sounding a bit jealous. You may be the current bridegroom but I'm under the impression that both you and Daphne are in agreement in wanting this annulment as soon as possible." Claringdon took a swallow of his drink.

"*After* the mission," Rafe clarified, pulling the top off the decanter of brandy.

"Of course," Claringdon replied, eyeing him curiously.

Rafe needed to change the subject. He turned his attention toward Swifdon. "As for the mission. I intend to come for Daphne tomorrow night after dinner. She should be prepared and in costume."

"You mean dressed like a cabin boy?" Swifdon replied.

Rafe splashed brandy into his glass. "Yes."

"I still can't believe Donald ever agreed to that." Julian set his glass on the desk.

"Your brother changed a lot after your father died," Rafe said. "He was quite a bit more carefree and daring than I'd known him to be previously."

Swifdon nodded, turned in his chair, and glanced out the window. "God knows Mother would have my hide if she knew I was agreeing to allow Daphne to go back out there."

Claringdon cleared his throat. "At the risk of offending either or both of you, why *are* you allowing it?"

The hint of a smile tugged at Swifdon's lips. "It's as I said, once Daphne's made up her mind about something, there's no stopping her. If I said no, she'd slip out the window while I wasn't looking. I'd rather have her go with my blessing."

Claringdon nodded. "I see."

"At the risk of offending you, Cavendish, I must say that I'm surprised Wellington is allowing you to take on this particular mission. You're not exactly impartial to this one," Swifdon said.

"I've already infiltrated their ranks. They know me. The men who held me captive in France had never seen me or known me as the ship's captain. There is no one better to do this particular mission."

"What is your plan?" Claringdon asked.

"The Russians know me as a part-time smuggler. Someone who trades goods for secrets on behalf of the Crown. They think I'm an informant to the War Office," Rafe explained.

"So you'll trade goods for the letters?"

"Yes. The letters should give us the French spies' latest whereabouts. As soon as I get them, I intend to sail for France immediately and find those bastards."

"I wish you nothing but luck, Cavendish," Claringdon said.

Rafe smiled wryly. "I don't need luck. I just need those letters."

"In the meantime, be careful," Claringdon replied. "For yourself and for Lady Daphne."

Swifdon nodded toward Rafe but spoke to Claringdon. "I trust Cavendish with my own life and my sister's."

"I will not let you down, my lord," Rafe replied. A lump had formed in his throat. Swifdon still had faith in him, after all that had happened.

"See that you don't," Swifdon said. "As for Daphne. She's going to go on this mission and then she's going to marry this Lord Fitzwell chap whether I like it or not."

Rafe downed the rest of his drink and growled.

CHAPTER SEVENTEEN

The drawing room was full. Apparently no one wanted to miss charades. Well, no one except Aunt Willie, who was taking a nap. Everyone else was present. Lucy and Derek, Cass and Julian, Jane and Garrett, Sir Roderick, Delilah, Lord Berkeley, Lord Fitzwell, and . . . Rafe.

Daphne made her way into the room and greeted Lord Berkeley. Berkeley was a friend of Garrett Upton's who lived in the north. On the occasion he came to town he was always a good sport at any party. Daphne liked him immensely.

"Good afternoon, Lord Berkeley," she said, smiling at him widely.

Lord Berkeley stood and bowed. "Lady Daphne, a pleasure."

"I was so glad you were able to join us for the party this weekend," Daphne said.

"Only just. I'm off to Northumbria on Monday."

"Not staying for the Season, my lord?"

Lord Berkeley shuddered. "The Season is not my favored type of amusement, I'm afraid. Despite my best efforts to attend events and be charming, I find that wife hunting has never been my most successful pursuit."

Daphne smiled at him. "I'm certain any young woman would be honored by your suit, my lord." She scanned her memory. She must know someone who would be suited for Lord Berkeley. The man was a catch. If he didn't live so far from London, he'd have scored higher on Daphne's list.

"Yes, well, please tell that to the young ladies," Berkeley said with a laugh. "Otherwise, I fear I'm a confirmed bachelor."

Daphne laughed, too. "I shall put in a good word for you, my lord."

Daphne took her leave from Lord Berkeley and scanned the room. Nearly every available seat was taken. Luckily there was one available next to Lord Fitzwell and Daphne hurried over to claim it.

"Good afternoon, my lord." She batted her eyelashes at Lord Fitzwell. Delilah had informed her that gentlemen liked that sort of thing. Lovely. She was taking courtship advice from a twelve-year-old.

Daphne glanced up to see Delilah standing on tiptoes searching the room. Delilah had asked for Mother's approval to attend the game and, much to Delilah's long-suffering governess's dismay, Mama had agreed. Delilah appeared to be looking for Captain Cavendish because the moment her eyes alighted on him, she drifted over to hover near him. Hmm. Daphne tapped her finger against her cheek. Perhaps Delilah was just what was needed in the battle against Captain Cavendish. Daphne would have to put her plan into action after charades.

"I trust you slept well," Lord Fitzwell asked Daphne.

Daphne nearly jumped. "Oh, I did, my lord. And you?"

Lord Fitzwell rubbed a hand across the back of his neck. "I have a bit of a cramp in my shoulder and the pillow was a bit lumpy and—"

Daphne wasn't listening. She was craning her neck to watch Rafe speak to Delilah. His infamous, arrogant grin was replaced by a softer, kinder smile. One that made his eyes crinkle at the corners. He glanced up and caught her staring at him. His grin widened and he inclined his head toward her. She quickly averted her gaze. Blast him. Not only did he intend to remain at the party, he also clearly intended to make her miserable while he was at it.

"That's nice," she said to Lord Fitzwell.

"It wasn't nice at all. It was a bit uncomfortable, actually," Lord Fitzwell replied, still rubbing his shoulder.

"Pardon? Oh, I'm sorry, my lord. Of course. It must have been terribly difficult for you." She turned fully to face him. What had he said? Oh, fiddle. Now she was allowing her preoccupation with that rogue Cavendish to keep her from being properly attentive to Lord Fitzwell. This wouldn't do at all.

"It was, it truly was," Lord Fitzwell replied.

"*What* a pity," Sir Roderick said from the seat on the other side of Daphne.

Daphne elbowed him.

Mother stood and made her way to the front of the room. She clapped her hands. "I believe we're all here. Who would like to go first?"

"I shall!" Lord Fitzwell piped up.

"Apparently, his uncomfortable sleeping arrangements didn't dampen his enthusiasm for charades," Sir Roderick drawled.

"Roddy, stop it." Daphne gave the knight her most stern

look, but she couldn't help but laugh when he waggled his eyebrows at her.

Meanwhile, Lord Fitzwell stood, tugged on his jacket, and made a grand show of walking in a wide circle before moving into the center of the room.

"Reminds me of a peacock," Sir Roderick breathed.

Daphne narrowed her eyes on the knight.

Lord Fitzwell began by pushing out his neck in what Daphne could only describe as a very odd manner. His arms were tucked up to his sides and his head ducked forward and back as if he were experiencing convulsions. From time to time he would cock his head to the side and open his mouth.

"A dandy," Cass guessed.

"The Prince Regent," Lucy shouted.

"Lucy!" Claringdon's voice rang out.

"Oh, sorry, darling," Lucy replied, tossing a black curl off her forehead.

"A madman," Sir Roderick offered, turning the room's attention back to the performance. Daphne elbowed him again.

Lord Fitzwell shook his head to indicate they were incorrect before continuing his same strange antics.

"Beau Brummel," Mother said.

"Pengree," Julian called, and quickly earned himself a frown from that very man who'd been standing at attention at the back of the room. "Sorry, Peng," Julian added with a shrug.

More head shaking from Lord Fitzwell.

Daphne glanced at Rafe. He sat with his arms folded, his eyes narrowed on Lord Fitzwell as if he were watching an escapee from Bedlam. He didn't bother to offer any guess.

"A bird!" shouted Delilah finally.

Vigorous nodding ensued from Lord Fitzwell.

"What type of bird?" Mother asked.

More nodding from Lord Fitzwell.

"An owl," Cass offered.

"A canary," Daphne said, wanting to contribute something in an effort to make the poor man stop.

"A rooster?" Upton offered.

"A *Phasianus colchicus,*" Jane called out.

"No one's ever heard of that, Jane," Lucy said, shaking her head.

"Honestly, Lucy, it's just a pheasant," Jane shot back, also shaking her head.

"Then say 'pheasant,'" Lucy replied. "Latin is uncalled for during charades."

"Don't make me stick my tongue out at you, Lucy," Jane replied.

"Please make it end," Sir Roderick murmured under his breath. "I already said it but"—he raised his voice so the room could hear—"a peacock!"

All of these guesses earned more head shaking from Lord Fitzwell. He continued to strut about in front of the fireplace with his arms tucked to his sides and his mouth intermittently falling open. Daphne cocked her head to the side and stared at him. Was that what a bird looked like?

"A popinjay!" Delilah shouted next.

Lord Fitzwell straightened up, smiled, and pointed at Delilah. "Exactly right, Miss Montbank."

"Ah, a popinjay, I was close." Sir Roderick shrugged.

Delilah looked exceedingly pleased with herself, her smile reached from ear to ear. Daphne had no earthly idea how the girl had been able to guess based on Lord Fitzwell's odd posturing. In fact, she shook her head to remove the memory of it.

Mother clapped her hands again. "Who's next?"

"I'll go!" Daphne announced, smiling brightly at Lord Fitzwell as he resumed his seat next to her.

She'd already decided what she would do. She would pretend to be a flower. A sunflower perhaps but any flower would do. It would be simple and dainty, certain to impress Lord Fitzwell. Not to mention easy to guess.

She hoped.

But just in case, she decided a bit of insurance was best. "If it goes on too long, I'm a sunflower," she whispered to Sir Roderick just before she stood.

She made her way to the front of the room, doing her best to keep her gaze from Rafe. She lifted her chin and concentrated on the rose-patterned wallpaper on the far wall.

She began by spreading her hands to the sides to mimic leaves and tilting up her head to the imaginary sun. She basked in the glow of the pretend sunshine.

"A statue," Lucy called out.

"An actress," Delilah called. Mother shushed her.

Daphne shook her head. Hmm. Perhaps a bit more was required of this particular charade.

She bent her knees and crouched low, then slowly raised herself up, this time trying to mimic the act of growing. If only she could use water and sun to grow in real life. Being the opposite of tall was not a pleasure. She nearly laughed at her own thought. Then she reminded herself that flowers didn't smile.

"An angel," Lord Berkeley called.

"A mole," Sir Roderick offered.

"A slow fish?" Cass asked, a frown on her face.

Daphne shook her head again. Hmm. They weren't getting it. What else were flowers about?

Standing upright again, she raised her face to the sky and opened her mouth. Then she used her hands to mimic a sprinkle as if rain was falling and she was drinking it. She leaned her head back, lifted her hand, opened her mouth, and pretended that she was pouring a drink into her throat.

"An Egyptian," Jane said.

"That makes no sense at all," Lucy pointed out.

"I'm trying," Jane replied with a shrug.

"No. Wait. She's drinking," Upton announced.

"The vicar!" Delilah offered. Mother shushed her more vehemently this time.

Daphne shook her head and scowled at her cousin.

"Oh, drinking spirits?" Lucy shouted. "I see."

Before Daphne had a chance to shake her head, Rafe's voice rang out across the room. "Surely not. The pristine goddess would never allow alcohol to touch her lips, not even imaginary alcohol."

Daphne lowered her gaze and faced him. How dare he? A sharp retort came to her lips. She opened her mouth and snapped it closed. She couldn't reply. And he knew it. No speaking during charades and all of that. He was purposely taunting her.

"But is it spirits?" Lucy pressed.

Daphne shook her head.

"Never think it," Rafe replied. "Lemonade perhaps, but the faultless Lady Daphne would never drink alcohol. Is it lemonade, Lady Daphne? For surely it is not a spirit."

That was it. She couldn't take it. He'd pushed her too far. She crossed her arms over her chest and tapped her foot on the carpet. "Better to never drink imaginary alcohol than to drink far too much of the real stuff."

The assembly fell quiet. Everyone's gazes darted back and forth between Daphne and Rafe.

Sir Roderick's bark of laughter was the only sound.

"How would you know how bad it is to drink too much when you've never had so much as a taste of the stuff?" Rafe countered.

Mother stood and wrung her hands. "Why don't we all—"

"No, no, Mother. That's quite all right. Let's continue. I shan't allow Captain Cavendish's poor manners to ruin the fun," Daphne said.

Cass gasped.

Daphne finally looked at Lord Fitzwell. He was frowning, the sides of his mouth decidedly turned down. She had to do something quickly to divert the attention away from her war of words with Rafe.

She tried to resume her flowerlike stance but couldn't manage much. She wanted to run from the room. She glanced desperately at Sir Roderick and gave him a pleading look.

"A sunflower!" he shouted.

Daphne expelled her breath. Thank heavens for Roddy. She nodded quickly.

"Well done," Lord Berkeley said to Sir Roderick, clapping him on the back.

"I'll go next," Lucy gamely offered.

"Yes, please do," Daphne replied, moving away from the center of the room. She cleared her throat and stopped next to her cousin's chair. "Delilah, may I please speak to you in the next room?"

CHAPTER EIGHTEEN

"Let me ensure that I understand you correctly," Delilah said, pacing slowly across the rug in the drawing room next door to where the charades game was still taking place. Delilah's hands were folded behind her back and her gamine little face was pulled up in a knowing smile. "You want me to *distract* Captain Cavendish?"

"Precisely." Daphne nodded.

"And how exactly do you suggest I go about doing such a thing?"

"You know? Talk to him, follow him about, keep him from showing up every time I'm speaking with Lord Fitzwell. He seems to take great pleasure in causing me trouble and I'd like to see him stopped."

"And in return for this service, you'll give me what in exchange?" Delilah unfolded her arms from behind her back and tapped one finger against her plump little cheek.

Daphne sighed. Before this weekend was over, she

might as well give her cousin all of her worldly possessions. "Name your price."

Delilah's eyes rounded. "Ooh, that is tempting."

"Go ahead, you little urchin. What is it that you want?"

The finger continued to tap against Delilah's cheek. "I want that new bonnet you purchased on Bond Street last week. *J'adore* it."

"Done."

"And . . ."

"And?" Daphne rubbed her temples. The girl knew how to bargain, she'd give her that.

"And I want you to—"

An unexpected rapping on the door interrupted their conversation. Rafe's head appeared. "I do hate to interrupt, but it seems your poor Lord Fitzwell has become afflicted with a nosebleed. Your mother has called for some linens and he's lying on the settee in the next room but the game of charades has decidedly come to an end."

Daphne whirled to face Rafe. "Oh, heavens. Is he all right?"

"I expect him to be. It is only a nosebleed after all." The scoffing in his voice was quite apparent.

"Yes, well, I'll just allow you two to chat. Seems you may want to apologize to each other after that nastiness over charades. I'd begin with that." Delilah trotted past Daphne.

"Where are you going?" Daphne called to her cousin. How could the girl even think of leaving now? "I thought we had an agreement," Daphne added in a singsong voice.

"Nothing has been settled," Delilah replied in the same singsong voice. "Besides, I've never seen a nosebleed before. I must go look." She swept out the door and shut it behind her.

Daphne crossed her arms over her chest and glared at Rafe, who had entered the room and was even now looking down at her.

"I'm willing to accept your apology," he said.

"My *what*! Oh, how magnanimous of you. The only problem is, I haven't *offered* an apology."

"Go ahead. I'll wait."

"You'll be waiting till Hades has turned to ice. I have no intention of offering an apology."

Rafe folded his hands behind his back and rocked back on his heels. "That's exceedingly rude of you."

Daphne's mouth fell open. "You just called *me* rude?"

"If the bonnet fits. You're the one who essentially announced to the entire drawing room that I drink too much."

She tossed a hand in the air. "That's hardly news."

Rafe cupped a hand beneath his chin and studied her. "You know what your problem is?"

Arms still crossed, she tapped her fingertips along her elbows. "I'm on tenterhooks to hear this."

"Your problem is that in addition to being far too judgmental, you're also far too coddled. Never a blow that hasn't been softened for you by your family. Never a blow that won't be softened."

Daphne clenched her elbows so tightly they ached. "You don't know anything about my life."

"I think I do. Your every moment is planned to the smallest detail. Your clothing, your hair, what you'll wear tomorrow and the day after and the day after that. What you'll be doing next week and the next. You wrote a list of men to marry, for God's sake, and scored them."

"Who told you that?"

"Do you deny it?"

She simmered but kept her mouth firmly shut.

"You pretend to be outraged but if you're angry it's because you know there's truth to what I'm saying. You're more interested in titles and lineage than happiness."

"That's a lie!"

"Is it?" He sauntered over to her and leaned down. He was a scant inch from her face and Daphne's damned traitorous knees weakened at the scent of him. "Tell me, Lady Daphne. Is my name on that list?"

The door opened again and Delilah stuck in her head. "Daphne, Aunt says to come quickly. Lord Fitzwell's nosebleed is worsening and they're discussing having the footmen carry him up to his room."

CHAPTER NINETEEN

Rafe jumped. Something, or more precisely *someone,* had pinched him. He was standing in the Swifts' ballroom, wearing his uniform, formally dressed for the ball that was being held tonight in Daphne's honor. Daphne and Lord Fitzwell's honor, more precisely, but apparently the man hadn't quite offered for her yet. Delilah had informed Rafe earlier that the nosebleed had been stopped by some additional pressure with linens after the footmen had carried the bore up the staircase to his room. Too bad.

Who had pinched him? Rafe looked behind him, half expecting to see Delilah grinning up at him. Instead, he found Daphne's Aunt Wilhelmina waggling her gray eyebrows in a manner he could only describe as unsettling.

"Captain Cavendish?" The older woman's voice was sharp and accusatory.

"Yes," Rafe replied, rubbing the offended spot on his rump.

"With you in the room, I have absolutely no heavenly

idea why my niece is looking twice at that Fitzwarton fellow."

Rafe hid his smile behind his fist, which he coughed into. "Surely you're not implying that I am a suitable suitor for Lady Daphne's hand?"

"Suitability has nothing to do with it, Captain. I'm strictly speaking about looks. Lord Fitzwell is handsome but you are both handsome and dashing."

What was this family's preoccupation with being dashing? "I'll take that as a compliment." Rafe inclined his head toward the wicked old widow. Pinching him had been egregious, but he'd heard that about her before.

"I'd settle for your upending their engagement. I can't say I highly approve of Fitztottle. The man seems to be more interested in Daphne's connections than Daphne."

"With all due respect, my lady. Isn't that the way of your, er, class?"

"My nephew Julian was able to find both love and rank. I expect Daphne can do the same."

"A baron isn't good enough for you, my lady?"

"Pish-posh. I don't give a fig about his title. Fitzwhobert isn't good enough for me. Or more specifically, my niece." Another eyebrow waggle. "Now might I suggest you ask Daphne to dance."

Daphne peeked into the ballroom. The space was magnificent. It looked as if an arboretum had been brought inside. Mother and Cass had surely outdone themselves. Daphne stood on the threshold to the ballroom, clutching Julian's arm, pressing her hand to her middle, and taking large gulps of air. Tonight was the night. Lord Fitzwell would ask her to marry him tonight. He had to. And she would accept. Yes, there was the small matter of her annulment that would need to be settled before the actual marriage could take place, but that was a detail she intended to see to immediately after completing Rafe's mission.

She held her breath. The conveyances of the guests who had not been invited to the house party arrived in a steady stream at the front entrance. The *ton* was abuzz tonight and this was her engagement ball. That was all there was to it. Now the potential bridegroom merely needed to do his bit and propose.

She'd finally reached an agreement with Delilah, that little thief, before the ball tonight. The girl promised to occupy Rafe's attention and keep what she knew to herself in exchange for another month's pin money, Daphne's new light pink bonnet, a second fan, and a new pair of gloves. Daphne had no idea how she'd explain all of that to Mother. But she'd worry about that later. Tonight she had more pressing concerns, like securing an engagement with her husband in the room.

She certainly looked more confident than she felt. She wore a sparkling silver gown that made her feel like a diamond. A string of sapphires laced through her hair and a sapphire shrug draped around her shoulders. Her hair was up in a chignon with curling pieces framing her face. She'd pinched pink into her cheeks per Delilah's suggestion just before she'd left her bedchamber. Delilah and her maid had both assured her that she was a vision. But Daphne didn't feel like a vision. She felt like a roiling mass of nerves. Yes. It was definite. She looked much better in the looking glass than she felt on the inside. That was certain. Inside, she felt as if she might just cast up her accounts.

Daphne took one last deep breath and nodded to her brother.

"You are stunning tonight, Daph," Julian said from her side as they waited at the top of the stairs to be introduced.

"Thank you," she replied in a shaky voice. "I only hope Lord Fitzwell thinks so."

Julian's gray eyes met hers. His were filled with concern. "Are you sure, Daphne? About Lord Fitzwell, I mean. If you have any doubts, you don't have to go through with any of this."

Daphne pressed her gloved fingertips into Julian's fine black sleeve. "What do you mean?"

"I was speaking to Cavendish earlier and he said—"

Daphne's breathing hitched. Despite the gloves, she dug her nails into her brother's coat. "You're listening to Captain Cavendish when it comes to my marital prospects?"

Julian arched a brow. "It is a bit ironic, isn't it?"

Daphne shook her head. "I was quite deliberate, Julian. I made a list. Lord Fitzwell is eligible and—"

"Being eligible and being correct are two different things."

"The Earl of Swifdon and Lady Daphne Swift," Pengree intoned, announcing them to the masses in the ballroom. Without saying another word, Julian stepped forward, bringing Daphne with him. All eyes turned to stare at them. Daphne searched the crowd. It wasn't until moments later that she realized she'd been looking for Rafe, not Lord Fitzwell. Blast it.

She and Julian made their way into the room together and Daphne kept her smile pinned to her face. It hurt to smile so much. She'd never realized it before. People greeting her were a blur. The room spun. She clutched at Julian's arm to steady herself. Thank heavens for her tall, composed brother.

"Daphne," her mother's voice rang out. A bit of space

opened up and Daphne followed her mother's voice over to their small group where Mama and Aunt Willie stood near the French doors that led out onto the terrace.

"I'll leave you here with the ladies," Julian said. "I'm off in search of my wife."

Daphne reluctantly let go of her brother's sleeve, reminding herself that she could hardly find herself engaged by the end of the evening if she clung to him all night. As soon as Julian glided away, Daphne took a deep breath and turned to the other ladies. Before she could say a word, Delilah came skipping up to them.

"Good evening, Cousin Daphne," she said, curtsying prettily.

Daphne curtsied back. "Delilah, what are you doing here?"

"She wouldn't stop begging me to make an appearance tonight," Mama explained. "I'm only allowing her in here because I know well and good that if I didn't she'd be hiding behind a door and peeking out in her night rail." She turned to Delilah. "But as I said, miss, you're only here for bit. Then, it's off to bed with you. I mean it."

Delilah nodded. "I know. I know."

"Oh, let the girl have her fun," Aunt Willie added. "I daresay being here is preferable to being cooped up upstairs with that sour-faced governess of hers."

"She is sour-faced isn't she, Aunt?" Delilah replied with a long-suffering sigh. "I often think so."

"Well, you certainly look pretty tonight, Delilah," Daphne interjected before anything more could be said about the poor, sour-faced governess.

Delilah was wearing a smart white gown with a turquoise sash around her waist and a matching turquoise bow on the top of her head . . . of the large variety as usual. She spun in a small circle. "Thank you. I smell good, too."

"Turn around, Delilah," Mama said. "I believe your skirt is hitching up in the back."

Delilah turned, trying to look at her backside in a maneuver that reminded Daphne as nothing so much as a puppy chasing its tail. "It's not the skirt, Auntie. It's me."

A footman walked by carrying a tray of champagne glasses. "Here, young man." Aunt Willie swiped a drink from the tray.

"Care for one, Daphne?" Aunt Willie waggled her eyebrows.

"No, Aunt." Daphne shook her head and waved the tray away.

"Ah, so Captain Cavendish was right about you?" Aunt Willie smiled at her, lifting the drink to her mouth.

Daphne pressed her lips together, hard. Captain Cavendish was *not* right about her. Why, of all the—

"I'll take one!" Delilah piped up.

"No, miss," Mama said to Delilah. "You may be at a ball, but you're still a bit too young for champagne."

"*J'adore* a ball. *J'adore* champagne," Delilah declared, her hands clasped together near her ear.

"That's just silly. How many balls have you been to?" Mama replied, shaking her head.

"Only just this one," Delilah replied, spinning to allow her skirts to swirl around her ankles. "But I am enjoying myself immensely and I'm certain all balls are as enjoyable."

"I refuse to ask how many glasses of champagne you've had."

"That's probably best, Auntie," Delilah replied.

"You look adorable," Daphne offered, smiling at Delilah and patting her on the head.

"Well," Aunt Willie said, motioning to Daphne with her champagne glass. "You're not going to get yourself engaged standing here with the three of us. You'd best be off in search of a gentleman to ask you to dance. If I were you I'd begin with Captain Cavendish."

Aunt Willie waggled her eyebrows again. Eyebrow waggling seemed her favorite pastime.

"Oh, ignore her," Mama said. "I believe Lord Fitzwell is over by the refreshment table. I'm certain he'll be along presently."

"I'll just go and greet Cass," Daphne said, spotting her sister-in-law across the room.

Daphne took leave of the small group and dashed over to where Cass, Lucy, and Jane were standing together in the corner. Cass was wearing a gorgeous lavender gown. Lucy was dressed in deep emerald, and Jane looked stunning in ice blue.

"Ah, Daphne, dear," Cass said, holding out a hand and pulling Daphne into their little circle. "You look absolutely breathtaking."

"Thank you." Daphne pressed a hand to her churning stomach. "I certainly don't feel breathtaking."

"Whatever do you mean?" Lucy asked, sipping from a champagne flute.

Daphne closed her eyes. "What if Lord Fitzwell doesn't offer for me tonight?"

"Then he's a fool," Jane stated loyally. Daphne smiled at that. Jane had a book in her hand and while she was tapping her foot in time to the music, Daphne knew she'd much rather be off in a quiet corner somewhere reading.

It was nice of Mrs. Upton to come to the ball tonight, for Daphne's sake.

Cass searched Daphne's face. "Do you have any reason to believe Lord Fitzwell won't offer for you?"

Daphne shook her head. "No, but I have yet to see him tonight. Perhaps his nosebleed was more serious than we thought."

Lucy winced. "Yes, that was extremely unfortunate, but don't worry, dear. I'm sure he's fine and you've only just arrived. You have all evening."

Daphne twisted her third finger. "I know. I know. But . . ." She glanced around. "Where's Julian? The last time I saw him he said he was coming to find you, Cass."

"Oh, he found me." Cass laughed. "He stopped by briefly after escorting you in but I do believe he's already retired to the study."

"With my husband, of course." Lucy snorted.

"And mine," Jane added, pushing up her spectacles on her nose.

"It's funny how married men aren't particularly keen on dancing." Cass shook her head.

"Yes. Quite unfortunate," Lucy replied. "As they tend to make the best partners."

All of the ladies laughed at that.

"It's a pity we don't have some sort of plot to keep us occupied these days," Lucy said, tapping a finger against her cheek.

Daphne was barely listening. Instead, she was standing on tiptoe and craning her neck. "Where's Captain Cavendish?" She returned her attention to her friends in time to see the three of them exchange a knowing glance. Daphne tugged at her necklace.

"Do you mean Lord Fitzwell?" Lucy asked Daphne, a sly smile on her face. Cass gave Lucy a warning look. Daphne pressed her hand to her middle again. She just might cast up her accounts after all. Did Cass know? Daphne hoped the duchess hadn't told what she saw in the library the other night but perhaps she had changed her mind.

"I was merely wondering if Captain Cavendish was in the study with the other gentlemen." Daphne did her best to answer the question with nonchalance but even she heard the edge to her voice. "I cannot afford to have him poking his nose into my courtship with Lord Fitzwell. He behaved quite outrageously today during charades."

"That's true enough," Lucy allowed. Her champagne glass dangled from her gloved fingers.

"I do believe Captain Cavendish is in the study as well. Though I haven't seen him," Cass added.

Daphne began to breathe a sigh of relief but stopped herself. Why wasn't Rafe out here trying to cause more trouble? Had he given up? Did he no longer intend to keep an eye on her? Did he no longer think she needed him? Or was he merely sufficiently chagrined by his own rude behavior during charades this afternoon? And how dare he say that she'd had every blow softened for her by her family. It was preposterous. It was outrageous. It was . . . The memory of her asking Julian to throw Rafe out of the house and secure the annulment flashed through her mind. Very well. Rafe had a small—very small—point. She would stop asking Julian for help. She didn't need him to handle Rafe. She could deal with him herself. The memory of her asking Delilah to help her keep him distracted flashed through her mind. Fiddle. Why was she thinking about Rafe at any rate? She needed to find Lord Fitzwell.

"I think it's high time we went into the study and brought the menfolk back out," said Jane. "They may be enjoying a bit of brandy and some male talk but I, for one, would like a suitable dance partner."

Cass nodded. "You're perfectly right, Janie. Not to mention Julian needs to remain available if he's to entertain a proposal from Lord Fitzwell." She patted Daphne's arm.

Daphne gulped. This was it. The night of the engagement.

"Don't worry, Daphne," Lucy said. "We'll help you. Just leave everything to us."

CHAPTER TWENTY

The night was more than half through by the time Daphne found herself standing in a group with Julian, Cass, Lucy, and Derek. "Has Lord Fitzwell asked to speak with you alone, Julian?" she asked, twisting her ring finger.

"Not since the last time you asked me. What was that, twenty minutes ago?" Julian replied. The men had been summoned from the study by their wives and had danced, laughed, and drank their way through the evening. The only problem was, every time Daphne caught a glimpse of Lord Fitzwell, he seemed to disappear.

Cass nudged her husband. "Be kind. Daphne is having a difficult evening."

Cass was correct on that score. Not only had Lord Fitzwell not yet asked to speak to Daphne's brother, let alone her, she'd only ever danced with him once and they'd barely said two words to each other. What was happening? He intended to offer for her, didn't he? He'd been courting her for weeks. They'd gone on rides in the park. He'd introduced her to his mother. They'd talked. They'd laughed. They'd enjoyed each other's company. Or so she'd thought. He'd accepted the invitation here this weekend. She couldn't be wrong about it. She just couldn't.

"Perhaps you should have a drink, Daphne." Lucy plucked two glasses of champagne from the tray of a passing footman.

"Daphne doesn't drink," Julian replied.

"Oh, that's right," Lucy replied. "Captain Cavendish said as much earlier."

"Excuse me, please." Daphne couldn't keep the edge from her voice as she left the small group. The night was turning into a colossal disaster and she had no idea how to salvage it.

The only good thing about this evening was that she'd managed to evade Rafe so far. Since he'd emerged from the study with the other gentlemen, Delilah had kept him occupied. The girl was like a hound with a scent. She hadn't let the man out of her sight all evening. Good girl, Delilah. At least she was earning the king's ransom Daphne had promised her. But Delilah would be sent to bed soon and then Daphne might have to contend with Rafe herself. If only Lord Fitzwell would offer for her. They could make the announcement and this whole awful charade could be over. Well, after Rafe granted her the annulment.

An hour later, Delilah had gone to bed, Daphne had danced with nearly every gentleman in the room (except Rafe), and Lord Fitzwell remained nowhere to be seen. She was just finishing her second dance with Sir Roderick when Julian strolled up. She thanked Roddy for the dance and excused herself to speak to her brother.

"Nothing from Lord Fitzwell yet?" Daphne asked.

"My dear sister, has it occurred to you that if the chap does ask me for your hand, I'd be offering them both? One is already taken at present."

Daphne glanced around to ensure no one could overhear them. "Only temporarily taken. Quite temporarily."

Julian slid his hands into his pockets. "Very well. I'll say yes if it's what you wish but the truth is I haven't even seen him tonight."

Daphne scanned the ballroom. She wished she had a chair to stand upon. It wasn't easy to see over the sea of coiffures and pomaded heads. "Wait. There he is. Over there." She pointed a gloved finger.

"Ah, yes, there he is," came a familiar voice over her shoulder.

Daphne spun around. Rafe was standing not a foot behind her, holding two champagne glasses.

Julian cleared his throat. "Yes, well, I'll just go make myself available should Lord Fitzwell have anything to discuss."

Daphne's smile at her brother faded as he left her alone with Rafe.

"I'd offer you one of my drinks," Rafe drawled. "But I know you wouldn't take it. I'd say it's a pity, but more for me."

That was it. Daphne had had enough. Enough of this wretched night. Enough of everyone's preconceived notions about her drinking habits. And enough of Rafe Cavendish jabbing at her with his words. She reached out and plucked the glass from his hand, brought it to her lips, downed the entire contents, and shoved it back into his hand.

Rafe's brows shot up. He whistled. "Impressive."

A footman carrying a tray of bright, gleaming champagne glasses walked by just then and Daphne took another. She downed its contents quickly.

"Be careful, love."

"I'm not your love." Daphne marched over to a table against the wall and discarded her empty glass. Rafe followed her.

"Aren't you, Grey?"

"I can drink, sometimes, if I choose to. I just don't normally choose to. That is all."

"Ah."

She folded her arms over her chest. "I'm not a goddess."

"Ah."

"I'm not pristine."

"Ah."

"Stop saying 'ah.'"

His grin was unrepentant. "Why are you choosing to drink tonight, then? Disappointed that Fitzwell isn't holding up his end of the bargain?"

Daphne glared at him. "You'd know about not holding up bargains, wouldn't you?"

Rafe casually sipped his own glass of champagne. "Ouch. Have a care, love."

She curled her hand into a fist. "Stop calling me love, and Grey—don't call me that, either."

"What would you prefer I call you then?"

"I prefer you not call me anything. I prefer you leave." She ground the toe of her slipper against the parquet floor.

"And miss seeing how this evening turns out? After you've had two glasses of champagne? Not a chance."

She stuck her nose in the air and turned her face away

from him. "You think you know me so well, but you don't. You don't know me at all."

"So it seems," he drawled. "What else don't I know about you?"

"That I'm about to have a third glass of champagne." She turned on her heel and left.

CHAPTER TWENTY-ONE

One hour later, Rafe was smoking in the gardens. The hedges and flowering bushes formed a bit of a maze and provided a great deal of privacy. He'd gone to the far end of the property and had propped one booted foot upon a stone bench that sat next to a small fountain. He breathed in the cool night air and glanced up at the stars. Stars had been some of his only friends when he'd been a child. They'd been some of his only friends while he'd been a prisoner in France, too. He had a relationship of sorts with the stars. They might be cool and distant, but they were good listeners.

Rafe took a deep breath. He didn't know why he'd stayed here these last two days when Daphne obviously wanted him to go. Something about her desire to get him to leave caused his competitive nature to take effect and then he'd be damned if he'd go. But it was true that he didn't have a good feeling about this Fitzwell chap. Why Swifdon was allowing his sister to consider the man's suit,

Rafe would never know. No. He knew why. It was because Daphne wanted him. And Lady Daphne got what Lady Daphne wanted. She always had. Which was exactly why Rafe and she could never be together. He couldn't offer a young lady like Daphne a life of luxury. He certainly wasn't rich, and blue blood did *not* flow through his veins. No. Daphne was meant for a member of the *ton*. But not Fitzwell, for God's sake. Couldn't she see that she'd be running rings around him before the honeymoon was over? Rafe shook his head. No doubt, that's exactly what she wanted to be able to do.

Why Rafe had asked her to kiss him, he'd truly never know. It was something about the way she'd seemed so ready to dismiss him, seemed so unaffected by him. She'd been affected by him once. And God knew, he'd been affected by her, too. Swifdon would pummel him if he'd known the thoughts that had raced through his mind last spring, let alone the liberties Rafe had taken in the library last night, but by God those few seconds before the Duchess of Claringdon had come in, they'd been worth it. Rafe popped the cheroot from his lips and grinned. He tossed the nub to the grass and ground it under his boot. He turned to head to the house just as a peculiar sound reached his ears.

Singing.

It was Daphne. Singing. Her voice was high, and happy, and sweet. He found himself smiling at the noise. Until he realized what she was singing. Good God. It was a bawdy song. One he'd heard in taverns more than once.

Alas, my fair maiden. Alas, alas.
Why do you roam so free?
Your hair, your hips, your nose, your lips.
Are irresistible to me.

She turned the corner around the hedge and stopped singing abruptly upon seeing him. A hiccup escaped her lips. She clapped her hand over her mouth.

A grin spread across his face. "Why, Grey. I don't think I've ever heard you sing before."

Her hand fell away from her mouth. She gave him a catlike grin, then she twirled in a circle, her silvery satin skirts swinging around her dainty ankles. "Alas, alas, alas," she sang.

He narrowed his eyes on her. "Grey, how many glasses of champagne did you drink?"

"Only two."

"Only the two I saw you drink earlier?"

"Only two more in addition to those two and one more."

"Good God."

"What?" Her eyes blinked and then rounded.

"You mean to tell me you've had *five* glasses of champagne this evening and you've never had spirits before?"

"Ha! I've had spirits before. Just goes to show what you know." She picked up her skirts and curtsied to the hedge. "Good evening, sir."

Rafe shook his head. "When have you had spirits before?"

"When I left finishing school. Mrs. Pennyhammer served us each a thimble of wine."

Rafe shook his head. "A thimble of wine couldn't get a mouse drunk. I think you should sit down." He moved to take her arm and escort her to the stone bench, but she sidestepped him and leaped up onto the top of the bench. Standing like that, she was a head taller than he.

"Aha!" she said. "I can see things much more clearly from up here. Do you know how dreadfully inconvenient it is to be the opposite of tall?"

"You mean short?" He moved to stand in front of the bench to help her down.

"No, sir, I do not. I don't care for that word."

He needed to distract her, not argue with her. "What can you see so clearly from up there?" He raised his hand to assist her.

She lifted her head to the sky and spread her arms out to her sides. "Why, I can see the moon. I can see the stars. I can nearly see over the top of the hedges." She giggled at herself.

"Come down from there before you trip and hurt yourself." He moved even closer to the bench and stood directly in front of her. Instead of taking his hand, she looked down at him and braced both her palms on either of his shoulders.

"I can see *you*," she breathed, staring into his eyes.

"What can you see about me?" he asked, suddenly serious.

"That you're far too handsome. Far, far too handsome. The kind of handsome that could get a young lady into a great deal of trouble."

Rafe eyed her carefully. She found him handsome, did she? She was quite inebriated but still . . . That was nice to hear. He lifted his arm to her. "Allow me to escort you back inside."

"I shall allow you to escort me back inside upon one condition," she announced. She curtsied to the rosebush beside the bench.

He groaned. "You and your family and your blasted conditions."

"That's it, take it or leave it." She sang the words instead of saying them.

Rafe cleared his throat. He couldn't very well leave her

out here alone in her condition. She might trip and fall into a bush. She might break her leg trying to descend from the bench. She might be accosted by some untoward chap. Any number of things could happen. "Fine. What is the condition?"

She put her hand on his cheek and fire leaped between them. "You must tell me a secret."

Rafe pulled her hand away and offered his arm. "I think we've had enough conditions for each other for one weekend." He tugged her hand lightly, hoping to help her from the bench safely.

Daphne didn't budge. Her slippered feet remained firmly planted on the stone bench. "Fine, then. I'll tell *you* a secret."

Rafe's head snapped up. She'd certainly got his attention. "What's your secret?"

She leaned down and the softness of her breath was a strawberry-scented whisper against his ear. "I liked kissing you the other night. I thought it was exceedingly *memorable*."

"Is that so?" he drawled. He briefly considered kissing her again. A sober Daphne Swift was tempting to be certain. An inebriated one, also tempting, but he wasn't about to take advantage of a young lady who was obviously going to have the devil of a head come morning. He didn't envy her.

"Yes, that's so," she announced, straightening back up again and eyeing him down the length of her nose. "What do you think?"

He shook his head. This couldn't end well. "I think you're a bit worse for drink and I'd better get you back to the house."

"So much for being adventurous, *Captain*." She

laughed. Before Rafe had a chance to ask her what exactly she meant by that, Daphne leaned down again. For a moment, he was certain she was going to kiss him. But there were footsteps on the gravel path coming toward them. The odds of it being Lucy Hunt again were far too low. They could not be seen kissing. It would ruin Daphne. Rafe took a step back to avoid her kiss and she tumbled off the bench onto him. They both fell onto the soft grass, Daphne completely splayed atop him.

Just as Lord Fitzwell came around the hedge.

CHAPTER TWENTY-TWO

"Lady Daphne? What is the meaning of this?" Lord Fitzwell demanded, hands on his hips.

Daphne turned her head and looked up at him and began to giggle uncontrollably. "I . . . I fell off the bench."

"Directly onto Mr. Cavendish?" Fitzwell's eyes were narrowed and suspicious.

"That's *Captain* Cavendish," Rafe said, struggling to pull Daphne off him and stand up without hurting her. "And yes, it was entirely an accident."

"It looked like a bit more than an accident," Lord Fitzwell said, pulling at his lapels, a deep frown on his face.

"What is that supposed to mean?" Rafe maneuvered himself to his feet and helped Daphne up as well. She continued to laugh, which was not helping things. Not in the least.

Daphne turned and bent over, apparently searching for something in the hedge. "I've lost my reticule," she said. She clearly wasn't comprehending the import of her would-be groom's presence, nor his insinuations.

"Daphne, stop," Rafe said.

Daphne swung around, her giggling ended, a surprised look on her face.

Lord Fitzwell raised his brows in total effrontery. "You're calling her by her Christian name?"

Rafe straightened to his full height and assumed his rigid army-captain stance. "I assure you, Lord Fitzwell, absolutely nothing untoward happened here tonight between Lady Daphne and myself."

Fitzwell turned to Daphne. "Lady Daphne, is this true?"

Daphne raised her nose in the air. "Lady Daphne, is this true?" she echoed, and then burst out laughing again.

"Lady Daphne, please," Lord Fitzwell said. "Why, I, if I didn't know any better, I'd wonder if you were . . . intoxicated."

"There's no need to wonder. I am intoxicated," Daphne said, still giggling. "I'm ever so intoxicated and at present I'm wondering why I haven't been intoxicated more often."

"No. No," Rafe said. "She's not intoxicated. She's just—"

"I am intoxicated!" Daphne insisted, stamping her foot.

Rafe groaned.

She brushed a bit of grass off her sleeve. "I am quite pleasantly intoxicated. And I have one question for you, Lord Fitzwell."

"Daphne, don't," Rafe warned.

"I'll thank you to stop using Lady Daphne's Christian name," Fitzwell added.

Rafe gave the baron a condemning glare.

"I have one question for you," Daphne repeated, pointing a finger high in the air.

"What's that?" Lord Fitzwell said, still tugging on his lapels.

"What does your backside look like?"

Lord Fitzwell's face contorted into a look of such utter confusion and horror that Rafe wondered if his nose would begin spontaneously bleeding again.

"Pardon me?" Lord Fitzwell asked. His valet would never get that coat right again after all the tugging the baron was subjecting it to tonight.

"I asked what your backside looks like. Please turn around. I'd like to see it, to compare."

"Lady Daphne, you're not well. Allow me to escort you back to the house." Rafe grabbed her elbow. If she said another word there would not only *not* be an engagement, but Daphne's reputation might be shredded past all repair.

"I am perfectly fine," Daphne said, struggling to pull herself from Rafe's grasp. "I would like another glass of champagne, actually."

"You cannot possibly mean that," Fitzwell said.

"Why not?" Daphne asked, blinking at Lord Fitzwell. "Would you like to hear a song?"

Rafe smothered his smile.

Lord Fitzwell tugged at his cravat this time. No doubt the man was sweating. So was Rafe. "I came out here to— Well, I'll just say it. I came from your brother's study, where we had a talk, came to an understanding. He provided his blessing in my asking for your hand. Your cousin told me I might find you here."

Daphne lifted her hand in front of her face and stared at it. "My hand? I thought Delilah was asleep and I can't imagine why you would want my hand. It's a funny expression, isn't it?" She waved her hand in front of her face, still staring at it.

"Lady Daphne, have you or have you not been drinking?" Fitzwell demanded, stamping his booted foot.

Daphne lifted her skirts and performed a simple three-step. "I have indeed. Quite a lot. Champagne, you know. It's ever so delicious."

Fitzwell frowned at her. "I must have your word that you'll never drink to excess again if we are to marry."

"Never? Never again?" Daphne asked, one hand clutching her necklace and her nose scrunched adorably.

"That's right. And I'd also like your word that nothing untoward happened between you and Captain Cavendish here tonight."

Daphne's face instantly sobered. She plunked her hands on her hips. "What did you *think* had happened?"

"I certainly don't know but it looked quite bad," Fitzwell replied.

Daphne's hands remained firmly planted on her hips. "So you just assumed that we had what? Been rolling around on the grass together on purpose?"

Fitzwell puffed up his chest. "I didn't know what to think."

Daphne raised her nose in the air and drew herself up to her entire five-foot height. "Lord Fitzwell, you are judgmental."

The baron's eyes nearly bugged from his skull. "Why, I—"

"And not only are you judgmental, you're also quite wrong."

Fitzwell's face turned an alarming shade of red. Rafe slid his hands into his pockets and whistled. There was nothing left to do here but to let this little drama play out.

A scattering of pebbles announced someone else's arrival as Claringdon came around the hedge. "Is something the matter? I was out for a walk and I heard a commotion."

Lord Fitzwell's eyes lit up. "No. Nothing. I was just

about to ask Lady Daphne here for her hand in marriage. I do hope you'll be able to attend the ceremony, your grace." Another obsequious bow from the baron. Rafe rolled his eyes.

Claringdon's shrewd gaze covered the three of them. "If Lady Daphne wishes it."

"I do *not* wish it," Daphne announced.

Rafe scratched the back of his neck.

"Lady Daphne, you cannot mean to exclude the Duke of Claringdon from our wedding," Lord Fitzwell said, sounding entirely shocked. He turned to Claringdon and bowed again. "I'm sorry, your grace. She's not well this evening and—"

"I don't mean that at all," Daphne interjected. "I mean that I do not wish to marry you, Lord Fitzwell."

Fitzwell's head swiveled to face her. "What? Why?"

"I do not think we suit. Nor fit . . . well." She couldn't help breaking into a new round of giggles over that one. Rafe bit the inside of his cheek to keep from laughing too.

Fitzwell's face was quickly turning a mottled shade of red. "I cannot imagine what you mean. I was under the impression that you would welcome my suit. I thought that we—"

"That was before I realized how judgmental you are," Daphne announced.

"I don't know what to say." Lord Fitzwell's hands returned to savagely grip his lapels. "I am in shock and am entirely without words."

Ah, finally, his opening.

"That may be for the best." Rafe flashed the baron a grin. "The lady has spoken, my lord. Might I suggest you leave?"

CHAPTER TWENTY-THREE

The soft knock at her bedchamber door the next morning didn't wake Daphne. She was already wide awake and had been all morning. Most of the night, too, if she was honest. Last night, Julian had sent a maid with some concoction a friend of his had invented for people who'd had too much to drink. She'd downed the noxious stuff and then, a sputtering mess, had fallen fitfully to sleep. But she'd been up with the sun, biting at the tip of her thumbnail and replaying the whole awful sordid night in her head.

"Who is it?" she called toward the door.

"It's Cass, dear. May I come in?"

Daphne sighed. No doubt her sister-in-law had heard all about her foibles last night. "Of course," she called back.

Cass came sweeping into the room wearing a pretty peach day dress and a wide smile on her lovely face. She made her way over to the bed, pulled the chair from the writing desk next to it, and took a seat. "How are you feeling, Daphne?"

Daphne groaned and rubbed a hand to her forehead. "Like I was run over by the mail coach."

Cass winced. "I'm so sorry." She reached out and patted Daphne's hand.

Daphne pressed a knuckle to her forehead. "Ooh, I knew alcohol was evil. I knew it. I cannot imagine why I thought it was a good idea to have any."

Cass's cornflower-blue eyes were filled with sympathy. "In moderation, it isn't so bad. But I hear that moderation was not with you last night."

Daphne heaved a sigh. "It wasn't. Not a bit. Oh, Cass, I completely ruined my life last night."

Cass gave her a slight smile. "Don't you think it's a bit of an exaggeration to say you ruined your *entire* life?"

Daphne put the back of her hand to her forehead. "Very well. Perhaps not my *entire* life, but a good portion of it. Certainly my plans for the future."

Cass smoothed the bedsheets with one hand. "You mean your engagement to Lord Fitzwell?"

"Yes. Not to mention my reputation. If Lord Fitzwell tells anyone what he saw, I'll be a disgraced spinster the rest of my life." Daphne bit her thumbnail again.

Cass patted her knee above the blanket. "Don't worry about that, dear. Julian had a nice long chat with Lord Fitzwell before he left."

Daphne blinked. "Lord Fitzwell left?"

"Yes."

"And Julian had a chat with him?" Daphne gulped.

"Julian made it quite clear that he'd better not hear a word against your character or he'd take it up with Fitzwell privately."

Daphne breathed a sigh of relief. Julian was a crack shot. No one in his sound mind would want to face him in a duel. "I'm glad to hear that, but if I hadn't acted so reck-lessly Julian wouldn't have had to threaten poor Lord Fitzwell."

"Don't worry about Fitzwell. I think he was extremely—how did you say it?—judgmental last night."

Daphne whimpered. "Were you there, too?"

Cass shook her head. "No. I heard about it afterward from Julian."

"Was Julian there?" Daphne groaned.

"No. He heard about it from Captain Cavendish."

"Well, Captain Cavendish certainly was there. That much I remember. I blame him for this."

Cass shook her head. "Why?"

"Because he's . . . he's just so . . ."

"Kissable?"

Daphne let her head fall into her hands. She groaned again. "Lucy told you?"

"Yes, but she swore me to secrecy, I promise."

Daphne pulled the pillow over her head and buried her face in it. "I'm ruined."

"You're hardly ruined, dear. You drank a bit too much and ended up in a seemingly compromising position with a handsome gentleman, your husband, I might add, in the garden under the moonlight. Many a girl has done much worse. But I'm afraid you cannot blame Captain Caven-dish for your behavior last night."

Daphne rubbed her forehead. "I know. It was all me. I'm the one who drank five glasses of champagne. I'm the one who jumped up on a bench. I'm the one who— Oh, I just wish Rafe had left when I asked him to. He refused, you know. If he hadn't been there last night, I wouldn't have had the opportunity to fall on him and tumble about in the grass in front of Lord Fitzwell."

Cass laughed aloud at that. "It was an unfortunate incident, to be certain, dear, but I've never known you to be much for rules. If I remember correctly, aren't you the same young lady who once tried to sneak out the window at the Hillboroughs' ball?"

Daphne lifted her eyes and blinked at her sister-in-law. "You remember that?"

"I most certainly do. You never told me. Why were you trying to sneak out that night?"

Daphne hung her head. "It's too humiliating to tell."

"A midnight assignation?" Cass's eyes sparkled.

"Something like that." Daphne sighed. "Actually, the truth is that I was sneaking out to see Rafe."

Cass's blond eyebrow arched at that. "Is that so?"

"Yes. That's when word had just come about how hurt he was and I desperately wanted to see him and I—I intended to hire a hack and visit him. Oh, Cass, I'm so ashamed of myself."

Cass patted her hand again. "You've little to be ashamed of, Daphne. It seems to me you're quite in love with Captain Cavendish and you happen to be conveniently married to him. I don't see the problem."

"I am *not* in love with him!" The words were a bit too vehement even to her own ears.

Cass gave her an understanding smile. "Aren't you?"

Daphne sniffed. "Maybe just a little, but I fully intend to rid myself of it. You don't know what he's done."

"Love is not like a cold, Daphne. You cannot wait for it to go away. It seems to me Lord Fitzwell did you a favor last night, leaving here."

Daphne groaned and flopped back against the pillows. "There I can agree with you. He obviously wasn't right for me if a bit of champagne and some rule-breaking scared him off. Mother's sure to be angry with me for making such a mess of things. After all of the work and planning you and she did for the party. I'm so sorry, Cass."

"On the contrary, I believe your mother was quite relieved to see Lord Fitzwell go. I know Aunt Willie was, and I can't say I'm particularly displeased."

Daphne sat up again and searched her sister-in-law's face. "You're not?"

"Admittedly, I didn't know him well, but I don't believe Lord Fitzwell ever had your heart, Daphne. Believe me when I tell you how important that is."

Daphne reached out and patted Cass's hand. "Cass, you're so sweet. You've loved Julian since you were a girl. But for most of us, it doesn't happen that way. We must be methodical about finding a proper husband."

"Forgive me for disagreeing, but I don't think 'methodical' and 'husband' should be in the same sentence."

Daphne gave her sister-in-law a resigned smile. "Then we shall agree to disagree. I must consult my list again. I put it up in the cabinet. Do you mind fetching it for me?"

"What list?" Cass asked, her brow furrowed.

"My list of eligible gentlemen."

Cass's eyes went wide. "You made a list?"

"Of course I did."

"See, even that? It's not like you to be so . . . planned. So . . ." Shaking her head, Cass stood and made her way over to the cabinet.

"Methodical?" Daphne offered with a small laugh.

"Yes. You've always been so free-spirited and fun, Daphne. Finding the right man, your true love, shouldn't be the equivalent of a business proposition."

"It's just up on the top shelf," Daphne said, completely ignoring her sister-in-law's entreaties.

Cass, being several inches taller than Daphne, was able to reach it without a chair. She put a hand on the shelf and felt about. She pulled out the stationery and the box with the ship replica came tumbling down. Cass caught the box but not before the lid flew off.

"What's this?" she asked, staring at the little ship.

Daphne covered her face with her hands and groaned again. "*That* is my engagement present from Captain Cavendish."

"Your *what*?"

"Rafe sent me an engagement present when he heard that I was soon to become engaged to Lord Fitzwell."

"A tiny ship?" Cass's brow remained furrowed.

"It's a replica of the ship we were on for a fortnight together."

Cass brought the stationery and the ship and came back to sit next to Daphne again. "Daphne, dear. I do believe there is a story or two you haven't told me. Start from the beginning, if you please."

Daphne closed her eyes, allowing the memories to come flooding back. "Captain Cavendish and I—Rafe—we spent two weeks on the *True Love* at the docks last spring."

"I had heard a rumor that you were missing for two weeks, dear, but I never credited it."

Daphne sighed. "I wasn't missing. I knew exactly where I was the entire time. So did Donald. The story Mama and Donald told everyone was that I was visiting Aunt Willie, but obviously rumors spread regardless."

Cass patted her hand. "Go on."

"Donald wanted me to help Rafe. He allowed me to go with him, pose as his cabin boy. Interpret Russian."

"Did anything happen between you, dear? You and Captain Cavendish, I mean?"

Daphne closed her eyes again. "Not for a lack of trying on my part."

"Oh, dear. You *must* tell me what that means."

Daphne shook her head. It was too embarrassing to tell. But she had to tell someone. She had to rid herself of it somehow. Perhaps Cass, kind, sweet, loving Cass, could help her sort all of this out.

"I hired a hack and met Rafe at the docks. Donald knew about it, of course, but I wanted to be independent. We spent nearly two weeks on the ship. Two nights before we were to leave, I—" She covered her face again. She just couldn't look at Cass while she said it.

"Go, on, dear," Cass prompted.

"I . . . I . . . Oh, Cass, I tried to kiss him."

Cass's eyes rounded even further if that were possible. "You did?"

"Yes. I thought we'd been getting closer. I thought he had . . . developed feelings for me. And, after all, we were married and I . . . I made a complete fool of myself."

"Captain Cavendish didn't kiss you back, I take it?" Cass asked.

"No. He not only didn't kiss me back, he told me he thought of me as a *sister*."

Cass grimaced. "No!"

"Yes!"

Cass shook her head softly. "Well, that is unfortunate."

"Two days later, I found a blond doxy in his bed at the inn and— Oh, that's an entirely different story, but suffice it to say that Rafe never once acted inappropriately toward me during that entire fortnight."

"You can hardly blame the man for being a gentleman, darling. Though the sister comment is disturbing. I think I need to hear the story about this blond woman."

Daphne told her. The whole awful thing. When she was finished Cass gave her a sympathetic smile. "That doesn't sound good, does it?"

"No, it doesn't. It wasn't and I—" Daphne slapped her palm to her forehead and groaned in pain. "Oh, fiddle! Fiddle! Fiddle!"

"What?" Cass touched a hand to her throat.

Daphne squeezed her eyes shut and scowled. "I just remembered. I tried to kiss him again last night in the garden. He stepped away from me. That's why I fell on top of him."

"You fell on top of him?"

"Yes."

"Because he moved away when you tried to kiss him?"

"Yes. Oh, Cass, Lord Fitzwell was right to leave me. I am a shameless hussy. A harlot. A wanton."

Cass was obviously fighting a smile.

"Don't laugh at me, Cass," Daphne said miserably.

"I'm sorry, dear. Truly I am, but I think you're far from a wanton for trying to kiss Captain Cavendish in the garden. You must remember, you are married, dear. You keep forgetting. And he may have stepped away from you last night but he kissed you in the library, didn't he?"

"Yes."

"Well, then. He may have had other reasons for stepping away last night."

"I know Julian threatened to murder him, but—"

"What?"

"Julian told me. He had two conditions for allowing me to go with Rafe tonight. The first is that I remain safe. The second is to not touch me."

"Well, no wonder. Captain Cavendish is trying to do the honorable thing. He wouldn't be much of a gentleman if he kissed an intoxicated lady, would he? Not to mention he'd promised her brother to keep his hands to himself."

"But I don't want him to keep his hands to himself," Daphne groaned.

A gasp sounded from the other side of the closed door and Cass turned wide eyes to Daphne.

Daphne simply shook her head and rolled her eyes. "Don't worry. I suspect it's just Delilah. She has her ear pressed to the door."

"I do not!" came Delilah's disgruntled voice.

"You might as well come in, Dee," Daphne called. "And please mind the door slamming. I have the devil of a head."

The door opened and Delilah, a huge white satin bow in her hair and a fresh white day dress on, came prancing in. She closed the door with extreme care. "Very well, I might have been listening, a little."

"I never doubted it," Daphne replied.

Delilah came to stand at the foot of the bed. "What does it feel like to have a devil of a head?"

Daphne groaned again. "It's dreadful and I hope you never find out."

"I'd have the devil of a head in an instant if it meant I would end up rolling about in the grass with Captain Cavendish."

Daphne's jaw dropped. "Delilah, I swear, if you tell anyone—"

"I know. I know. Don't worry. I intend to remain entirely silent on the matter."

Daphne laid her head back against the pillows and rubbed her temples. A memory pushed itself through her hazy mind. "Did you tell Lord Fitzwell where to find me last night, Delilah?"

Delilah had a foxlike smile on her face. "Perhaps."

"I thought you'd gone up to bed. How did you know?"

"You cannot possibly think I would remain in bed with all of the interesting things happening in this house last night."

"What interesting things?" Daphne asked, pressing her fingertips to her temples.

"Things like Lord Fitzwell finding you outside in the gardens with Captain Cavendish."

"But that only happened because *you* told him where I was. How did you know, by the way?"

"I can't be held responsible if I happened to help along the interesting things. And I knew because I was the one who pointed you in the direction of the gardens last night. Don't you remember? You were singing a song I taught you. I knew Captain Cavendish was out there."

Daphne sat up straight and then groaned and rubbed her skull again. She'd moved far too quickly. "Delilah Montbank, tell me you did not orchestrate that entire set of madness that occurred last night."

Delilah put her hands on both hips. "Well, I like that. You're welcome."

"You did it all on purpose?" Daphne groaned. "Why?"

"Because Lord Fitzwell is not meant to be my cousin."

Daphne turned a pleading look toward Cass. "What do you think about this?"

Cass shrugged. "I can't say I blame her. And I'm quite impressed by her ingenuity."

Delilah beamed and executed a haphazard pirouette before bowing to Cass. "*Merci*, my lady."

"Did Aunt Willie know what you were about?" Daphne asked her cousin.

"Oh, Cousin Daphne." Delilah rolled her eyes. "Aunt Willie is the one who informed me that Captain Cavendish was in the gardens alone. Now, I had better get downstairs before Mrs. Upton eats all of the teacakes." And with that, Delilah skipped back to the door and left.

Daphne gave Cass a dejected look. "My entire family is plotting against me."

"It's not as bad as all of that. I promise you," Cass said. "I think you should just take the day and rest, dear. There's no need to make any hasty decisions."

Daphne shook her head. "No. No. There's no time to rest. Read me the list of eligibles, won't you? I may have made a mess of things with Lord Fitzwell but he's not the only gentleman in London."

"I don't think—"

"Please, Cass. Read them. After I get back from the mission with Rafe, we'll have another party. There will be another engagement. And by then I'll have my annulment so all will be well."

"I swear. I've never known you to sit still for so much as a minute," Cass replied. "Fine. I'll read them to you. And after you pick your next potential bridegroom, what then?"

"Then, I prepare for tonight. Rafe is coming for me after dinner. I must transform myself into a convincing cabin boy."

CHAPTER TWENTY-FOUR

Rafe rapped on the back door to the Swifdon house. He'd maneuvered his mount through the streets, around the mews, and through the alley behind the Earl of Swifdon's Mayfair residence. No one would see Lady Daphne Swift leaving the house dressed as a boy.

He'd left last night soon after Claringdon had escorted Daphne back inside. First, he'd found Swifdon in his study and informed him that his little sister was very much the worse for drink. He'd told Swifdon that he believed Lucy Hunt was ensuring that Daphne got tucked into bed without her mother being any the wiser. Swifdon had thanked him for his discretion, asked to speak with Lord Fitzwell privately, and told Rafe that he would send him a letter in the morning informing him of Daphne's condition. Apparently, Swifdon knew of a concoction that was said to quickly cure a sick head. Good thing, because worse for drink or not, Rafe still desperately needed Daphne's help.

Later, Rafe had watched with an unabashed smile on

his face as Lord Fitzwell ordered his coach and left the Swifts' house, jamming his hat atop his head, and ripping his coat from Pengree's grasp.

Then, Rafe had left. He'd returned to his rooms in a less fashionable part of town. He'd been relieved, actually, when Swifdon's letter had arrived this morning saying that Daphne had made a full recovery thanks to the concoction and was intent upon fulfilling her promise. Rafe had been a bit too relieved, perhaps. He'd expected Daphne to be angry with him, perhaps use her failed engagement as an excuse to back out of their agreement. He'd been wrong about her.

The back door swung open and Pengree was there. Clearly, the butler had been expecting him. "Captain Cavendish. Lord Swifdon wishes to see you."

Rafe followed the butler through the back of the house, up a small staircase, and through a series of corridors until they came to the familiar space in front of the doors that led to Swifdon's study.

Swifdon stood as soon as Rafe was announced. He moved to the sideboard and made Rafe a stiff drink. He turned and thrust it in Rafe's hand. "Down it. You'll need it."

Rafe accepted the glass with a smile and a nod. "For the mission?"

"No, for dealing with Daphne" was Swifdon's reply.

Rafe snorted. "I'm glad to hear she's feeling better. She was three sheets to the wind when I left."

"Yes, Cass tells me she was a bit green this morning."

Rafe set the drink aside. "I can only imagine. I'm pleased to hear that she's agreed to go through with it."

"Daphne is one of the most noble people I know. She's dreamed her whole life of being of use to the war effort.

Now the wars are over, of course, but this is exactly the type of thing I'd never be able to talk her out of."

"I understand, my lord."

If Swifdon thought it odd that Rafe wasn't drinking, he didn't indicate it. Swifdon tossed his own bit of brandy to the back of his throat. "I trust Daphne and I trust you, but I don't need to remind you what will happen to you if she is harmed."

"No." Rafe folded his hands behind his back and bowed. "Her life will be more important than my own."

"I've no doubt." Swifdon nodded. "Now, for a few specifics. Cass has taken Mother to the opera tonight to get her out of the house so she won't see Daphne leave. Mother thinks Daphne is going to Lucy Hunt's country house for several days to get over her disappointment about Fitzwell."

"Is she? Disappointed about Fitzwell, I mean?" As soon as the words left his mouth, Rafe silently cursed himself for asking them.

Swifdon grinned at him. "That's a question for Daphne." He rang for Pengree again. The butler appeared soon after. "Please ask Lady Daphne to join us."

The servant nodded and left the room.

Rafe lifted his brows.

"I have a similar warning for Daphne," Swifdon explained.

When Daphne entered the room moments later, Rafe sucked in his breath again but for an entirely different reason this time. She was wearing tight buff buckskin breeches that outlined every curve of her sweet backside, a plain, serviceable white shirt with a tight waistcoat that was obviously hiding the fact that she had breasts, however bound they might be. She wore small black top boots and her hair was coiled tight atop her head and hidden underneath a cap that completed her attire.

It was standard dock clothing, but no cabin boy could make it look as good as Daphne did. Anyone else would only see a slight boy but Rafe knew better. Her tiny waist accentuated, her glorious backside highlighted. Rafe glanced away before his own breeches tightened. For his part, he was dressed like a ruffian ship's captain. A white shirt, dark gray breeches, black boots, and a navy-colored coat, white cravat, and a tricorn.

Daphne gave him a once-over. He had to struggle to keep from doing the same to her . . . again.

"Captain," she said simply, barely allowing her lips to part. They quickly resumed their thin line.

"Grey." He nodded at her.

"I'd offer you a drink, too, Daphne, but something tells me you'd turn it down tonight," Swifdon said.

Daphne pressed her hand to her middle. "Ugh. I can barely countenance even seeing that vile liquid."

"I understand," Swifdon said to his sister. "Now, listen to me."

She quickly turned her head toward her brother. Her face took on a serious demeanor.

"I know you've been angry with Cavendish, but emotions can get you killed in situations like this. You and Rafe must treat each other like cohorts. Your life may well depend on it."

Daphne nodded once. "There is nothing emotional about this. I am entirely prepared to be nothing but proficient and do my duty." She lifted her chin, her face reflecting her pride. "For the Crown."

Rafe nearly let out a sigh of relief. He trusted this about Daphne. She wanted to find the men who killed Donald as much as he did and she would do what she must regardless of what had happened between them over the last two days.

"You can do this, Daphne," Swifdon said. "I have no doubt. I would not allow you to go if I thought you were in danger. Cavendish will keep you safe."

"I will keep myself safe," Daphne replied, her face blank and determined. "Don't worry for me, Julian." She stepped forward and hugged her brother tightly. "I love you."

Still hugging her, Swifdon said, "I love you, too, Daphne."

She let go of her brother, cleared her throat, and turned to Rafe, obviously shaking off the tears that had threatened to spill from her eyes. "Shall we?" The tears had been quickly replaced by a glint of steel that told him she'd completely shut him out of her emotions. Good. It was better this way. They needed to treat each other like nothing more than two spies on a mission working for the greater good of the country.

He nodded once. "Let's go."

"Be safe, both of you," Swifdon said.

Rafe and Daphne nodded.

Rafe held open the door and Daphne made her way through it, not acknowledging him. He followed her down the corridor, the steps, and toward the back door.

"Cousin Daphne!"

Daphne turned at the childlike female voice that came from behind them. "Delilah? What are you doing out of bed? You shouldn't be down here."

"I couldn't allow you to leave without saying good-bye." Delilah shook her head. "I mean, good luck. You'll be a hero, Daphne. I know it."

Daphne smiled at that. She squeezed the child's

shoulder. "Take care of Mother for me, Dee. And Cass and Julian." She lowered her voice to a whisper. "Just don't let Julian *know* you're taking care of him."

Delilah nodded and her dark curls bounced. "Consider it done. And please come back with many harrowing stories. *J'adore* a harrowing story."

Daphne shook her head. "I'll see what I can do."

"Oh, Captain Cavendish," came Delilah's sweet voice.

Rafe turned back to look at the girl. "Yes?"

"I do hope you'll be a gentleman while in the company of my cousin."

Rafe struggled to keep the smile from his face. "Of course, Miss Montbank. I give you my word."

"But not *too* much of a gentleman." And with that, Delilah was gone.

CHAPTER TWENTY-FIVE

Daphne marched out of the back door of her brother's town house. Rafe followed her, but as soon as they entered the alley, she felt the shift in him. She was no longer Lady Daphne Swift to him. She was Thomas Grey, the cabin boy.

Rafe didn't wait for her to precede him to where his mount was tied to a post near the mews. Instead, his long strides devoured the pebbled ground while she raced to keep up with him, pressing her cap onto her head to keep it from flying off.

Rafe had untied the horse by the time Daphne joined him. He swung up onto the animal, turned to her, and gave her a quick, unfeeling boost up, pulling her up behind him. Daphne quickly wrapped her hands around his hips as Rafe wasted no time sending the horse into a gallop. Daphne clung to him, praying her hat didn't wing off into the night sky. She clenched her hands around his middle, and desperately tried to ignore the outline of Rafe's flat muscled stomach beneath his coat and how good he smelled. Oh, fiddle. She was sniffing at his back. *Idiot.*

She needed to control herself. After all, she was going to be stuck with him in close quarters for up to a sennight. She needed to put a stop to these ludicrous thoughts. Julian had been right. There was no time for anger or pettiness. There was also no time for unwanted lust. They had a mission to accomplish and accomplish it, they would. This wasn't about her. It was for Donald. And the Crown.

Rafe spoke to the horse and kicked at its flanks as they rode through the streets, headed for the docks at a brisk clip.

The ride was not long and Daphne soon noticed the change in not only the inhabitants of the streets, but also the sights and smells. The docks were full of sailors on leave, whores, mongers, and a general riffraff of folk she would never have been exposed to in her life as Lady Daphne. It smelled like brackish water and alcohol and what Daphne feared was urine. She remembered all of this from the last time she'd been here. Despite the unpleasant smells, a thrill shot through her. Being here again was an adventure. It was entirely different from her staid, laced-up life in Mayfair. Anything could happen here. Anything. Her blood sang through her veins with excitement.

Rafe maneuvered the mount down the narrow wooden planks of the docks. Daphne remembered the drill. They would tie the mount to a post at the dock where Salty, Rafe's first mate, would see to it. Rafe quickly dismounted and Daphne tried to ignore the warm feel of Rafe's hands on her sides as he helped her down from the horse. He had only touched her momentarily, the way he would a cabin boy, certainly not in a way that could be described as sensual, but still, the feel of his skin against hers made her suck in her breath.

She shook her head. She must concentrate on the mission. Nothing but the mission.

"There's the rowboat." Rafe pointed to a tiny craft barely bobbing above the waterline.

"And the ship?" Daphne turned and looked out into the darkened waters. Several hulking vessels rested hunched in the brackish water.

"There." Rafe pointed to the farthest one.

Daphne looked at it. There she was. The *True Love*. Not a particularly fine vessel or a large one with its crew of only seven, but one that made sense for a small-time captain dealing in a few bits and goods here and there and dabbling in smuggling—the role Rafe was playing for the sake of the Russians and the French spies. The lopsided sloop had seen better days, but she remained sturdy and shipshape. Staring out at the vessel, Daphne swallowed the lump in her throat. The last time she'd left that ship, all her dreams had been dashed against the side of the dock. This time she was no longer the naïve young girl who'd been here before. She was older, more experienced. And had already had her heart broken. It could never hurt more than the first time.

If she were Lady Daphne Swift, Rafe would have carefully helped her into the small vessel. But as Thomas Grey the cabin boy, Rafe could do nothing but allow her to precede him and then hop in after her. She'd perfected getting in and out of the small boat the last time, however. She needed no help.

She braced her right hand on the right side of the tiny boat, her left hand on the left side, and stepped carefully toward the center, being certain not to rock too much. With a self-satisfied smirk on her face, she lifted her head to Rafe. Was that admiration in his eyes?

"Nicely done," he murmured under his breath. He maneuvered easily into the boat in front of her and grabbed an oar.

Daphne lifted the other oar. "You don't have to take care of me, you know."

"Good, because I won't have time," he tossed over his shoulder. "Now, on my count."

Rafe poised the right oar above the water, Daphne poised the left one, and together they rowed out to the sloop anchored in the harbor.

Rafe had taken off his coat to row. Daphne tried not to look at his muscles outlined in his shirtsleeves by the light of the moon and stars. Instead, she concentrated on keeping her oar strokes on pace with his.

Her mind wandered to their exchange from a few moments ago. "Good, because I won't have time," he'd told her. Never let it be said that Captain Cavendish wasn't blunt when he needed to be. Fine. But she'd meant what she'd said, too. She didn't need him to take care of her, nor did she expect him to. They were playing a dangerous game now, one in which lives were at stake. Julian had asked Rafe to take care of her and she knew how Rafe truly felt. He thought of her as a child. Someone whose family had taken care of her her whole life, pampered her, treated her like a princess. Softened every blow. Certainly not a useful creature. Certainly not someone who could be of help to him, the man who never needed help from anyone. She knew what he was thinking. She might have successfully climbed into the rowboat on her own, but he didn't believe for one second that she didn't need him.

She clutched her hands tighter around the oar and stroked harder, faster. She'd show him.

By the time they came alongside the sloop, Daphne had

already begun to break a sweat and was breathing heavily. Rafe, however, who'd matched her stroke for stroke, appeared completely unaffected. He'd even started whistling. He grabbed the rope that hung from the side of the ship and secured the small boat alongside it. Then, he nodded to Daphne to climb up first. There might not be any handholding or help, but he was allowing her to go first in case she should slip. She knew that.

She took a deep breath and jumped up to catch the bottom of the rickety wooden ladder that hung haphazardly from the side of the ship. It had always been a bit too high for her. But height challenges be damned. She grabbed it on the first try and smiled a bit to herself. She still could do it. She wiggled up the ladder as quickly as possible and vaulted onto the deck, where she landed with her booted feet braced apart. She sucked in a deep draught of sea air. Ah, she remembered that smell. She'd never forget it. Nor would she forget the feeling of being so free on the ship. Wearing breeches was absolutely delightful. It felt so delicious, as if she could do anything. Run. Jump. No inconvenient skirts to trip her. It was liberating. It was intoxicating. It was adventurous. Just like Calliope Cauldwell.

Daphne braced her hands on her hips and stared across the wide wooden deck, taking in the sights and sounds. It took a moment for her sea legs to come back under her. The gentle rhythm of the waving and swaying of the wood had a cadence all its own. There was an art to it, a craft to being able to keep one's balance on the deck of a ship. She'd mastered it once before. After a few moments, it was as if she'd never left.

Her eyes scanned the deck. The other men were there. The crew. She'd met them all before. They were also spies.

She knew them only by their false names and they knew her only as Grey. In addition to Salty, the first mate, there was Grim, the second mate, Holby, the bosun, Greggs and Peterby, the deckhands, and Cook, who was approximately forty years of age with dark, kind eyes and dark curly hair. She didn't see Salty. Perhaps he was still ashore. Salty was the opposite of his name, surprisingly young and handsome. In fact, with his light hair and blue eyes, he looked a bit like Rafe. Not half so domineering, however.

Daphne liked the entire crew. They might be a small operation but they were a large enough group to man the *True Love*. In her free time, Daphne liked to let her imagination run wild as to the real identities of the crewmates. Of course, she had no idea what the men did when they weren't on this ship. A few of them had been chosen for their deep tans and weathered faces. Men who spent their lives at sea must look the part. But they were in service to the Crown. Salty and Grim knew her true identity. The rest did not. For her part, she had no idea if Salty and Grim were in the military and, if so, what their rank was. For all she knew, she was standing next to important officers. But it was truly more fun this way. They all had their secrets.

"Tommy," called Grim, who was about thirty and handsome with brown eyes and brown hair, a medium build, and a quick smile. He came marching over and clapped Daphne on the back. She grinned at him. "Ah, lad, you look far too clean to be on the *True*." He swiped his thumb down her cheek and Daphne had no doubt that a streak of grit remained.

"Thanks for that, Grim," she said, still grinning.

Rafe was behind her then and after he'd greeted everyone, he led Daphne down toward the stern, into the companionway, and down a small flight of stairs that led to the captain's cabin.

"I would have liked to have stayed out there longer and talked to everyone," Daphne said, as soon as the door to the cabin shut behind them.

"It's not a good idea. One or two of those men haven't been officially on leave for months. And you're looking particularly . . ."—he cleared his throat—"good in those breeches."

Daphne gaped at him. Then, she turned toward the wall to hide her little smile. "Don't tell me you think my honor is at risk with the crew of the *True Love*."

"No, not your honor; I'd slice off a man's hand for touching you. It's my honor that's at stake. I'd hate to have to explain to Wellington why one of his most trusted spies is handless."

Daphne's eyes rounded. "You wouldn't truly do that, would you? Slice off their hands?"

Rafe lowered his voice. "On this ship, we are a real crew. I would do that and more."

Daphne swallowed. This was real. All of it. Adventurous, yes. Fun, perhaps. But quite real. Donald had lost his life dealing with the same men they were soon to deal with. Rafe had come close to death. This was all quite, quite real.

She nodded solemnly. "What's the plan? Will the smugglers be here tonight?"

"They've anchored out tonight. That's why the *True Love* is already here. We wanted them to see us when they came in. We've yet to spot the men themselves, but tomorrow we'll go ashore and I'll look for them."

Daphne nodded again. She glanced around the sparse room. "What about the sleeping arrangements?" She gulped, barely able to push the words past her dry lips. "Same as before?" She turned to make her way next door to the tiny closet-sized room where Rafe had made her a small but tidy bunk last time.

"No." The word sliced through the air. "We must sleep in here together. I can't risk letting you out of my sight. I promised your brother."

Daphne froze, her hand midway inside her bag. Sleeping in the same room with Rafe? That certainly wouldn't help matters much. She'd already been thinking about his shoulders and his muscles and . . . She turned in a circle, her eyes wide. There was only one bed in the captain's cabin. "But where—"

"Don't worry." His irresistibly wicked grin returned. He crossed over to the cupboard, opened it, and pulled out a mash of wooden sticks and a crisscross of fabric. "I'll take the hammock."

CHAPTER TWENTY-SIX

Daphne slept fitfully. She dreamt of spies, and smugglers, and torture, and murderers. She dreamt of being swallowed up by a giant sea creature. And then, after all the bad dreams fell away, she dreamt of being tangled in the hammock with Rafe, and that was perhaps the most disturbing dream of all. She was wrapped up as if in a cocoon in the captain's bunk, tossing and turning, sweating in the breezeless room while Rafe appeared to be contentedly sleeping, swinging with the sway of the ship, hoisted up in his hammock between the two wooden posts in the cabin.

He was completely unaffected by her presence, she thought with some chagrin as she pushed at her flat pillow in an attempt to make it more comfortable. She'd forgotten about the awful little pillows on ships. Rafe had explained to her last time that most of the crew didn't even have a pillow and she should stop behaving like a princess if the pillow wasn't good enough for her. She frowned into the darkness. She wouldn't make the same mistake again. Nothing. *Nothing* would be too uncomfortable that would make her complain. Not even her bound breasts that were far from comfortable. The moonlight that shone through the small window at the far end of the room provided the only light. It fell across Rafe's high cheekbone. The man was beautiful. It was really too unfair. His dark eyelashes brushed his cheeks as he calmly swung to and fro. He was snoring slightly but even that wasn't annoying. Donald used to snore so loudly he'd nearly wake the entire house, but Rafe's snores were barely discernible. *That* was what was annoying. The man was nearly perfect, like an angel come to life.

She stared up at the dark wooden ceiling. She needed to stop having such petty thoughts. Their mission was much more important than all of that. Even what had transpired between them last time. Even the blond doxy.

Daphne rolled onto her side and closed her eyes. What would tomorrow bring? Would they find the smugglers? Get the letters? Eventually avenge Donald's death? That was the most difficult part. Not knowing. But she would try. She would do whatever she must. Even if it involved torture. Or death. She gulped and counted three. Yes, even death.

The sun rose bright and shining the next morning and Rafe was up with it. Daphne remained huddled in her bed. He left her but not before pulling out the chamber pot from under the bunk so she'd have access to it when she woke. She'd had quite an experience of it last time, adapting to the ways of the ship, but after Rafe had explained to her that it was usually the job of a cabin boy to dispose of such refuse, she seemed relieved and did that duty for herself quite happily. He spared her his own chamber pot of course, but it still made him chuckle to think of her taking on such a task even for herself. But she'd done it gamely and with no complaints, if only a slight blush on her cheeks.

Rafe had slept fitfully. He'd drifted to sleep with the sound of the waves slapping along the side of the ship and the moonlight streaming through the widow. He hadn't been on a ship in months. Normally, the sea was like home to him. But the vision of Daphne's tight little arse scurrying up the ladder to the deck in front of him would not remove itself from his mind. It was as if it was burned there. Indefinitely. Last time they'd been together on this ship, he'd thought her pretty, certainly. But there was something about her now, her attitude, her poise, her bravery. The memory of their scorching hot kiss in Swifdon's library. It had been a complete surprise to him. Not to mention that alluring little smudge of dirt on her cheek. He'd had to stop himself twice from reaching out and wiping it off.

Rafe scrubbed his hands viciously across his face as if he could scrub away the memory lurking in his mind. This type of thinking would merely serve to drive him mad. It didn't matter how alluring she was or that her engagement to Lord Fitzwell hadn't happened. Daphne Swift was off limits for a dozen other reasons and Rafe would do well to remember it.

By the time he returned to the cabin an hour later, Daphne was up and the chamber pot was securely tucked underneath the bunk once more.

"Care for some breakfast?" he asked, handing her a small plate with a biscuit and some jam.

"Jam?" She arched a brow.

"We're close to shore. You may even get tea with milk if you ask Cook nicely."

She made an adorable little squealing noise in the back of her throat.

She sat at the small desk that was attached to the corner of the room and took delicate bites of her biscuit. "When will we go ashore and meet the smugglers?"

Rafe grinned at her. "First of all, you need to remember to prune your vocabulary of words like 'smugglers' and 'spies.' No one around here uses those words except the authorities."

She nodded. "Understood."

"And second we'll leave in due time. You seem eager."

"I am." She glanced out the window where a seagull looped overhead. "I've hated these men for months, years really."

Rafe crossed his arms over his chest and leaned against one of the wooden posts that held up his hammock. "Remember what your brother said. You must not allow your hatred for them to get the best of you."

She set her jaw and picked up her biscuit. "I understand."

"And the men we're meeting today aren't the men who killed Donald."

The biscuit dropped to the plate. "But you told me—"

Rafe lifted a hand, palm first. "Hear me out. They are the men who work for the men who killed Donald. To get to the others, we must first get through these men."

"I see." Daphne calmly picked up her biscuit again. "Will you explain it to me?"

Rafe nodded. That was something else he liked about Daphne. She could be reasoned with. That's why he'd known he could take her on this mission and not have to worry about whether she was angry with him. He liked how she'd calmly asked for an explanation. She deserved one.

He sat on the bunk. "Of course this is highly confidential information," he began.

Daphne nodded. "You have my word that I won't tell anyone."

He nodded back. "The men who killed Donald are a group of spies in France. The men here are a small group of Russians who have been working for the French. Frankly, these particular men will work for anyone who gives them enough coin. They have no loyalties. Though Russia has no great love for France, these men were playing both sides of the war. Making money and connections wherever it was convenient for them. Simply put, they led the French to us in exchange for coin and now we intend to get them to lead us to the French in exchange for goods that they want."

Daphne finished swallowing the bit of biscuit that she'd taken. "No loyalty. Those bastards."

"Yes, but it's not uncommon. Once Napoleon had been sent to Elba many of the French attempted to get back into the good graces of the English. Of course when the emperor returned, they were only too happy to pretend they had never left his employ. These Russians are the same. There are always men who can be bought . . . for a price."

"Go on," Daphne said, taking another bite.

"After Adam Hunt was captured in France, his brother, Collin, returned to find him. But Donald and I had already set out on the same mission. It's true that we were asked to find Adam if we were able, but our real mission was to find these men who were traitors to both England and France."

Daphne nodded. Adam and Collin Hunt were Derek, the Duke of Claringdon's, younger brothers. "Julian always believed Adam's disappearance in France had been the reason for Donald's mission."

"So it was, but I also needed the use of his knowledge of Russian to find the men who had Adam. I'd spent months here at the docks trying to infiltrate the group of men in France. The leaders never came here. They only had their Russian lackeys working for them. They believed Russians would be less suspicious than Frenchmen."

"The smugglers we're going to meet are the Russians? The ones we met last time I was with you here?"

"Yes. Exactly. They work for the men in France."

"But how do you intend to find the men in France if they never come here?"

"That's just it. If we can trade for the letters they've sent, we can trace their last known whereabouts in France."

"Why can't you follow them when they go to France to meet their French allies?"

"Donald's death put an end to their meetings with the Frenchmen. They know they're being watched. At least they suspect it. They limit their interactions now to closely guarded letters. The Russians believe we're trading secrets to the English government for money and goods. They don't know we *work* for the government. If we can make these men trust us enough to give us the letters, we can go to France and find the men they work for."

Daphne's voice trembled. "The men who tortured you and . . . killed Donald?"

"Yes." Rafe clenched his jaw. "I never forget a face. Or a voice. I'll know them immediately. In the meantime, I need you to interpret if their allies say anything important in Russian."

"I'm ready, Captain," she said solemnly. "Let's go."

CHAPTER TWENTY-SEVEN

The Dancing Pig tavern was a seedy place indeed. It was populated by an unruly misfit group of drinkers, gamblers, ladies of questionable repute, and not a few patrons who were wholly incapacitated at far too early an hour in the day. A few of them had passed out under broken tables and stools and were being licked by dogs who'd wandered in from the streets in search of their leftovers and meat-stained clothing.

Daphne fought the urge to daintily step over the refuse and old food that was strewn across the filthy floors. Instead, true to her role as a cabin boy, she pretended she didn't even notice it. She let her boots slide through the muck, maintaining a blank face as she and Rafe made their way to a table on the far end of the place away from the windows. Apparently smugglers (or whatever they were called) disliked windows.

"Sit behind me. Pretend you're not listening. Concentrate on your drink. And don't say a word," Rafe ordered under his breath, calling to the barmaid to bring over two mugs of ale.

"I remember," Daphne whispered back.

The barmaid soon arrived. She whistled when she saw Rafe. "My, aren't ye a good-lookin' one, eh?" Daphne was just about to roll her eyes when she realized the barmaid was talking about *her*. "Ye'r a pretty boy, ain't ya?" The woman batted her eyelashes at Daphne.

Heat rushed to Daphne's cheeks. She ducked her head and pulled her cap down over her forehead. Rafe's laughter followed. "You'll have to excuse my friend," he said. "He's not particularly, ahem, experienced."

Daphne's face grew even hotter and she tugged her cap down farther.

The barmaid giggled. "Oy, but I'd like ta teach 'im a thing o' two." She must have turned toward Rafe. "Ye ain't too bad-looking yerself, guv. Interested in a quick tumble?"

Daphne pressed her lips together and counted ten. Granted, the blond she'd found in Rafe's bed had been a sight better looking and more refined than this tavern barmaid but it still brought back the memory to poke at her. It would be just like Rafe to take the barmaid up on it. If they weren't just about to meet the smugglers, no doubt he would. He hadn't allowed his work to stop him last time.

"No, but thank you for the offer, kind lady," Rafe said. "My friend here will be certain to let you know if he changes his mind."

Rafe laughed and Daphne slunk lower in her chair. The barmaid sashayed off and Daphne pulled her mug of ale from the table in front of her. She peered down into the dark liquid.

Ale was revolting. This Daphne already knew from the

last time she'd falsely ordered one, which had also been the last time they were in a dockside tavern. She'd tentatively tasted it and promptly wished to spit it out. It wasn't as if spit wasn't commonplace in such an establishment. But even pretending to be a cabin boy, she couldn't bring herself to spit on the floor. Instead, she'd just ever-so-carefully lifted the mug to her lips again and deposited the contents back inside. Later, she'd pretended to accidentally knock the mug to the dirt floor and shrugged when Rafe gave her a why-the-hell-did-you-do-that glare.

This time she didn't even bother with a sip. She still wasn't entirely over her bout with alcohol from two nights ago. She had no intention of downing more of the hideous stuff. She shuddered. Then she concentrated on assuming her role as a bored cabin boy hanging around a tavern waiting for his captain to finish his business. She'd spent a fair amount of time before their last mission studying the actions of young boys. She'd even asked Donald for suggestions. Donald, of course, had been quite a different sort of boy than a cabin boy would be, but one thing she learned was that boys loved to lean on the two back legs of their chairs whenever possible. She'd practiced quite a bit and nearly perfected the art at home, though Mama had walked in on her once in the breakfast room and gave her a look as if she'd taken leave of her senses, then warned her that she could break her neck doing such a thing. Daphne had smiled bashfully and thanked her mother for the warning.

But now, here in the tavern, she kicked away a small pile of leftover bones, and set about balancing on the back two legs of her chair with great aplomb. By the time the two men they were meeting arrived, she'd managed to perfect her balance and hold her mug in the air without spilling.

When the Russians entered the tavern, Rafe darted a look her way and then toward the doors. Daphne continued to balance on her chair but her gaze briefly touched on the two swarthy-looking men and then she looked away. She barely nodded back at him to indicate that she'd seen them.

It didn't take the men long to locate Rafe and they came marching over soon after. Rafe inclined his head toward the two chairs next to him. The men grabbed the rickety wooden chairs, turned them around, and straddled them. Daphne made a mental note. She'd do the same if she ever pretended to be a swarthy smuggler. Men seemed to like to have their legs spread quite a bit. Fascinating really. Even Rafe, who sat facing forward, had his legs spread open at the knees, boots firmly planted on the dirty floor in front of him.

"Gentlemen," he said smoothly as soon as the two had taken their seats.

"Captain," one of the men said gruffly in a thick Russian accent.

Rafe nodded at them both.

"Who's that?" The second man, who seemed barely taller than Daphne, jabbed a fat finger in her direction. He, too, spoke with a heavy Russian accent.

"You remember my cabin boy, Grey?"

The taller man grunted his apparent approval. But Shorty kept staring at her with beady eyes.

"Grey, say good morning to Anton and Viktor," Rafe prodded.

"Mornin'," Daphne mumbled. She pulled at the visor of her cap in greeting and went back to pretending to drink her ale. She remembered them. The taller one was Anton and beady eyes was Viktor. She wouldn't forget.

The two men barely nodded at her in return greeting and then Rafe leaned forward. Anton and Viktor followed suit. They talked in hushed tones that Daphne struggled to hear. Rafe had warned her that it would be difficult. They were discussing their trade and it would be odd for Rafe to speak of such things in a loud voice. That's why she'd positioned herself closer to the Russians' seats than Rafe's. Still, she'd hoped they would be louder. She held her breath to hear better while trying to appear as if she was *not* leaning toward them. Spying was downright difficult.

Thankfully, she was able to pick up some of the conversation.

"I can have everything to you tonight," Rafe finished. "I just need to return to my ship and make the preparations, hire a wherry."

"After we get it, we'll need a few days to examine it, for quality," Anton grunted.

"Of course," Rafe replied. "How long do you need?"

The two spoke in hushed tones but Daphne made out "Friday."

"Agreed," Rafe answered. "But if I wait till Friday, I expect to get the full price immediately. I won't countenance any last-minute shortages or delays."

Daphne knew the "price" was the letters Rafe wanted, but they obviously weren't speaking about it in those terms.

Viktor kept glaring at her with those dark beady eyes of his. She tried to look as if she were whistling a tune to herself. She could only hope he believed it.

"Do we have an agreement?" Rafe finally asked.

The men turned toward each other and began speaking quietly in their native tongue. Daphne caught her breath. This was it. The reason she had come. She continued her balancing act, staring straight ahead of her, desperately hoping the look on her face indicated she was nothing more than a bored cabin boy waiting for her captain to finish his business. But her senses were on high alert. The hair on the back of her neck stood up and her ears prickled. Sweat trailed down between her bound breasts.

She continued to hold her breath, listening intently, fighting against the urge to squeeze her eyes closed she was listening so attentively. And she heard every word.

A few minutes later the men stopped talking and Anton turned to Rafe. "Agreed. Have your men send everything to us. We'll see you back here on Friday."

CHAPTER TWENTY-EIGHT

Rafe waited until they were well on their way back to the *True Love* in the rowboat before asking Daphne. "What did they say?"

"Taller, I mean . . . Anton, said the price would depend on the quality of the goods."

Rafe laughed. "Taller?"

"Yes, that's my nickname for him. Viktor is Beady Eyes."

"Good names."

"He also said Gabriel wouldn't like it. Who is Gabriel?" Daphne asked.

Rafe's voice grew tight and angry. "He's the leader of the Frenchmen who captured us. He also speaks Russian and often spoke it in our presence. That's why I needed Donald there with me."

Daphne nodded. "Gabriel's the man who tortured you?"

"Yes," Rafe said through obviously clenched teeth.

Then his voice relaxed. "At any rate, the quality of the goods won't be a problem. They're coming directly from the English government."

"What exactly are you giving them?" Daphne asked.

"The usual things. Spices, tea, fabrics, pottery. Anything they can sell for more in France. Which right now is nearly anything. What else did they say?"

"Viktor said he didn't trust you and Anton explained that they'd keep an eye on you all week."

"I like that," Rafe said with another laugh. "They're about to get our goods. We should keep an eye on *them* all week. And speaking of being untrustworthy . . ."

Daphne pulled her oar in time with Rafe's. "Why does it take a week to check them out? What are they checking for?"

"They're making certain the goods aren't stolen from anyone who's going to trace them. They want to ensure the government's not involved. That we're not spies."

Daphne snorted. "But we are spies."

"Yes, but the War Office knows how to make the goods untraceable. They'll never know. Did they say anything else?"

"Viktor said he didn't remember me. He was suspicious. Anton said he did. He said I was a, ahem, pretty boy."

Rafe growled under his breath. "Was that all he said?"

"For the most part."

Rafe's voice turned lighter. "Well, that's two admirers in one day, Grey. Not bad for a lad of sixteen, I'd say. Not bad at all."

Rafe's laughter was drowned out by the rowboat clunking against the side of the ship. Daphne didn't wait to hear more of it. Scowling, she jumped up, grabbed the ladder, and climbed as fast as she could. "I'll see you in the cabin."

The rest of the day stretched out interminably. Daphne had straightened up every possible thing that needed straightening. Which, in a very tidy captain's quarters, wasn't much. Rafe had taught her how to pull the bedsheets so tight she could bounce a coin on them. Wearing gloves, she scoured the wooden floor on her hands and knees with water and lye. Rafe hadn't come into the cabin since they'd returned to the ship. No doubt he'd been making arrangements to get the goods to the smugglers.

"I didn't think a lady would know how to clean a floor."

Daphne jumped. Rafe had entered the cabin silently like a wraith. Unsettling that. Spies were exceedingly quiet when they wanted to be.

"Shows how much ye know, Cap'n," she drawled in the voice that she'd been practicing so that she'd sound more like a cabin boy and less like an aristocratic lady should she be required to speak in front of Anton and Viktor.

Rafe laughed out loud at her accent.

"Me mum always said idle hands are the work o' the devil," Daphne continued.

"How are you so easily able to speak in that accent?" Rafe asked softly.

"I'm not certain. Somehow I've always been good at voices," she replied in her normal tone. "I used to have Julian and Donald in stitches by imitating Father's voice. We have a stable boy at our country estate who speaks this way. I spent a bit of time talking to him. He's a nice boy. His mother died when he was just a lad. I taught him how to read."

Rafe narrowed his eyes on her. "You did?"

Daphne scrubbed the brush against the floor with all the strength in her right arm. "Yes. I was speaking to him one day and he said he didn't know how. I asked him if he wanted to learn. After that I'd go to the stables every afternoon for an hour or two and teach him in between his chores."

"The stable master didn't mind?"

"Mr. Griggs? Oh, no. He didn't mind at all. He said the boy would be much better off in life if he knew how to read."

"That was kind of him." Rafe paused. "And of you."

"It wasn't kind. I'd do that for anyone who wanted to know how to read. Why should I know and he not know simply because he wasn't born to privilege the way I was? Reading is one of life's greatest pleasures. After I taught him, I asked Donald if the boy could come in and borrow books from the library from time to time. Of course Donald agreed."

Rafe shook his head. "I didn't think blue bloods had it in them."

Daphne stopped scrubbing and looked up at him with one hand on her hip. "Not all of us are pompous fools, you know?"

"Like Fitzroyal?"

Daphne finished scrubbing the floor, splashed water across it, sat up, and peeled off her gloves. "Fitzroyal *is* a pompous fool."

"Were you disappointed that the engagement didn't happen?" Rafe's question was low, soft.

Daphne shrugged. "Mother and Aunt Willie like to re-mind me that there are plenty of eligible gentlemen to be had. Besides, I've already chosen the next man on my list. Cass helped me."

"Ah, yes. Your list. And I suppose the *ton* is full of worthy gentlemen."

Daphne tossed the brush into the bucket. Still sitting on the floor, she turned to look at Rafe and tucked her knees up to her chest. "You don't like my class very much, do you?"

Rafe walked over to the bunk and sat on its edge. "Honestly, I haven't seen much to like."

Daphne wrapped her arms around her knees. "You like Derek and Julian."

Rafe nodded. "Claringdon was born the son of soldier like I was. He was only awarded his dukedom after his bravery in battle. And Swifdon, he may have been born to privilege, but he's a soldier through and through. And he wasn't meant to inherit until . . ." Rafe glanced away, biting his lip.

"Donald died," she finished.

"Yes." Rafe nodded.

Daphne tapped her boots against the wooden planks of the floor. "So that's it? No one is worthy of your respect unless they are soldiers and don't belong to the aristocracy."

"No. That's not true. Not at all."

Daphne narrowed her eyes on him. "Name one person you respect who isn't a soldier and who is part of the aristocracy?"

"You."

Daphne blinked. Her hands dropped to the floor. "You respect *me*?"

"Of course I do."

Her brow furrowed. "How? Why?"

"You're here, aren't you? Putting yourself in danger for the Crown, for your brother. You didn't have to do this, Daphne. You still don't have to."

"It surprises you to see someone of my class being brave, being noble?"

"I think your family is special."

"What about Lucy? What about Garrett?"

Rafe smiled. "Lucy is one of a kind. Anyone who meets her knows that. And Upton is going to be an earl only because his cousin died. It's not the same thing."

Daphne groaned and shook her head. She pushed at the bucket with the tip of her boot. "Talking to you is impossible."

"Then let's not talk. Let's do something else."

Daphne turned to look at him and swallowed. A thrill shot down her spine but she concentrated on keeping her face blank. "What exactly did you have in mind?"

Rafe stood up and walked over to the desk where he opened the drawer and rifled inside. "Would you like to play cards?"

"Oh." Daphne swallowed. "Cards."

"Yes, how about vingt-et-un?"

"Perfect." She gave him a shaky smile. "That's Delilah's favorite."

"Delilah plays cards?"

"Only when she can sneak away from her governess, which is essentially always. She should be the spy in the family. The girl is a master at evading capture."

Rafe laughed. "Yes, I witnessed that particular skill of hers myself."

He made his way back over to the bunk and plopped down on it, then he patted the space across from him. "It's tight quarters but there are few other places to sit."

Daphne looked down at the wet floor. She tossed a towel over it and scrubbed so it wouldn't stay wet and warp. She supposed she was responsible for the tight quarters. She could sit in the bunk with him. They were already far beyond inappropriate, they might as well play cards in a bunk. She stood and dusted off her backside with both hands. Then she climbed up onto the bunk next to him, allowing her booted feet to dangle off the front.

Daphne watched with wide eyes as the cards sprang to life in Rafe's hands. He shuffled them, snapped them, and began to deal two at a time.

"Let's make this more interesting, shall we?" he said.

Daphne wiggled backward on the bunk so that her back rested against the wall. "What do you suggest?"

"Whoever wins each hand gets to ask the other a question. And get an honest answer."

"We're not allowed to fib? How disappointing." Daphne smiled at him.

He returned her smile with a knee-weakening grin. "Well?"

Daphne tapped a finger against her cheek as if she were thinking about it but there was little to consider. "Very well. I have nothing to hide. You're the one who should be worried. You're a spy with, I'm certain, a great many secrets."

His grin widened. "Yes, but I'm quite good at vingt-et-un."

Daphne shook her head at him. "And modest, too, I see."

The first round was over quickly and Daphne lost soundly. "Very well. Ask your question."

"You never answered me earlier. Were you disappointed about Lord Fitzwell leaving?"

Daphne pressed her cap to her head and scrubbed her hand over her face. She had to answer honestly. She'd promised. She thought for several seconds. "No," she finally said softly. "It would be a lie to say I was. I think I was more disappointed by the idea of losing an engagement than the reality of actually losing Lord Fitzwell."

"I have to say that I think you were magnificent when you were telling him how judgmental he was."

"Well, he was."

"True, though I must admit I found your diatribe a bit ironic given how judgmental you've been about me."

Daphne's gaze snapped to his face. "When have I been judgmental about you?"

"Not believing me about the blond who just happened to crawl in my bed."

Daphne sucked in her breath, prepared to unleash a steady stream of rebuttals at his head.

"Or whenever I've had a drink, for example," he continued, without letting her speak.

That stopped her. "Why do you drink so often?"

"Ah, ah, ah. You didn't win the hand. No questions for you."

He dealt again and won again. Daphne sighed. "What's your next question?"

"Delilah told me she had a trick up her sleeve."

"She did, did she?" Daphne scowled at the thought of her cousin's orchestrations the night of the ball.

"Yes. Was she responsible for Lord Fitzwell coming out into the gardens?"

Daphne eyed Rafe carefully. "Very astute of you, Captain. Yes. That little urchin admitted it to me the next day. She sent him out there. It seems she was never a proponent of my marrying Lord Fitzwell."

"I can't say I blame her," Rafe replied.

Daphne laughed. "I daresay she's the most opinionated twelve-year-old in the kingdom."

Rafe shuffled the cards again. "I must agree with you there. I'd learned as much only having spent a brief time in her company."

Rafe dealt again and won again.

Another sigh from Daphne. "You *are* good at this," she admitted.

"I've had far too much practice," Rafe replied. "In fact, I need to think of a question."

He tugged at his lips and Daphne tried to ignore the memory of kissing those same lips. She looked up at the ceiling, over at the door, anywhere to keep her eyes from his handsome face.

"Here's one," he finally said. "Who is the next lucky gentleman on the list?"

Daphne furrowed her brow. "You mean the next one I chose? With Cass?"

"Yes."

"It doesn't matter, does it?"

"It does to me, your husband."

Daphne's gaze snapped to his face. She took a deep breath. "I know you tried to help me, Rafe. I've had time to think about it since that night and I remember you tried to get me to stop talking, to salvage the engagement with Lord Fitzwell."

Rafe glanced down at the cards that he'd gathered back into his hands. "I thought it was what you wanted."

"I was a fool that night. But losing Lord Fitzwell. Well, it obviously wasn't meant to be."

For some reason, Rafe didn't press her for the name of the next man on her list. She may have decided. But it didn't feel right, either. She'd worry about that after she returned home. Instead, Rafe shuffled the cards soundly again and dealt them. This time he lost.

"Ah, seems my luck is running out," he said. "What is your question?"

"Will you teach me how to be a spy?"

"What? Why?"

"You yourself just finished telling me how brave I am and how you respect me. I could be risking my life on this mission. I think I deserve to be trained in order to protect myself if I have to."

Rafe was silent for a moment as if he were considering her words. "You're right," he said quietly.

Daphne's eyes widened. "You're going to teach me?"

"Yes. There's no reason not to. First lesson, hand signals."

Daphne sat up straight and watched him intently. Rafe rubbed the side of his nose. "This means I understand."

Daphne rubbed her nose, too.

"You've got it," he said.

Next he wiped his brow.

"What does that mean?" Daphne asked.

"It means watch your back."

Twenty minutes later, Daphne felt as if she had a good understanding of a dozen different signals. She'd done them all more than once and practiced to remember each clearly. "Thank you," she said softly to Rafe. "For teaching me."

"Thank you for coming with me," he replied. He shook his head and the casual devil-may-care Rafe was back. "Shall we play one more hand?" he offered, shuffling the cards again.

"Why not?"

Rafe dealt and Daphne won for a second time. She inhaled deeply and met his gaze. She knew exactly what she would ask him. "Why do you drink so much, Rafe?"

Rafe blinked as if surprised by the question. "I haven't had a drink since we came on this ship. I didn't touch my ale yesterday. Nor the drink your brother offered me the night we left his house."

Daphne searched his face. "That didn't answer my question. I've seen you go to the clubs with Derek. Always with a brandy glass in your hand when you visit Julian. I know you've been drinking too much for too long."

"I'm not certain I know the answer to your question," he admitted with a shaky laugh.

"I do," Daphne said solemnly.

He rubbed a hand through his hair. "I wish you'd tell me, then."

"You're trying to forget about Donald's death."

CHAPTER TWENTY-NINE

Daphne slept fitfully again. This time she dreamt of a blond woman in Rafe's bed. She hadn't imagined it back then. She'd seen it with her own two eyes. They'd been staying at an inn near the docks. They'd left the ship the final night thinking it was unsafe to be there. They'd got two rooms but they'd been adjoining so Rafe could keep an eye on Daphne and keep her safe. He barricaded her door to the corridor with a large armoire and helped her move it the next morning when she'd told him she wanted to go downstairs in search of some tea. Rafe had asked if she'd like him to fetch it for her, but she'd insisted on doing it herself.

When she'd come back upstairs, she'd brought him a cup, too. She'd pushed open the door to his room and there she was. The blond. Lying in his bed. Naked but for a sheet pulled up under her arms. Lavish and gorgeous and hair spilling around her shoulders. Heart pounding, Daphne had immediately dropped both teacups and turned and fled. She ran back down the stairs, and encountered Rafe coming up. Apparently, he'd gone downstairs to check on her.

Daphne woke in a cold sweat. She'd had that dream before, relived that moment time and time again. But it always had the same ending. The rest of it was a lot of denials and confusion. The blond was soon gone but it was too late. Daphne had been mortally wounded. Her and Rafe's marriage hadn't been consummated, that was true, but the least he could do was not flaunt his doxies under her nose until the mission was over and their annulment secured. Was that too much to ask? Apparently. And yes, there'd been a small, stupid part of her that had hoped, wished even, that their marriage would be real after all. That Rafe might actually fall in love with her. That small, stupid part of her died the moment she saw the blond. Actually it had begun to die the moment he'd said he thought of her as a sister and refused to kiss her two days earlier. Clearly, he had no *sisterly* feelings toward the blond.

But the worst part, the very worst, was that after he'd spent the better part of an hour denying that he even knew who the blond was, he proceeded to ruin all of his carefully worded denials. "I don't know why you're so angry, Daphne. It's not as if we could ever be together. What does it matter who I have in my bed?"

That had been that. The mission had ended soon after. That afternoon Rafe had got the names of the men he was searching for in France and he took Daphne back to Mayfair that same day. Mother had been beside herself with worry. Apparently, she'd been writing to her daughter at Aunt Willie's with no response and had even written to Julian in the war, telling him she feared Daphne had run off. Daphne had hugged her mother fiercely, telling her how sorry she was to have caused her such worry. But that night, back in her own bed with unbound breasts, and large fluffy, soft down pillows, she'd cried herself to sleep. "What does it matter who I have in my bed?" he'd said to her. And with that, she'd known all of it had been nothing more than work to him. Any tenderness or emotions she'd thought had developed between them had been nothing more than a figment of her imagination. She was angry with him, yes. But she was mostly angry with herself for being so gullible. How could an army captain remain married to the daughter of an earl? Why, it was unheard of. Of course Rafe had agreed to the marriage because Donald had insisted. There was no other reason.

Daphne had waited a year to let her heart mend a bit, before she'd decided to stop moping and write a list. Get on with it. Find a proper husband. One who was suitable, from the right kind of family, one who didn't have a penchant for keeping blonds in his bed. She'd thought Lord Fitzwell fit the bill. She'd been mistaken there, too.

She glanced over to where Rafe swung peacefully in the hammock, fast asleep. She pressed her head against her pillow. It didn't matter. All that mattered now was completing this mission and keeping Rafe at arm's length for the duration. She owed it to Donald. Rafe needed her for her language skills and keen hearing. She'd decided that she needed him for something else. And she'd ask him for it, in the morning.

"I want you to teach me how to throw a knife," Daphne announced the next morning after breakfast. The rest of the crew had been up with the sun scurrying around the decks as usual. Whether the men knew much about ships or not, they certainly made an impressive show of it for the sake of their mission. Daphne often watched them in awe. Stringing sails, scrubbing decks, picking oakum. They made it all look extremely convincing.

Rafe looked twice at Daphne. "A what?"

"A knife. I saw you throw one once, last spring. When that boy had stolen your purse and ran away. You pinned his shirt to the wall from thirty paces. I want you to teach me how to do that."

Rafe rubbed his hand across his chin. "It takes a great deal of practice, you know. You shouldn't expect to be that good at it right off."

Daphne swallowed a bite of her biscuit. She did indeed have tea and milk to go with it this morning, courtesy of Cook. "I'm certain. It's like reading. You can't expect to read the *Iliad* while you're still in leading strings but you get better. I want to learn the fundamentals of throwing a knife. I'll get better at it on my own."

"You've read the *Iliad*?"

"Of course," she replied.

Rafe whistled. "Fancy that, Grey."

She rolled her eyes at him. "Will you teach me to throw a knife or not?"

Rafe cupped his chin in his hand and considered her. "It might be useful for you to know how to do it. You may as well learn how to defend yourself."

She nodded. "Thank you."

"Of course I hope you never have an occasion to throw one at *me*."

She smirked at him. "What if I promise not to if you teach me?"

"I have your word?" he asked with a grin.

"Of course." She smiled at him sweetly and took another bite of her biscuit.

Rafe inclined his head toward her. "Very well. Meet me on deck at three bells. I'll teach you how to throw a knife."

At half past one, Daphne stood on the deck, her cap hiding her hair, a smile on her face. She was looking forward to this. Quite a lot, actually.

"I've gathered every knife I had and borrowed some from the crew," Rafe announced, laying a blanket on the deck and opening it. It was filled with an assortment of knives. He'd also brought a large wooden box.

"What's that for?" Daphne asked.

"This is our target," Rafe said, dragging the box over toward the deck rails. "If you miss, there will be enough room for the knife to fly before sailing off the side of the ship into the water."

"That sounds like a good plan," Daphne replied, pulling down her cap over her forehead farther.

"First, you must choose your knife," Rafe said. "And if you must use whatever knife is at your disposal, then the method of throwing it will vary."

Daphne nodded.

Rafe gestured toward the collection of knives splayed out in an arc at their feet. "See this one? Its handle is larger than its blade."

Daphne nodded again.

"And this one?" He pointed at a second knife. "Its blade is bigger."

"Which is the best one to throw?" Daphne asked.

"It depends." He hefted the one with the smaller blade in his hand and held it out to her, handle first. "A more balanced blade is usually best for beginners. But you'll have to see which one you feel most comfortable with."

He stood and moved behind her with his legs braced apart, the breeze slightly mussing his hair. "Stand this way." He demonstrated, widening his stance. Daphne mimicked him.

"You want the weight to be thrown first. So with this handle-heavy knife, you'd hold it by the blade to throw."

She carefully turned it in her hand so that she clutched the blade.

"Now, which is your dominant hand?" he asked.

"My right."

"Then grip the blade with your right hand." He placed his hand over hers. Hers seemed so small compared to his. "Hold it firmly, but delicately."

"What does that mean?" Daphne asked with a half-smile.

"If you hold it too tightly, it'll hamper the throw. But if you don't have a firm enough grip on it, it may fly out of your hand before you're ready and could hurt someone. Including you."

"I see," Daphne said with another nod. "Now what?"

"Take the knife like so." He moved his hand over hers to show her. "Put the blunt edge of the blade along your thumb like this." He moved her thumb into position along her palm. "Put your thumb along this side of the blade and your fingers on the other side."

Daphne furrowed her brow, and stuck out her tongue, concentrating.

"You look positively fetching that way," he said with a laugh. Daphne quickly popped her tongue back into her mouth and swallowed the smile that was in danger of spreading across her lips.

"Pinch the blade without pressing against the point or the sharp part," he continued.

Daphne did exactly as she was told, trying to ignore both his closeness and his familiar scent.

"Excellent," Rafe said.

"Now what?" Daphne asked, the tip of her tongue caught between her teeth.

"Now you must adjust your angle. It will determine how quickly the knife will flip. The angle, of course, depends on how far you are from your target."

"I see," she said, moving her hand at an angle.

"It's in the wrist," he added. "If your target is close, you must bend your wrist back as far as you can, which will allow it to flip more quickly."

"And if the target is far away?"

"Don't bend your wrist at all. It will keep the knife from turning too much," Rafe said.

"Very well."

"Next, you pick your target. I've already counted and it's ten paces to the target. See there?" Rafe pointed toward the wooden box.

Daphne nodded again. "Yes."

"Now, throw!"

Daphne pulled back her arm and let go. The knife flew through the air and glanced off the side of the box. *"Sacrebleu!"* she exclaimed, but she felt her cheeks heating. "Sorry. I've obviously spent too much time with a certain twelve-year-old who *adores* French."

Rafe whistled. "Actually not bad for a first throw. Most people hit entirely too wide of the mark. At least you connected with it."

Daphne smiled at the praise and Rafe glanced away.

"Speaking of Delilah," Rafe continued. "I can just imagine how easily she'd take to this particular sport."

"No doubt she'd excel at it. As for me, I'm rubbish at archery but this seems like much more fun." Daphne laughed.

Rafe bent over to pick up the next knife and Daphne caught a glimpse of his perfect backside. The man really should be awarded a medal for that particular feature. It was positively riveting. When he straightened again, he handed her a new knife and Daphne shook her head to clear it of her indecent thoughts.

After a bit of maneuvering she threw the second knife. This time the blade struck. Rafe whistled again. "You have a natural talent for this, Grey."

She bowed. "Thank you, Captain." She glanced up at him. The sun was in his hair, his shirt hugged his mus-cled chest, his breeches hugged his backside. She glanced away. His nearness had made her want to kiss him, she realized. He smelled so good and looked so handsome and— No. This was completely useless thinking. No more kisses between them. Ever. The one had been quite nice but there were still a score of reasons why kissing him was a bad, bad idea. Not the least of which was the mysterious blond, the sister comment, and the fact that they were set to get an annulment as soon as they finished this mission. The mission for which she must learn how to adequately throw a knife. She needed to concentrate on *that,* not how good the man looked in his breeches. And he did, indeed, look very, very good.

Rafe came up behind her again, jolting Daphne from her thoughts. "This blade is far larger than the others. Allow me to show you," he said.

His nearness caused gooseflesh to pop along the back of her neck. She swallowed. His large, warm hand covered hers. Why was her hand so cold? She'd never before realized how small her hands were. They were tiny compared to his. "Y . . . yes," she breathed.

His chin hovered just above her right shoulder. "Hold this one by the handle," he instructed.

He smelled like wood and ocean breezes. She closed her eyes. Oh, fiddle. She couldn't concentrate on his instruction. She was reliving their kiss over and over again in her mind. There was no help for it. She wanted to kiss him again.

". . . like this," he was saying, and Daphne bit the inside of her cheek to remind herself to pay attention. Rafe moved to the side to allow her room to throw. It was much easier to think when he wasn't so near. She pulled back her wrist and let the blade fly. It struck the box straight on and quivered in the wood. She expelled her breath.

"Well done," he said, grinning at her. She tried not to notice the alluring cleft in his chin. "I'll leave you to practice. I must see to a few things."

He was leaving? Why did the thought make her want to whimper?

"I'll ask Cook to bring you up a cup of tea," he added.

Tea. Spilled tea. Blond. Last night's nightmare came rushing back full force to squeeze Daphne's middle until she could barely breathe.

"Thank you for the lesson, Captain," she said in the most businesslike voice she could muster.

He tipped his hat to her but she refused to look at him. He turned on his heel.

He was leaving. Good.

Rafe made his way down to his cabin and shut the door firmly behind him. Good God, he'd nearly embarrassed himself out there on the deck, getting hard when Daphne had sidled her little backside up to him while he'd been teaching her to throw a knife of all things. Only she could give him an erection while he was teaching her how to use a deadly weapon.

He crossed over to the washbasin, dunked both hands into the cool water and splashed his face. He was tempted to upend the entire basin over his head. But Daphne would probably ask why there was water all over the floor when she returned.

It was a good thing, teaching her how to be a spy. Showing her the hand signals and teaching her how to throw a knife. She should be skilled, trained. She'd have a fighting chance to defend herself if the worst happened and they were found out. A memory flashed before his eyes. A painful memory of the day Donald Swift had been shot. He was useless to them, they decided. Nothing more than an aristocrat who knew no real secrets. Rafe suspected they'd kept Donald alive as long as they had only to make Rafe more compliant. They'd been right. Rafe would have done anything to save the earl. But in the end, they'd taken him out to the tree line behind their tents and shot him in the head. Rafe clenched his fist. The crack of that pistol would ring in his ears forever. The guilt would stay with him longer than that. He shook his head. Yes, Daphne should learn all she could in their short time together on the ship.

That night Rafe couldn't sleep. He couldn't get comfortable in his hammock at all. Daphne had remained on deck all day throwing the knives. She'd come back down late at night with a fetching amount of sun on her cheeks (no doubt *that* would be difficult to explain away next week when she was back in her Mayfair drawing rooms). She'd yawned and stretched and thanked him for teaching her how to throw the knives, reporting that she'd got so good at it by the end of the day that the crew had been placing bets on her throws. Rafe lurched in the hammock, nearly throwing himself onto the wooden floor. He cursed under his breath. Daphne was fast asleep, adorable little sighs coming from her throat like a relaxed kitten, while he was wholly unable to sleep because all he could do was remember her tight little backside pressed against him during their knife-throwing lesson.

He'd already decided upon tomorrow's lesson and there was nothing at all alluring about it.

CHAPTER THIRTY

"Today I'm going to teach you how to shoot, Daphne," Rafe announced the next morning after Daphne had finished her breakfast and was making the bunk. There wasn't much to do while they awaited the Russians' inspection of their cargo. They had to remain on the ship in case the Russians paid a visit, and Rafe was convinced they were being watched as well. They had to appear completely at ease, playing the role of a crew anchored in harbor.

Daphne whirled around to face Rafe. "I don't particularly care to learn how to shoot. I intended to spend the afternoon practicing my knife throwing."

"There will be time for that later. I've been considering it and I think it's important for you to learn how to shoot as well."

Daphne wrinkled her nose. She'd never much cared for pistols. Her father and Donald had gone shooting often. She followed them on occasion to watch and she remembered it being loud and smoky. Not a particularly pleasant way to spend the day if you asked her. But if Rafe thought it was important that she learn, she wasn't going to turn down the opportunity for a lesson. Not to mention, spending a bit more time in his company was not an unpleasant thought.

Daphne followed Rafe up to the deck to the far side of the ship where no other ships were moored off the starboard side. There was nothing ahead of them but open water, a perfectly safe place for shooting practice. He had set up a makeshift target using an old piece of flotsam he'd apparently dredged out of the water or retrieved from the hold. There was a crude bull's-eye painted on it.

She glanced at the bull's-eye and then back at Rafe. "You did this, for me?" She pointed at herself.

His characteristic grin appeared on his face. "How else do you expect to learn to shoot?"

Daphne bit the inside of her cheek to keep from smiling too wide.

Just as he had the day before, Rafe showed her how to stand, how to angle her hand, and how to hold the pistol. They stood together on the bow of the ship and shot off into the water, using the horizon as their guide. Rafe had two pistols and was obliged to stop and reload them each time they were used.

Twenty minutes later, Rafe declared, "You're much better at throwing knives than shooting pistols."

"I told you. I don't like pistols," Daphne said, squinting. "They're far too loud and a bit unpredictable."

"I must say, with two older brothers, I'd have thought they'd have taught you before now. I must speak to Swifdon about it when we return."

Daphne laughed and shook her head. "Julian did try to teach me when I was much younger, but I quickly tired of it. He and Donald used to have a bit of brandy and challenge each other to shooting matches."

"That hardly sounds safe."

"It wasn't. They were young lads when they did it. If Father had known, he would have beaten the tar out of both of them. Father taught Donald to shoot like a gentleman."

"He didn't teach Julian?" Rafe asked, his brow furrowed.

Daphne looked down at the deck and shook her head.

Rafe stepped closer to her and lowered his voice so the members of the crew who were on deck couldn't hear. "I understand. My father never taught me anything useful." Rafe cleared his throat. "At any rate, only a fool would drink and use pistols."

Daphne would have loved to hear more about Rafe's father. He never talked about his family. But he'd already changed the subject.

"I agree," she said with a laugh. "I shall endeavor not to drink spirits when I'm practicing my shot."

"Or when you're practicing your knife throwing, either," he added with a wink that made Daphne's belly flip.

"Good plan," she said. "I have to be honest. Until the other night when you told me you didn't drink while working, I thought you couldn't control your drinking."

Rafe looked up from reloading one of the pistols. "I know that, Daphne."

She pushed the tip of one of her boots along the wood-planked deck. "Why didn't you tell me it's not true?"

He raised both brows. "And ruin your bad opinion of me?"

She met his eyes. "Be serious."

Rafe rammed the shot into the muzzle of the gun. "My father drank, to excess. He became angry and unreasonable when he drank. I vowed years ago that I would never follow suit."

Daphne watched his profile solemnly. "I can't imagine you ever being angry or unreasonable."

Rafe shrugged. "My mother always said I didn't take after my father, in temperament at least. Good thing, that. But still. I refuse to allow alcohol to control me."

"Are you like your father at all?"

"No, I'm not, but—"

"But what?"

"I'm not like my father in any way that I can help. Mother always said I have his eyes. Other than that, I made my life a study of being the opposite of him."

"How so?"

"He left us, when I was twelve. I haven't seen him since."

Daphne gasped. "That's awful."

"The man wasn't responsible a day in his life. He was discharged from the army. He stole things, begged, got tossed in gaol a time or two. I was always ashamed of him."

Daphne took an unconscious step toward him. "But you're nothing like that, Rafe."

He slid the hammer back on the pistol and handed it to her carefully. "On purpose. I vowed to live a life I could be proud of. A life in service to my country and fellow man." He lowered his voice again. "I joined the army as soon as I could. I didn't have parents to buy me a commission like Claringdon or Swifdon. I had to work my way up."

She whispered, too. "And you became an officer? A spy?"

"Yes. After many years. My superior officers saw the potential in me. I was always good at talking myself out of any situation. I was stealthy, fast, blended in, got away quickly. Perfect spy material."

Daphne swallowed. "And brave, Rafe. You're uncommonly brave."

"I don't think of myself that way. I only think of doing my duty."

"Did you always want to be a spy?"

"Yes. I think so. I didn't know the word for it but I knew I had the ability to be in the military and do special work."

"You are quite good at it, Rafe."

Rafe ran a hand over his face. "Tell that to Donald."

Daphne shook her head. "No. Certainly not. Donald's death wasn't your fault. You must know that."

He rubbed the back of his hand against his forehead. He moved closer to her again and kept his voice low. "Enough about me. What about you? What did you always want to be when you were a little girl?"

Daphne aimed the pistol at the bull's-eye. The air seemed to suspend in her lungs. No one had asked her such a question before. It was popularly assumed that all young women of the *ton* wanted to marry well and produce offspring. No one ever asked them what they *wanted* to do. She took the shot and, like all the others, it winged off into the ocean, coming nowhere near the bull's-eye. "I should have known when I practiced archery with Jane at Julian's wedding party that I was no good at shooting things."

Rafe took the pistol from her. "You didn't answer my question."

"I'm not certain I know how to answer it."

"Have I confused you?" Rafe laughed.

"A bit," she admitted sheepishly. "I've just never been . . . No one's ever asked me such a question."

Rafe concentrated on reloading the pistol again. He shook powder into the muzzle. "That's a shame."

Daphne lifted her chin. "It is a shame, isn't it?"

He looked up at her and nodded.

She lifted her chin. "I do have an answer, though."

He met her eyes. "What is it?"

"You must promise not to laugh."

"I would never laugh at you."

She swallowed and glanced out at the horizon. "I always wanted to be a pirate."

Rafe's eyebrow quirked. "A pirate?"

"Yes. A pirate. I read about a lady pirate once. Well, she was more of a privateer, I suppose. I wouldn't want to actually break the law. But adventures on the high seas, sun, and wind and rain, and . . . freedom. It always sounded so wonderful to me."

Rafe shook his head. His brow furrowed. "You surprise me, Grey."

"Do I?" She rubbed the bottom of her boot along the deck. "You expected me to say something about embroidery or charities?"

"Perhaps."

"That is mighty boring, Cap'n," she said in her best Thomas Grey voice, doffing her cap.

"Agreed," he answered. "For I, too, always longed for adventure."

CHAPTER THIRTY-ONE

"Tonight's lesson involves being tied up," Rafe announced that evening after they'd said good night to the rest of the crew following dinner and retired to the captain's cabin. He drew a long piece of rope out of the cabinet above the desk.

Daphne swallowed hard. "Pardon me?"

"I thought you wanted to learn how to be a spy," Rafe replied.

"Oh yes. Yes, I do." She brushed her hands across her thighs. "And . . . spies are often . . . tied up?"

"Upon occasion," Rafe replied with his infamous wicked grin. "I was tied up in France more often than not."

Daphne swallowed again and ducked her head. Of course. This was serious and if Rafe had something to teach her about being tied up, she was ready to learn it.

"Of course, sometimes allowing your captors to think you're tied up is part of your strategy."

"Did you do that?" she asked tentatively. "In France?"

"Nearly every day. I kept my hands behind my back and the rope around them, but often, I was only seconds away from being free."

The breath caught in her throat. "What should I do?"

He motioned to the bed with his chin. "Get on the bunk, Grey. I'm going to tie you up."

A thrill that was a mixture of fear and anticipation shot through her. "Y . . . yes, Captain."

She climbed up onto the bunk and sat watching him carefully.

"Lie on your stomach."

She did as she was told.

"Put your hands behind your back," he ordered.

She rested both hands, palms up, over her buttocks. Did Rafe swear under his breath?

"This may hurt a bit. I'll try to be gentle. Of course if the French were doing it, it would hurt like hell. They aren't careful. On purpose."

"I understand," she murmured into the pillow.

He wrapped the length of rope around her wrists. It scraped at the tender skin there but otherwise there was no pain.

"This is the type of knot that's not easy to get out of," Rafe said.

"And you're going to show me how to get out of it?" she breathed.

"Yes," came his sure voice. "But you've already failed your first lesson."

She turned her head sharply to the side on the pillow. "What? How?"

"The first lesson of being tied up is to ensure your wrists are at an angle when they're being tied. An astute captor will notice this but you should always try in case you're dealing with an amateur."

"What does the angle have to do with it?"

"If your wrists aren't pressed together, you'll have a better chance of tugging one free."

Daphne pressed her cheek against the pillow. "Ah. Are you going to untie me so I can try again?"

He'd leaned over her and she felt more than saw his smile near her cheek. "Not a chance. I'm an astute captor."

"Are you?" she whispered into the pillow. Was it getting hot in the cabin all of a sudden?

"That's right."

She closed her eyes and tried to concentrate on the lesson. "What should I do next?"

"What is your instinct, Grey? Being a competent spy is often about instinct."

"My instinct is to try to pull my wrists free from the rope."

"The exact wrong thing to do," he answered matter-of-factly.

Daphne frowned. "Why?"

"Because all you'll do is chafe them and then they'll be bloody and sore, which will make it more difficult to escape."

"What should I do then?" she whispered, wishing she couldn't smell his musky scent.

"That's the trick. If you are not in imminent danger . . . In other words if you think your captors mean to hold you and not immediately kill you, you should remain still and wait for them to leave you alone. They usually will at some time or another."

"And once I'm alone?"

"Look around your environment." He pushed his arms under her and flipped her over so that she was sitting in an instant. She tried to ignore the fact that he had touched the side of her breast just a little. "Look for something that could cut the ties," he said.

Daphne hesitated. "In here?"

"Yes."

She carefully moved to the edge of the bunk and stood on shaking legs. "How am I supposed to get anything with my hands tied?"

He nodded. "That's the question, isn't it? Use your imagination."

She glanced around the small room. The washbasin, the hammock, the door handle. Nothing that would cut a rope. Her gaze fell on the small writing desk. She tried to recall its contents. An ink pot. Some paper. There was a letter opener in there! She hurried over to the desk and stared at it, then she turned and carefully pulled open the drawer using only the touch of her fingers to guide her way. It was more difficult than she'd even guessed it would be. Being the opposite of tall didn't help, either. She kicked out the chair and climbed up on it to sit on the top of the desk then turned again to rummage in the contents of the open drawer. It took several moments but she finally felt the handle of the letter opener and she grasped it upside down in her palm. A sheen of sweat was on her forehead and her tongue was tightly clenched between her teeth as she attempted to saw at the rope.

"This could take all night," she breathed.

Rafe stood, folded his arms across his chest and stalked toward her. "It could indeed. Time is always of the essence. You must work as quickly as possible. And remember, your captor may come back at any time. What would you do if I walked through that door and stopped you right now?" He pulled her off the desk and into his arms, kicking the chair out of the way.

She gasped as she collided with his broad chest. "I'd—I'd—"

His breath touched her cheek. "You'd better hide the letter opener as quickly as possible, whether that means pushing it up the back of your shirt or sliding it back into the drawer as quietly as possible."

"What letter opener?" she asked, blinking innocently.

Rafe glanced over her shoulder and looked down into her empty hands. "Your shirt?" he asked with rakish grin.

"My breeches," she whispered.

His mouth was only mere inches from hers and the feel of his hard body pressed to hers was making her feel hot and wet in places she didn't want to think about at the moment. His hand moved to her back and pushed down to her backside to the outline of the letter opener that she'd slid into the back of her breeches. He tucked his fingers into the top of her breeches, his knuckles brushing against her heated skin there. She closed her eyes and concentrated on breathing. He slowly slid the device out of her breeches and held it up in front of her. "Well done, Grey."

His face changed then. Became blank. He spun her around and quickly untied her hands. "That's enough for tonight. Tomorrow I'll show you how to use the angle of your wrists to get out of a knot if you must."

Minutes later he was swinging peacefully in his hammock, while Daphne rubbed at her slightly sore wrists and replayed that moment when he'd pulled her forcefully against his chest again and again in her traitorous mind. Sleep was not going to come easily tonight.

CHAPTER THIRTY-TWO

Daphne spent the entire next day throwing knives. She'd decided her pistol-shooting future was dim, her knot-foiling ability was bleak, but her knife-throwing talent could be cultivated if given enough practice. Her arm ached, her legs turned to jam, and she felt as if she might fall to her knees, but she remained on the deck, hurling the knife at the wooden box over and over and over again as the morning turned to afternoon and the afternoon faded into evening.

Instead of using the group of knives that Rafe had provided her with to practice, she'd decided on one knife in particular. Her favorite one. It had a smaller blade than handle and she threw it, retrieved it, and threw it again. Over and over again. She'd reached the point where she never missed. Not even when she was tired. But she didn't allow herself to take a break and she didn't allow herself to stop. Her father's words from her childhood echoed in her ears. *If you want to be perfect at something you must practice perfectly.* Father had kept Donald out in the field jumping his horse again and again and again. If the horse tired, they got another mount, but Donald was never allowed to stop, never allowed to quit. Father had never treated her like that. He'd never treated Julian like that, either, since he was not the heir. Father had specifically never asked that of her because she was female, of course, but Daphne had watched and listened and learned. She knew the way to excel at something was to never give up. It was why she'd been successful at learning Russian. And Daphne intended to excel at knife throwing. She wiped the sweat from her brow and resettled the cap on her head. Then she retrieved the knife and threw it again.

Rafe had surprised her yesterday when he'd told her about his childhood. What sort of a father left his wife and twelve-year-old son? It made her angry on his behalf. Outwardly, Rafe appeared to be unaffected by it, but she'd heard a note of pain in his voice, seen a flash of anger in his eyes. Apparently she'd surprised Rafe, too, when she'd told him that she'd always longed to be a pirate. She'd never admitted that to anyone before. Not Donald, or Cass, and especially not her mother. Not even Julian. Mama would probably have an apoplectic fit if she knew her well-bred little Society miss of a daughter had dreams of sailing the high seas and swashbuckling. But somehow Daphne had known she could tell Rafe, probably because nothing could shock him. The man seemed unshockable. Which made it quite freeing to talk to him actually.

It was true that she wanted to become proficient at throwing the knife. But if she were being honest, she stayed out on the deck all day for another reason, also. To avoid Rafe. He was too handsome, too witty, and he smelled too good. In short, he was too tempting. Last night's lesson had taught her more than how to look for a way to get out of a knot. It had also taught her that her attraction to Rafe was quite real and quite dangerous. When she chose a man with her head (as she had with her list) instead of with her nose and her eyes (that both highly favored Rafe) she would be much better off. Yes, perhaps Fitzwell hadn't been the best choice after all, but still, the list was certain to find her a better match than a rogue like Rafe.

The sun went down and Daphne continued to throw the knife. She didn't quit until Cook came up to the deck and insisted she have something to eat. Cook pulled over a stool for her and handed her a bowl of stew. She nearly fell onto the stool and just lifting the spoon to take a bite was nearly too much for her weary arm. It felt as if it was on fire. She waited a bit before finishing the bowl using her left hand to lift the spoon, which proved a bit awkward and slow going.

The next thing she knew, she'd fallen asleep on the deck. She awoke to see the moon hanging high in the black velvet sky. She was curled into a ball near a length of rope. A bit of a tarp had been pulled over her and the stool and her stew bowl and spoon were gone. Cook must have cleaned up and left her here to sleep. That was nice of him. Nice of him, indeed.

Daphne pushed the tarp away and sat up and stretched. She was exhausted, actually. She rubbed her throwing arm. It felt much better than it had when she'd been trying to eat earlier, but no doubt it would be sore come morning. She decided to sneak into the captain's cabin. Perhaps Rafe was already asleep in the hammock.

She made her way through the companionway, and down the steps to the cabin as quietly as possible. She tip-toed to the door. She turned the handle slowly and softly pushed open the door without making a sound. She stuck her head inside.

Luck was not on her side tonight. Rafe was sitting at the desk writing a letter by the light of an oil lamp. His cravat was untied and his boots were off but otherwise he was fully clothed, thank heavens. Or perhaps not . . .

He looked up and smiled at her lazily and her stomach did a little flip when she looked at the cleft in his chin.

No longer concerned with noise, she pushed the door wider and walked inside, doing her best to ignore how good he smelled, like candlewax and wood shavings. Or maybe that was the cabin. Either way, it reminded her of him. She shook her head and trotted over to the washstand in the corner.

"How's your knife-throwing skill coming?" Rafe asked.

"Improving greatly, thank you." She pulled a bit of linen from the nearby cabinet and washed her face. Then she cleaned her teeth using toothpowder that she also retrieved from the cabinet. Once she was finished with her ablutions, she sat on the edge of the bunk and shucked first one boot, then the next.

"Tired?" he asked.

"Exceedingly so," she answered, rubbing her sore feet through her stockings. Breeches might be freeing, but slippers were ever so much more accommodating than boots. How did gentlemen stand them? "What are you writing?" she ventured.

"Some long overdue correspondence," he answered. "How's your arm?"

She squeezed her throwing arm and winced. "Sore."

He dabbed his quill back into the ink pot. "I don't doubt it."

She set her boots on the wooden plank floor next to the

bunk and climbed wearily under the covers. She stretched and sighed. "Is this what men do all day on ships? It seems quite boring."

"When the ships are at sea there is quite a bit more work to be done," he answered with a laugh.

She propped her arms underneath her head and stared up at the ceiling. "What do you normally do at night? Like now."

"Sleep."

"And?" she ventured.

"Write letters. I could teach you how to use your wrists to get out of a knot."

She held up her hands. "No. No. No. Not tonight." She didn't think she could take that again. Another lesson being tied up. She'd go mad with lust possibly.

"Very well. Sometimes there is drinking and card games," Rafe offered.

"We already played cards," Daphne said on another sigh.

"Well, then." He snickered. "Care for a drink?"

She sat up, bracing her palms behind her. "I thought you said you didn't drink while you're on duty."

He sanded his letter and began to fold it. "Everything in moderation. Besides, the workday is done."

She narrowed her eyes on him. "You think I'm going to say no, don't you?"

He covered the ink pot and put the quill back in the drawer, where he placed the folded letter as well. "I'm convinced of it."

She arched a brow. "So it would shock you if I said yes?"

He turned in his seat to face her and braced his palms on both knees. "Entirely."

"Then, yes, I'll have a drink." She stuck her nose in the air and gave him a triumphant smile.

Rafe inclined his head toward her. "As you wish." He pushed back the chair, stood, and opened a small cabinet above the desk. "Brandy?"

"Brandy!" She lurched up.

He flashed his infamous grin and Daphne's belly did another unceremonious flip. "You said you longed for adventure, didn't you? And you are a cabin boy, not a lady, at present."

The man had a good point. "Fine, then. Brandy it is."

He pulled two glasses from the shelf and splashed the amber liquid into both of them.

"Mr. Grey," he said, moving toward the bunk, handing her a glass, and bowing.

Daphne took the glass from Rafe's hand and stared at the thing as if she were holding a five-day-old fish. Her nose was still turned up and she sniffed at the contents as if they might make her retch at any moment.

"Never had brandy before?" he asked, eyeing her carefully.

She turned the glass slowly in her hand, still studying the liquid. "Can't say I have."

"First time for everything." He lifted his glass in salute.

She raised hers in the air and smiled at him sweetly. "To adventure!"

"To adventure," he echoed, his glass still hoisted high.

Daphne tentatively put the snifter to her lips and tipped it slowly. She took a tiny taste, barely enough to wet the tip of her tongue. She scrunched her face into a grimace.

"Come now, that was hardly a sip, let alone a drink," Rafe said.

She shook her head violently. "How can you stand this vile brew?"

"This isn't tavern ale. It's delicious, actually, once you acquire a taste for it."

She made a gagging noise. "I don't wish to acquire a taste for it."

"You've barely given it a try. Surely you should hold your opinion until you've at least had enough of it to give a good, solid review."

"Ugh." She glared at the glass.

He tsked at her. "Not very adventurous of you, Grey."

Daphne narrowed her eyes at him. Then she glared at the glass again. The best way to do things one wanted to have done with was to do them quickly. She remembered a trick from childhood when her governess had forced her to drink quinine when she was ill. Perhaps it would work with brandy, too. There was only one way to find out.

She pinched her nose, hoisted the glass to her lips, and took a large, quick swallow.

Fire shot down her throat. She released her nose and gasped and gagged, pressing her hand against her chest and desperately trying to draw air into her burning lungs. "Good God, it's going to kill me," she choked.

Rafe quickly poured her a bit of water from the pitcher near the washbasin and handed it to her. She tossed it into the back of her throat and coughed even more. "It's awful, absolutely vile, entirely—"

"It's only water." He laughed.

"I was talking about the brandy, not the water. I—"

Daphne stopped, and blinked. Already, a delicious warmth was creeping through her veins and her head began to buzz with a pleasant sensation. She closed her eyes and leaned her head against the wall behind her. "Perhaps I might take one more tiny little sip."

She tentatively touched the glass to her lips again and tipped it back. The liquid seeped into her throat more slowly this time. It burned again but this time she cared less. The delightful warmth in her limbs was spreading further.

Rafe pulled the glass from her quickly numbing fingers. "Oh no, you don't. You cannot get drunk as a wheelbarrow. I need you with me tomorrow when we go ashore to meet the Russians, not to mention I've no idea how to formulate that concoction your brother makes to cure such things."

Daphne lay back on the bunk and let the delicious warmth spread through her limbs. "I don't think I mind brandy after all."

Rafe laughed. "Don't you?"

"No, it's quite . . . warming and . . . pleasant, actually."

Rafe downed the rest of the contents of his own glass and placed the bottle back inside the cabinet. "That's quite enough for both of us."

Daphne braced both hands under her head. "I never drank a drop of alcohol before I met you, you know. You're a horrible influence on me."

His face was skeptical. "Oh, really? What about Mrs. Pennyhammer and the thimble full of wine?"

She giggled. "That hardly counts. I certainly hadn't been inebriated before I met you and now I've been so twice in one week. I hope you're proud of yourself, Captain."

Rafe's voice held a note of amusement. "I believe you are currently experiencing what is commonly referred to as a fuzzy head."

"Fuzzy head?" She lifted one hand and pressed it against her forehead.

"Yes. Not entirely drunken but not quite sober, either."

She patted herself atop her head. "I like my fuzzy head. Quite a lot. And I quite like brandy as well." She stretched and splayed her legs and arms across the bed like an X.

"I'm glad to hear it," he replied with another throaty laugh.

Daphne snapped her fingers. "Let's play a game."

Rafe's eyebrows shot up. "Cards?"

"No. No. Let's play that game we played the other night but without the cards. I cannot concentrate on maths with my fuzzy head."

"What game?" he asked, his brow furrowed.

She waved a hand in the air. "You know. The question game."

"Pardon?"

She turned to face him. "I'll ask you a question and you must tell the truth and then you ask me a question and I must tell the truth."

He shoved his hands in his pockets. "That's not precisely how it went."

"Don't be so stuffy. I'll even allow you to go first."

"Stuffy?" His voice was full of effrontery. "Me?"

"Yes, now go on. Ask me something, anything. I promise to answer truthfully."

"Very well." He paused for a few moments. "Why did you pick Lord Fitzwell? From your list?"

Daphne blinked dumbly. Her head was fuzzy indeed. "Why would you ask something like that?"

Rafe's grin was downright devilish. "That's not an answer, and you promised to answer truthfully."

She sighed and stretched again. Better not to look at

him. Yes. Much better. Er, safer. "So I did. Let's see . . ." She tapped a finger along the tip of her nose. "I picked him because he met all my requirements."

"Your requirements?"

"Yes. On my list."

"And what requirements were those?" Rafe leaned against one of the posts and crossed his stockinged feet at the ankles.

"You know, titled, rich, handsome, *loyal*."

"So, it's safe to say, I'm not on your list. I only have two of those four requirements."

She shrugged one shoulder, steadfastly ignoring his claim and vowing not to guess which two he thought he had. "It's the type of list a lady must make when looking for a suitable husband."

Rafe narrowed his eyes on her. "But you don't even know Lord Fitzwell."

"I knew him as well as most ladies know their future husbands. I knew his family. I saw him from time to time at various events about town. We even went riding in the park once or twice." She punctuated her sentence with a firm nod.

"Once?" Rafe's voice dripped with skepticism.

"Or twice. With the promise to do it again sometime."

"How exciting." This time Rafe's voice dripped with sarcasm.

"I knew enough about him. I knew he doesn't drink much. He doesn't gamble to excess. And he would never be found with a blond in his bed."

"He sounds like a dead bore." Rafe unbuttoned his shirt.

Daphne swallowed. Why was he unbuttoning his shirt? Had he done that the other nights? Slept shirtless and she hadn't noticed? How had she *failed* to notice that? "That's exactly the sort of thing I'd expect someone like you to say," she replied.

"Someone like me?" He pulled his shirt over his head.

Daphne nearly gulped audibly. "Yes," she managed to answer him, but her eyes were devouring his muscled chest. Good God. How had she missed this little nightly ritual? Or was she only imagining it due to her fuzzy head? "Do you have your shirt off?" she asked, clearing her throat.

He chuckled. "Yes. My apologies if I am offending your ladylike sensibilities. But I need a fresh one."

"I shouldn't be looking."

His gaze met hers. Sparks leaped between them. "Then why are you?"

Her face heated. Her cheeks boiled. She turned away toward the wall.

"Please do explain," Rafe continued.

"Explain what?" Daphne's voice was muffled against the wooden wall.

"Who 'someone like me' is? What did you mean by that?"

She wiggled under the sheets and forced herself to turn back to face him. He was standing directly next to the bed. Daphne's head swam. Her eyes locked to his bare chest. Fuzzy brain, indeed. She took a deep breath. "I only meant that you're everything he's not. You drink. You gamble. You—"

"Kiss you?" He captured her wrist, brought it to his lips and kissed it. Daphne couldn't stop her shudder.

She snatched her hand away. "Don't."

"Why?" he said, looking down at her, his voice growing louder, laced with a bit of anger. "Afraid you might actually feel something? You're right. I'm everything he's not and I'm also much more. Do you think your Lord Fitz-well has an adventurous bone in his body? By God, the most excitement the man has had is an unexpected nose-bleed. Do you think your Lord Fitzwell has fought for his country? Watched men die for his country? He hasn't. The most he's done is read about it in the papers and shake his head. You say I don't know you, Daphne, but I do. I know you pretend to want to plan everything, and maybe you do, but deep down you're adventurous, just like I am. Draw-ing rooms are too stuffy for you. A man like Fitzwell would bore you to tears in the space of six months. But if you want to waste your beauty and intelligence and talents on him or someone like him, by all means, don't let me stop you."

Tears shimmered in Daphne's eyes. She sat up and braced herself against the wall again. "What did you say?"

"I said, 'Don't let me stop you.'"

"No, before that. The part about my beauty and intel-ligence?" Her heart hammered in her chest. She could barely breathe.

He braced both of his hands on the wooden plank that hung from the ceiling above the bunk and stared down at her still. "You heard me. You deserve better than Fitz-well. But you're so damned stubborn and certain of your-self, you can't even see it. You need to take your bloody list and rip it into a thousand pieces just to see what's standing right in front of you. The thing that never made it onto the list."

"You?" she whispered.

"Me." Rafe let go of the plank and his mouth swooped down to capture hers.

CHAPTER THIRTY-THREE

Daphne shuddered. Rafe's mouth shaped hers, owned hers, while lust shot through her entire body in sharp, shooting sparks. He had moved down to where she sat on the bed and she wrapped her arms around his neck, leaning into the kiss with everything she had. Who cared how this had started? All she knew was that she wanted it to continue. She wanted to make love with Rafe. She wanted to be his wife in every way.

What happened next was most likely the doing of two very fuzzy heads because five moments later, Daphne's shirt was over her head, her breeches unbuttoned and yanked free of her body, and the linen wrapping her breasts was gone. She lay in the bunk naked. She was completely exposed in a way she had never been in front of any man before but all she could feel was . . . happiness and excitement.

Rafe was gazing at her, his eyes full of desire, his breathing completely unsteady. His hand rested on her knee, hot, heavy. His fingers traced up the inside of her thigh, the outside of her hip, along her rib cage.

He gently, lightly touched the outside of her left breast. Then his fingertips skimmed over her nipple and she shivered with desire. His hand traveled up to her collarbone, her neck, her cheekbone. Daphne closed her eyes and reveled in the feel of his rough touch along her sensitive skin. He had the hands of a man who had worked for a living. Not the soft hands of Lord Fitzwell. Rafe had actually done things like throwing knives and shooting pistols and riding horses and nearly dying for his country. He was right. He was nothing like Lord Fitzwell. Nothing at all.

Rafe groaned deep in his throat and lowered himself over her. He was still wearing his breeches and stockings. His hot bare chest pressed intimately to hers and made Daphne moan. The friction between them was so good. She wrapped her arms around his neck again and he kissed her deeply. Daphne's head remained fuzzy and she was a swirling mass of lust. The spot between her legs ached and throbbed.

She pushed her legs apart and clenched her eyes shut. Cass and Lucy had mentioned that the first time would hurt a bit. "I'm ready," she announced, scrunching up her nose and bracing a hand against the wall.

Rafe's laughter was the last thing she expected. But it was there, loud and melodious, bouncing off the wooden sides of the small cabin. She cracked open an eye. "What's funny about this?"

He nudged at her with his nose and kissed one eyelid, then the other. "Nothing, my darling."

"Why are you laughing?" she asked, chagrined, but she couldn't quite bring herself to push him away. His hot hardness between her legs and the warm heat and weight of his chest against hers were too compelling.

He cleared his throat. "It doesn't quite— Let's just say there's more to it than my pouncing on you. Not to mention if I were to make love to you, I might find myself in a thousand little pieces once your brother finds out."

She wiggled against him and Rafe closed his eyes briefly. "Daphne, please," he whispered.

"I didn't expect you to pounce, but aren't you supposed to . . . ?" She trailed off in abject embarrassment, not even certain of the right words to use in such a circumstance. She wasn't worried about Julian. She had no doubt that getting Rafe to this point was all she needed. There'd be little chance he'd stop if they continued to do what they were doing. "I have no intention of telling Julian anything about this," she said with a coy smile.

Rafe leaned down and kissed her again and all the thoughts fluttered straight from her brain. "Whatever we do, it's supposed to feel good . . . and happen naturally," he said. "Most importantly, feel good."

"I like the sound of that," she admitted, kissing the cleft in his chin softly.

He pushed a curl away from her ear and leaned down and traced the outline of it with his tongue. Daphne bucked against him. "Let me make you feel good, Daphne," he whispered.

"Yes" was her only reply.

He moved down, his lips a hot brand against her cheek, her neck, her collarbone. Daphne wrapped her arms around his shoulders. How could his mouth on her neck feel so good? She'd never imagined it. His lips moved lower, next. They nipped at the top of her breast. Then Daphne gasped as the hot wetness settled over her nipple.

"Oh my God," she moaned. His smile burned against her soft skin. His mouth played with her, biting and tracing small patterns against the fevered skin of her breast. "You're perfect, do you know that?" he whispered.

"No I'm not."

"Yes you are." He sucked her nipple deep into his mouth and Daphne decided she was done arguing with him. The wet heat between her legs was driving her mad and the sensations in her breast were zipping through her body and pulling at the juncture between her thighs. She wanted him on top of her. She wanted him inside of her. "Please, Rafe," she whispered, her lower body squirming against him.

"Wait, Daphne. Just wait for it."

His mouth continued its gentle assault on her breast while his left hand moved down to her wet warmth. Her chest rose and fell with each of her labored breaths. His hand teased her, barely touching the springy curls between her legs. He traced her cleft, running one long finger down her center. She pressed up against his hand, wanting more, but not knowing exactly what.

Rafe parted her and pressed a finger between her legs. He moved it into a spot that made Daphne cry out. He stroked her there, slowly, so slowly. Then he began to circle the spot, using only his fingertip, and Daphne cried out. "Rafe!"

He covered her mouth with his other hand. "Shh. We don't want the crew to hear."

"At the moment I don't give a damn," Daphne breathed against his neck.

"Just feel, Daphne. Don't think."

Daphne moaned. All she was doing was feeling. And the feeling made her want to sob. His finger circled her again and again and again. Her hips moved of their own accord in a primal rhythm along with his finger. The tug of his mouth against her nipple and the circling of his finger between her hips made her want to scream. She bent her head to his hair. He smelled so good, like soap and rugged man. He nudged at that perfect spot between her legs, again, again, again. Daphne squirmed beneath him. Her legs were taut, open to him, but clenching with all her might to feel more of the sensation he was offering. Her hands were tangled in his hair. His mouth still owned her breast. He nipped her one more time.

"Rafe, I want—" But she didn't know how to finish the sentence.

"Just wait, Daphne."

His mouth left her breast and moved down, down, down. Her mind in a fog, she didn't realize what he intended until his finger left its spot between her legs. She sobbed, but nearly as quickly as it had left, his mouth replaced his hand and this time she moaned for an entirely different reason.

"Oh God, Rafe, no," she cried.

"Yes," he breathed against her most intimate spot.

Her face was aflame with embarrassment but the moment his tongue began tracing the little circles where his fingers had been, Daphne ceased to care. There was no more embarrassment, only raw, hot, wanton *need*. She needed him. In a way she had never needed anyone before in her life.

His tongue circled her again and again. The tip poked at her most sensitive spot and she cried out. "Rafe, I'm going to—" But she didn't know how to finish that sentence, either.

"Yes, Daphne. Yes." His hot breath covered the nub between her legs, and when he licked her in deep, wet strokes, she fell over the edge of an abyss she'd never known existed. "Rafe, oh, Rafe," she called, clutching the back of his head to her, never wanting him to stop and not caring if the entire harbor heard her.

She surfaced from her lust-induced haze several minutes later and looked down to see Rafe's face at her belly. He grinned up at her with the most self-satisfied smirk she'd ever seen.

"Proud of yourself?" she asked, on a laugh, but zigs and zips of pure pleasure were still racing through her body.

"Yes," he answered, his grin unrepentant.

She grinned back at him. "You should be. If I had known you were capable of doing *that*, I would have demanded my marital rights long, long ago."

He heaved himself up to kiss her lips. The kiss was long and deep and Daphne wrapped her arms around his neck. Rafe wasn't satisfied. She knew that. He'd ensured that she was satisfied before he saw to his own pleasure. The thought stoked something deep within her—protectiveness, caring, love?

She shook her head. She didn't have long to contemplate the thought because Rafe was making her wet with lust again by stroking between her legs once more. She parted for him. She wanted to feel him . . . inside of her. She had never wanted anything more in her life.

"Daphne, I—"

"I know it's uncomfortable, the first time," she admitted with a shaky smile. "Cass told me."

"No. It's not that."

"I told you, I won't tell Julian."

Rafe smiled at her and traced her ear with the tip of his finger. He kissed her nose. "It's not that, either. If we do this, I'll have to be man enough to face your brother. I can do that. But I want to make certain it's . . . what you really want."

Daphne stared up at him. She hoped he couldn't see all the emotions she felt for him in her eyes. At the moment she didn't care. She didn't care about Julian, or the blond, or even their future. All she cared about was being in Rafe's arms. Giving herself to the man she had always wanted. "I do want it Rafe. Truly," she promised him.

"Are you certain?"

She wrapped her arms around his neck and nodded.

He kissed her cheek gently. "I'll do my best to keep from hurting you."

"I know you will." She lifted up and brushed a kiss to his forehead.

Rafe sat up and quickly divested himself of his breeches. Once they were gone, he moved back and settled atop her. He kissed her deeply, his mouth shaping hers. With his knee, he pushed her legs wider. Daphne held her breath. Then his hard hotness was between her legs, nudging at her wet warmth, seeking its place.

Thump. Thump. Thump.

Daphne's eyes went wide. The knock on the door shocked her. "No!" she whispered fiercely against his strong neck.

Rafe groaned and rolled to his side.

"What is it?" he growled. "And by God, if it's anything other than this ship being on fire, I'm going to—"

"Captain," came Salty's voice. "The men from the tavern. They're here. They rowed out and have asked to speak with you immediately."

Rafe's second groan was painful. He vaulted from the bed in a lightning flash. "Daphne, I'm sorry but there's no time for you to dress. You must hide in the closet." He pulled his shirt over her head to hide her nakedness. "I'd meet them on the deck but if they say anything you can interpret—"

"I understand." She nodded jerkily.

"Show them in," Rafe commanded Salty. Rafe grabbed his breeches and yanked them up over his hips. Then he ripped the hammock from the beams and shoved it into the cabinet.

Daphne moved from the bed on legs that felt like water. Somehow she managed to gather her clothing from the corner and rush into the closet with the wad of fabric in her arms. Just before she pulled the door shut behind her, she saw Rafe jump into the mussed bed. Apparently he would pretend he'd been sleeping.

She held her breath. She knew what she must do. Not draw attention to herself. If the Russians opened the door and discovered her hiding and holding boy's clothing, the entire ruse would be up and she and Rafe might be killed on the spot. Not to mention she must listen to hear if they said anything to each other in Russian. But standing there in the closet, shivering and fearful, was hardly conducive to spying. She held her breath so tightly she thought her ribs might crack.

She heard the door to the cabin open and the footsteps of the two men entering the room. "Good evening, Captain." It was Anton's voice. "We do hope we're not interrupting anything."

CHAPTER THIRTY-FOUR

"Not at all, gentlemen," Rafe replied, waving the two men into the room. "I'd retired for the evening but I can always make time for two of my best customers." He pushed himself up against the wall. He glanced around furtively but kept his eyes hooded so the men couldn't see. Daphne had managed to gather all of her clothing, thank God.

Anton plopped himself into the chair. Rafe leaned back, still trying to calm his breathing. Viktor sauntered over and leaned against the door to the closet, which didn't help Rafe's breathing one bit. He could only hope Daphne was completely silent in there.

"We thought we'd come out and see your rig," Viktor explained.

Rafe didn't believe it for a moment. They weren't in the habit of paying friendly calls. They wanted to make certain that the crew was a crew and the ship was a ship. Which meant they were suspicious and that wasn't good.

"Where's your boy? What's his name, Grey is it?" Viktor asked in his heavy accent.

Rafe matched his gaze calmly. "He's asleep with the rest of the crew, I expect."

"I would like to see the hold," Anton added.

"Absolutely," Rafe answered, knowing full well that they wanted to see the hold to ensure there were actually more goods on the ship. Another sign they were suspicious. They wouldn't be disappointed. The War Office had packed the hold tightly. Not a detail left to chance in this ruse. "I'll take you there momentarily," Rafe said. "But first, what of the letters?"

"We've got them," Viktor said. "If we like what we see in the hold, we'll bring them to you tomorrow. At the tavern."

"Very well. Let me get the key." Rafe tossed back the sheet and stood. He made his way over to the desk. Anton stood and moved out of the way and Rafe rifled inside his desk drawer for a bit too long. They were speaking in Russian and he hoped Daphne could hear.

Finally, he turned to them, the key in his hand. "Ah, here it is. Follow me, gentlemen."

Daphne counted one hundred before opening the closet door and tentatively stepping out. She dressed more quickly than she ever had in her life. Her heart still beat like a drum in her chest. She'd been holding her breath in there. Her ear pressed to the wood to hear the two smugglers speak.

Her head was no longer fuzzy. She crawled back into the bed, shaking a bit at the memory of what had almost happened here not an hour earlier. She didn't allow herself to think about it, though. Instead, she concentrated on re-membering what the two men had said to each other. Be-cause she had heard. Every word.

Rafe returned over a quarter of an hour later, and by then, Daphne's heartbeat had returned to normal and she had restored a semblance of calm to her face. She was lying in the bunk, staring at the ceiling and repeating the Russians' words over and over again so she wouldn't for-get them.

Rafe opened the door and eyed her cautiously.

"Are they gone?" she asked, pushing up on her elbows to look at him.

"Yes, I watched their rowboat go." He closed the door behind him.

"Thank heavens." She gave a shaky laugh. "That was . . . close."

Rafe raked a hand through his hair and gave an equally shaky laugh. "An understatement, to be sure."

"I heard what they said."

Rafe cocked his head to the side. "And?"

"They're suspicious, but they do intend to bring you the letters. At least they said they do."

"Traitors have no loyalties, to anyone. Even their sup-posed cohorts," Rafe said.

"That's good for us, though."

"You're right," Rafe replied. "They were impressed with the hold. They told me they'd see me tomorrow night at the tavern again. We must meet them. They're bringing the letters. This is it."

CHAPTER THIRTY-FIVE

Daphne awoke with a splitting headache and a bundle of nerves in her belly. She hadn't slept well. What had happened with Rafe last night kept replaying itself over and over in her mind. The bedsheets still smelled like him. Maddening, that. She snuggled into them and breathed deeply.

His speech had sounded heartfelt and sincere when they'd been drinking, but that was the problem with drinking, wasn't it? It confused things. Gave you a fuzzy head. Hadn't he said as much himself?

The truly frightening part was she'd nearly given herself to him last night. She had no doubt if they hadn't been interrupted, she would no longer be a maiden. Rafe had apparently been so overcome that he was willing to defy Julian's edict and put himself in danger just to have her. But a night of passion wouldn't change the fact that he couldn't be trusted and they weren't suitable for one another. Yet another reason not to drink.

Daphne spent the day practicing with her knife, and by the time they loaded into the rowboat to go ashore, she had firmed her resolve in two quarters. She wasn't about to let alcohol touch her lips again when she was anywhere *near* Rafe Cavendish, and she was not—*was not*—going to kiss him again. Ever.

The ride to shore was mostly silent. In fact they'd barely spoken to each other all day. It was more of an awkward silence than anything else. They both seemed hyperaware of the enormity of the mistake they'd come so close to making last night.

They were in the rowboat alone but the rest of the crew had already come to shore. The men of the *True Love* were on alert tonight. They would blend into the crowd in and around the tavern to keep an eye on things.

Daphne breathed deep. The docks stank but she couldn't help but feel a certain exhilaration. This was the type of moment she'd never have sipping tea in drawing rooms, painting with watercolors, playing whist with the other ladies of the *ton*. She pulled the oar with all her might, matching Rafe's strokes.

As soon as the rowboat hit the dock, Daphne made to leap from the vessel, but Rafe's hand on her arm stopped her. "Be careful," he whispered.

Daphne nodded. She took her favorite knife out of her back pocket and slipped it into her boot.

CHAPTER THIRTY-SIX

Rafe glanced around the tavern. The hairs on the back of his neck stood up. Something seemed off tonight. Wrong. Daphne had assured him that all Anton and Viktor had said in their native tongue while they'd been on the *True Love* was that they had their suspicions. They'd further indicated that everything seemed legitimate before they left. The War Office team had done their research as far as the ship went. The two Russians might have believed that an unannounced visit to the ship would have revealed something, but other than nearly revealing him and Daphne in a state of undress, there was nothing suspicious about the contents of the sloop.

Daphne. Rafe didn't have time to think about the mistake they'd nearly made last night.

The Russians were nowhere to be seen. Rafe made his way across the large space to the same table where he'd sat the last time they were here. Daphne followed on his

heels. The same barmaid approached and Rafe ordered
two mugs of ale as usual.

"It's good ta see ya again, guv," the barmaid said, laughing, causing Daphne to pull her cap down and cross her
arms tightly over her chest. The barmaid soon left to get
their drinks and Daphne took her same place at the next
table. She didn't lean back on the chair legs tonight. She
seemed tense, alert. Just like Rafe was.

"There," Rafe breathed, as soon as the two men entered
the tavern.

Daphne glanced up and her eyes flared. She quickly
looked off into the crowd as if she hadn't even noticed.

Anton and Viktor came ambling toward them. They sat
backward in their seats again.

"Good to see you again so soon," Viktor said with a
laugh. He spat tobacco juice on the dirt floor. Rafe could
only imagine Daphne's internal reaction to that nastiness.
But she was doing a fair job of keeping her face blank. She
was on the far side of the men, so Rafe could see her. She
was glancing around the bar, nonchalant, as if she hadn't
a care in the world, seemingly quaffing her ale. But Rafe
knew better.

"You said the goods checked out." Rafe wanted to get
this over with as quickly as possible. No good could come
of this meeting being protracted. But most of all he wanted
what he'd come for. The letters, the whereabouts of the
men whom he would stop at nothing to find.

"They did," Viktor said. He turned to stare at Daphne.
Daphne pretended she didn't even notice. Well done.

"And do you have the agreed-upon payment?" Rafe
asked.

"*Da*," Anton said.

Rafe arched a brow. "Where is it?"

"We left them in a bundle, in a cart, in the alley. We didn't want to bring attention to ourselves hauling them in here. Too many eyes watching, you know?" Viktor said, still eyeing Daphne on occasion. He spat another wad of tobacco juice in a wide arc onto the ground.

Rafe narrowed his eyes on Viktor. In a cart in the alley? What was his game? "You wish me to accompany you to the alley?" Rafe asked. He made a move to stand but Anton stopped him with a hand in the air. "No."

"No?" Rafe's eyes narrowed further.

"We'll go get them. We wanted to make sure we weren't being watched first."

Rafe clenched his fist. They were up to something. "Being watched? That's preposterous. Go get them."

The barmaid walked past just then, holding a large tray full of ale tankards high in the air. She tripped near Grey's table, sending the tankards toppling and their contents spilling all over Daphne.

Daphne jumped up and pulled her shirt from her chest, clearly desperate to keep the fabric from becoming transparent.

"Oh me God. I'm so sorry, guv," the barmaid cried. "I've ruined yer clothes. Let me take ye in the back and fetch ye a new shirt. One of the boys will have one."

Daphne's gaze snapped to Rafe's. He touched the corner of his left eye. The signal for no.

"I'll be all right," Daphne said in her best Grey accent. "No need ta worry. It's not the first mug o' ale I've 'ad dumped on me and won't be the last, I'm certain."

Pride swelled in Rafe's chest. Daphne was playing her part perfectly. Though he could tell she was rattled.

The Russians laughed. "I think the maid likes your little friend," Anton said to Rafe, poking Viktor in the chest with his elbow.

Daphne tried to sit back down but the barmaid wouldn't let her. The woman kept trying to usher Daphne to the back. "Just come with me. I'll have ye fixed up in a trice. If ye don't want a new shirt at least let me get ye a towel."

Rafe touched his eye again. This was hardly the time to allow a tavern barmaid's flirtation to compromise their plans.

"Come on. Just a towel, guv. It's the least I can do after me mistake," the barmaid insisted.

Anton and Viktor both guffawed.

"Go on, boy. You're not afraid of a woman, are you?" Anton said.

"Or perhaps it's your master who keeps you here? Afraid to leave him, are you?" Viktor smirked at Rafe. "I think you're bit too close with the lad, English."

Rafe cursed under his breath. He had no choice but to let Daphne go. If he pressed it too far, they would no doubt turn suspicious and then the entire mission would be in danger of being aborted. They'd worked too hard and come too far. Rafe rubbed his right eye this time, the signal for yes. He could only hope Daphne returned quickly. Daphne's eyes met Rafe's and he saw the fear and hesitation in their gray depths. But he also saw her determination. She lifted her chin and gave him a barely perceptible nod. He knew from her face what her mouth could not say. She could handle this.

"Go on, Grey," he prompted, before turning his attention back to the Russians. "While he's gone, I'll wait for you to get the letters."

Anton and Viktor nodded and stood, heading for the door. "We'll be right back, Captain."

"No," Rafe said, pulling back his coat to reveal one of his pistols. "One of you will be right back. The other is staying with me."

CHAPTER THIRTY-SEVEN

Daphne allowed the barmaid to escort her to the back of the tavern. The woman fussed over her like a momma bird with her baby. She clasped her arm through Daphne's. The stench of sweat and ale wafted off her like perfume. A steady stream of apologies tumbled from her rouged lips as she ushered Daphne into a tiny room at the back of the establishment.

"I don't know wot came over me," she said in her overly loud voice. "I ain't never been so clumsy. Jimmy's sure ta take those tankards out o' me pay."

Daphne was barely listening. She was worried about leaving Rafe alone to wait for the letters. Something was going on. She'd seen the look in Rafe's eyes. He was suspicious. And so was she. Leaving the letters in the alley hadn't been part of the original plan. She racked her brain. Had either of the Russians said anything on the *True Love* last night that she hadn't remembered? Anything that could be interpreted as them having cottoned on? No. There was nothing. Or damn it. Had she missed it because her head had been fuzzy?

The barmaid quickly produced a towel of questionable cleanliness and tossed it to Daphne, who used it to blot the remaining ale from her cap and forehead and dry her shirt as best she could. She needed to get out of there as quickly as possible and back to the table.

"Obliged," she said, tipping her cap and moving around the barmaid.

"Wot's yer hurry, guv?" the barmaid said, plunking her hands on her hips.

Oh, not *this* again. Before Daphne could answer, a knock sounded on the door at the far end of the small room. The barmaid turned to open it.

A huge man stepped into the room. He handed the barmaid a wad of bills and she pointed at Daphne. "There she is, mate." She smiled, revealing cracked uneven teeth.

She? Before Daphne had a chance to run, the huge man lunged toward her. She turned to flee and was crushed under his enormous weight. She coughed, the breath knocked from her lungs. The giant swung her over his shoulder as if she were a dishcloth. Then the barmaid shoved a filthy rag into her mouth. Her arms pinned, Daphne struggled to breathe, as he moved toward the door he'd come through.

"Ain't nothing personal, guv, ya hear," the barmaid said. "I told these blokes ye was a lady and apparently that bit o' information was worth some money to 'em. I gots young ones ta feed, ye know, and I ain't never seen a boy as pretty as ye were pretending ta be." She laughed again and the sound screeched in Daphne's ears.

The door slammed behind them and Daphne and the giant were in the alley. It was dark and dank. The moon was hidden behind clouds tonight and its light was sparse. The alley smelled of urine and something Daphne desperately hoped she'd never define. The giant pulled her off his shoulder and she fell to the filthy ground in a heap. She only had a moment to look around. By the light of a swinging lantern, she made out a rickety cart sitting on the opposite side around the bend in the alleyway. Then the scene went dark as a scratchy burlap sack was yanked over her head. She tugged the rag from her throat but her scream was muffled by the giant's hand over her mouth.

"Don't scream or I'll stick my knife straight in your heart," her captor warned. He had a Russian accent, too. The man made quick work of tying her hands and feet while Daphne struggled in vain to get away from him. She desperately tried to remember what Rafe had told her about her wrists. He'd never completed that particular lesson. "Don't fight me. I can just as easily kill you as take you with me," the giant warned. Daphne went slack.

Once he finished tying her, the brawny man lifted her in a bear hug. Her ribs ached as if they would crack. Her feet dangled off the ground. She tried to kick but he shook her hard, making her teeth crack and her jaw hit her breastbone. She steeled herself for another fight but instead the man moved with her. Her entire body shook as he tossed her into something made of wood. It had to be the cart she'd seen. She rolled onto a bed of sticky, smelly hay as the cart took off down the alleyway.

CHAPTER THIRTY-EIGHT

Rafe tapped his fingers repeatedly against the mug of ale. His knee was bobbing up and down just as quickly as Viktor's was. Something was wrong. He could feel it. Anton had been gone less than five minutes and Daphne hadn't returned. It shouldn't be taking this long. One more minute and Rafe would whip out his pistol, kill this fool, and go in search of Daphne. His fingers rested on his pistol where it remained hidden in his coat.

"Worried, Lord Captain English?" Viktor asked with a smirk. "Is your boy bad with direction?"

Rafe narrowed his eyes on the other man. He clutched the pistol. "You've got me confused with someone else. I'm no lord. I'm merely a working-class lad from the streets of London."

"Your clothes are finer than mine have ever been." Viktor expelled a stream of tobacco.

Rafe was so on edge, he actually took a drink of the foul ale. "Perhaps you should work a bit harder."

Viktor growled at him.

"I should warn you," Rafe said. "If this is a setup—"

"You'll what?" Viktor asked through an evil, rotten-toothed grin.

"I'll see you and your cohort in hell," Rafe growled through clenched teeth. He banged his fist on the tabletop.

Viktor laughed then. It was loud and long. The sound sent chills through Rafe. When he looked up, Rafe saw the man nod nearly imperceptibly. Rafe turned his head to see a shadowy figure in the doorway.

"Was that Anton?" Rafe asked.

"No, Captain. That was another one of my comrades."

"Where's Anton?"

Viktor met Rafe's stare. "By now he's with Boris and Grey. Or should I say, your lady friend?"

Rafe jumped up from the table and spun toward the door, but the shadowy figure from the doorway was there directly behind him with a pistol half hidden in his giant meaty paw. "Sit down, Captain," the man commanded in a Russian accent. "Don't make a scene. Don't worry, your *cabin boy* is being held somewhere safe."

Rafe did as commanded, his mind spinning through all of the possible scenarios. His team was out there. Men he'd worked with for years. They'd been watching. They'd be following whoever had Daphne. They'd know where she was taken. But could they get to her in time before she was hurt? An icy cold sweat melted down Rafe's back.

Once Rafe was seated again, the meaty man pulled up the chair in which Daphne had been sitting only minutes before. Rafe braced his hands against his knees. "I'll tear you vermin limb from limb if she is hurt."

"Ah, big threats from someone who's in no position to

be making them, Captain," Viktor said. "Put your hands where we can see them, please."

Rafe did as he was told, pounding his fists against the tabletop. The mugs of ale bounced. "What do you want?" he demanded through clenched teeth.

"Why, you, of course, Captain English." Viktor's grin revealed all of his rotten, yellowed teeth. "Or should I say, Captain Cavendish?"

Rafe clenched his jaw. Damn them. This entire thing had been a setup. He'd been too anxious to get the letters. Too emotionally involved to see it for what it was.

"No more games. I repeat, what do you want?" Rafe slammed an open palm on the tabletop.

"We've got your lady friend," Viktor said. "And if you want her back, you'll turn yourself over so the men who pay us can finish what they started in France. It seems they want your head, Captain."

Rafe concentrated on his breathing. He slowly clenched and unclenched his fist. He wanted to wring their bloody necks right now, but if his team hadn't been able to follow Daphne for some reason, these two idiots might be the only people who knew where she was. "Why didn't you just let me go with you to the alley if it was me you are after?"

"And let you take a few of us with you? I don't think so, Captain. We much prefer you compliant. Taking that bit of fluff you had dressed up like a boy was the one way we knew we could keep you sane and us safe," Viktor said.

The man with the pistol kept his mouth closed. His eyes were trained on Rafe. Viktor was obviously the leader of this pack, though they'd made it out to seem as if Anton had been before.

Rafe clenched his jaw so tightly it popped. "If I go with you, you'll release her?"

"Yes."

Rafe stared at them out of the narrow slits his eyes had become. "How do I know you're not lying?"

"You don't, but what choice do you have? All I can tell you is that the men who employ us aren't interested in the girl. They want *you*."

Now *that* was believable. Especially since they didn't seem to realize that Daphne was a member of the aristocracy. At least that much remained a secret. Rafe stood. "Let's go."

These vermin were right for once.

His life for Daphne's?

There was no choice.

CHAPTER THIRTY-NINE

Daphne rubbed her chafed wrists and looked around the nasty little room she'd been tossed in. The bone-jarring ride in the wagon hadn't lasted long, thank heavens, and she could still smell the salty air of the docks. She wasn't far from where she'd been abducted, but wherever they'd taken her, it was a horrid place. Her abductor had hauled her out of the wagon, tossed her over his shoulder like a bag of hay, making the air whoosh from her lungs painfully, and carried her up three flights of stairs. She'd counted. A wooden door had creaked open, he'd removed her ties, and she'd been unceremoniously dumped in her current environment.

She glanced around. Not particularly hospitable. The room was perhaps ten feet square with a dirty wood floor and one tiny window at the top of the far wall. The window let in a bit of hazy moonlight but she was far too short to see out. One small wooden stool rested haphazardly in the far right corner. Some dirty remnants of food lay tossed on the floor and there was a—she gasped—fairly large rat gnawing on a piece of moldy bread near the stool. She willed herself not to scream. She'd never been particularly frightened of rats but she certainly didn't want to share a living space with one.

"Good day, Sir Rat," she said with a shaky voice. "What did you do to get put in here?"

She smiled at her own nonsensical behavior. At least she hadn't lost her sense of humor . . . yet. What had she thought earlier about wanting adventure? Rubbish. Utter rubbish. Though she supposed if she made it home, she'd have a harrowing story for Delilah.

Daphne scooted back against the door and eyed the rat nervously. "Let's make an agreement, you and I."

The rat merely blinked at her. He did not stop his nibbling.

"You remain over there . . ." She scooted to the right around the wall and slowly pulled the stool back over toward the door. "And I'll just stay over here. How about that?"

The rat blinked again but didn't move, thank heavens.

"I don't suppose you could give me the address of this place?" She smiled at herself again. Not that she'd be able to do anything with it if she had it. She was sorely lacking a carrier pigeon. Keeping on eye on the rat's location, she pushed the stool over to the wall with the window and stood on it. Still too short to see out. Blast. Being the opposite of tall was such a curse. She jumped. Nothing. She tried again. Only a sliver of the outside appeared. But the stool seemed in imminent danger of cracking into pieces so she decided not to try again. The tiny glimpse she'd got on the second jump had only been enough to see darkness. Reluctantly, her eye still on the rat, she scraped the stool back over toward the door to put as much distance between herself and her hairy little cellmate as possible.

"Nothing personal," she said to the rat.

Daphne glanced all around the small room. She wasn't about to just sit quietly and wait to be rescued. First, she tried the door. It was locked, of course. She jiggled the handle furiously. No movement. Screwing up her courage because proximity to the rat was involved, she backed up to the far wall and ran as hard as she could, tossing her body against the door with all her force. She bounced off the door and flew backward, knocking over the stool, which went skittering toward the rat. The rat narrowly escaped it, scurrying out of the way just in time.

"Ouch." Daphne rubbed her injured and no doubt bruised shoulder. "I beg your pardon," she said to the rat.

The door was obviously locked with a bolt from the outside and made of extremely sturdy wood. She glanced about again. There was nothing else. No cracks in the walls, no other entrances or windows. Just her and the rat. She had to think. There must be some way she could get out. Something she could do. She considered yelling for help but thought against it. If her captor heard her and returned, he would no doubt threaten her with stabbing again. She could only hope he hadn't heard her run at the door.

She sat with her back against the wall and pulled up her knees. The crew of the *True Love* had been in the crowd at the tavern earlier. They must have seen her leave. And Rafe. Rafe would soon realize she wasn't coming back and he'd come for her. He'd rip Anton and Viktor and probably that barmaid apart as soon as he realized they'd double-crossed him. Then he'd be on his way. She knew it.

In the meantime, perhaps her captor would return and

provide her with an opportunity to escape. The man seemed like a hulking mass, but she was small and spry. She just might manage to get around him and run. He wouldn't have the element of surprise he'd had earlier. She just might make it if she could find the staircase easily. Regardless, she had to try.

She let her head fall back against the dusty stone wall behind her and assessed her situation. She had two things going for her. One, Rafe and the rest of the crew would be searching for her and they wouldn't stop until they found her. She knew it. And two, she just so happened to have a knife in her boot. She slid her hand down to her ankle and patted the knife's handle. It had warmed against her skin and gave her confidence.

For now, or until she could come up with a plan, all there was to do was wait.

She'd drifted off to sleep a bit, lulled by the rhythmic sound of the nearby waves, when the bolt screeching against the door woke her.

"Who's there?" she whispered into the dark. She glanced over. The rat was gone.

The wide wooden door swung open and the huge man stood blocking the light from the corridor.

"What do you want?" she asked, trying her best not to cower against the wall from his sheer size.

"What's your name? And don't lie to me," he demanded.

"Ye don't know who ye kidnapped?" she said in her cabin boy voice.

The hulking mass kicked her leg, hard, and Daphne quickly decided against further antagonism. Earl's daughters were never kicked. Apparently, mouthy cabin boys, or whoever they believed her to be, were. Regardless, she wasn't about to give up her false identity. She rubbed her aching calf. "Thomas Grey," she said. "I'm the cabin boy from the *True Love*."

"I said don't lie to me." Spittle flew from the hulking mass's mouth.

"I'm not lying," Daphne insisted.

"Yes you are."

"Fine. Why don't ye tell me wot me name is then?" she answered, glaring at him, daring him to call her bluff.

"It's Daphne Swift. Or should I call you 'my lady'?"

CHAPTER FORTY

Daphne froze. Icicles pierced her veins. He'd obviously been told by the barmaid she was a female, but how did he know her name?

"Rat got your tongue, my fine lady?" the hulking mass said in his thick Russian accent.

"What do you plan to do with me?" she replied.

The hulking mass wiped a dirty arm across his cracked lips. "We're using you to lure Captain Cavendish."

More ice encrusted Daphne's heart. They had Rafe? They'd used her to capture Rafe? And they knew his real name, too? Had they already murdered him? Were they torturing him again somewhere? Perhaps in this very place? She scratched at her arms, frantic to get out of here and help him.

"But my friend and I, we thought we might have a bit of sport with you. Neither of us has ever been with a true lady." The hulking mass waggled his bushy eyebrows at her.

Daphne pulled herself into a ball in the corner. She was going to be sick. "Your friend?" she choked out.

The hulking mass didn't have to answer. Another man came barreling through the door. This man was much shorter, much smaller, and spryer, and leaner than the hulking mass.

"There you are, Billy. I've been waiting for you," the hulking mass said. "You should be thankful I didn't already have my way with her." He laughed a disgusting laugh.

Daphne shuddered. Bile rose in her throat. Rape. She hadn't considered rape. Pain, yes. Torture, yes. Death, even. But she'd been pretending to be a boy. The thought of rape hadn't occurred to her.

Though Billy was considerably smaller than his friend he was equally unkempt and still much larger than Daphne. His cloudy blue eyes darted around the room haphazardly. He looked a bit mad. "Aye, she's a fine one, just like ye said, Boris."

"I don't lie," Boris answered. "Have you ever known me to lie?"

"I can't say I has," Billy replied, drooling a bit from the side of his wide mouth.

Daphne backed away even farther. Her back and hands against the stone, she moved slowly toward the far wall. She only had one knife. She might manage to kill or wound one of them but the other might overpower her. Her heart hammered in her throat. *Think. Think.*

"Billy?" she asked. "Is that your name? Billy?"

"Aye." Billy nodded.

"What are you doing working with these Russians, Billy? Why would you turn against your own countryfolk?"

Billy wiped at his mouth. "Aye, don't think ye can talk to me about loyalty and kinship, me lady." He sneered. "I was wounded in the army and got nothin' from me country. Not even a kick in the teef. I works fer who pays me best now. That's wot I do. And if there's a bit o' fun ta be had whilst I'm at it, like a tumble wit ye, I'm all for it."

Daphne swallowed hard and continued her crawl toward the far wall. Clearly Billy wasn't going to be talked out of this.

Billy's wild eyes tracked her movement. They devoured her. "Where do ye think ye're going, me lady?"

"There's no place to run to," Boris added with a laugh that could curdle milk.

Billy advanced on her, his arms wide as if he would catch her if she tried to stand and run around him. It would have been no use at any rate because Boris's girth filled the doorway. He laughed and rubbed his hands together as Billy stalked toward her.

"Tell me something," Daphne asked, attempting to stall and wanting to know the answer.

"Wot's that?" Billy asked, grinning at her through rotten teeth.

"Did either of you . . . were either of you there when my brother, the Earl of Swifdon, was murdered?"

Billy laughed. "Can't say I did the honors, me lady, but I surely was part o' the gang wot turned him over to those Frenchies."

Daphne stood up, her back against the far wall now, and clenched her jaw. Just as she suspected. These two men *were* part of the group responsible for Donald's death. She hated them with every part of her body, mind, and spirit.

Billy continued to slowly advance on her and Daphne swallowed hard again. The closer he got, the stronger his smell. He reeked of sweat and rotting garbage. She pressed the back of her arm across her mouth, fighting against the bile in her throat. Billy jumped at her and caught her arm, pulling her down onto the dirty floor with him. She screamed and bucked, trying desperately to push him off her. He pinned one of her arms above her head and began unbuttoning his filthy trousers with the other. "Don't squirm so much, yer highness. It'll be better for both of us."

This was it. She might only kill one of them but she had to try. With her free arm, she reached into her boot for the knife. Billy was too preoccupied with his trousers to notice. The hulking mass didn't seem to, either.

Billy sprang free, his erection pressing against Daphne's leg. She fought her gag even harder. He yanked at Daphne's breeches, ripping the material at her waist.

"No!" she cried.

He lifted his arm and cracked her across the cheek. Her head snapped to the side and hit hard against the floor. Pain ripped through her face and neck. She gritted her teeth, turned her head, and curled her fingers around the hilt of the knife. She lifted the weapon in her hand and pushed him off her body with all her might. Billy fell to the side, off kilter because of his fight to remove her breeches. Daphne took one last deep breath and plunged the knife into his chest, just below his left shoulder, right where his heart would be. Blood spurted, dark and hot, out of the wound in his chest, coating Daphne's hands and splattering across her face and clothing.

"Gah!" Billy screamed and crumpled to the floor while blood continued to pour out of the large wound around the knife.

"She's kilt me!" he cried.

The hulking mass's eyes went wide, then they narrowed into beady black coals. "Damn you, bitch."

Daphne watched in horror as Boris advanced toward her with murder in his eyes. The giant was going to kill her. Rape her first, then kill her. She knew it, but at least she'd taken one of the two. She'd go to her grave knowing she'd taken a life for her brother's. And Billy was indeed dying. Blood trickled from his lips and he gurgled. He'd propped himself against the wall, staring unseeing into the room, each breath more shallow than the last.

"That was for my brother," she spat at the dying man.

Billy made no other sound.

"I'm going to snap your neck after I've had my way with you," the hulking mass snarled.

Daphne sprang to her feet and faced off with him. "You'll have to catch me first." She leaped over to Billy and yanked the knife from his chest with one solid move. More blood sprayed onto her breeches. Billy's eyes drained of life until they were completely blank.

She turned back to Boris, the knife clutched in her slick, bloody fist. The weapon may have given the giant pause, but not for long. He lunged at her. She aimed the knife at his heart but it slid into his shoulder instead. Groaning in pain, he tackled her to the ground, nearly breaking her back. She struggled for air. She would suffocate if he stayed on her for any length of time.

"No!" she screamed, but the knife was still lodged in his shoulder, pinned between them. She couldn't retrieve it. Her wrist was pinned to the floorboards. It felt as if it might snap.

"Aargh." With an unearthly cry, Boris groaned and collapsed atop her, his bulbous face falling to the side of her neck.

Daphne's eyes went wide. What had just happened?

The next thing she knew, the giant body atop hers was pushed over and fell away and Rafe was standing there, breathing heavily. His hands on his hips. She glanced over at the hulk's body. The handle of a knife was standing up in the back of his neck.

"And that was for me!" Rafe shouted at the hulk's quivering mass, viciously kicking him in the side.

"Rafe," Daphne cried, tears pooling in her eyes. She was still shaking so hard her teeth clacked.

Rafe fell to his knees beside her, his hands skimming her neck, her chest, her legs. "Daphne, are you all right? Have you been stabbed?"

"No, no," she sobbed.

"You're covered in blood." Rafe enveloped her in his arms, cradling her head against his chest. "Did they hurt you? Did they—?"

"I'm fine. Just . . . frightened." She wrapped her arms around his neck. "Rafe, how did they know? How did they find out? The barmaid told them I was female but . . . how did they know my name?"

Rafe didn't let her go. He stroked her head. "I don't know. They must have done some investigating after they discovered you weren't a boy. I can only imagine they paid enough money to the right person."

Daphne shuddered. It truly didn't matter how they found out. All that mattered was that she was safe. And Rafe was safe. "How did you find me?" she whispered against his chest.

"Those two idiots, Anton and Viktor, offered your life for mine."

Daphne gasped. She pulled back away from him slightly and cupped her blood-streaked hand over her mouth.

"I agreed of course and they brought me here. In shackles."

Daphne eyed him up and down. He clearly wasn't wearing any shackles on his wrists or his ankles. Her brow furrowed. "How did you escape?"

Rafe's infamous grin lit up his face. "You and I didn't quite make it to that lesson, but unfortunately for them, escaping shackles is one of my specialties."

Daphne had to smile at that. "Did you . . . are they dead?"

"No. Though not because I didn't want to kill them with my bare hands. The crew took them. They followed me here. They were unable to find where you'd been taken because they'd been watching the door to the tavern, not the alley, but when Viktor brought me out of the inn, they followed us."

Daphne shuddered at the thought of how close she'd come to rape and death. Thank God Viktor had brought Rafe here.

"What will happen to them?" she asked, while Rafe removed his coat and covered her shaking limbs.

"They'll both be tried for murder and espionage. And I've got the letters that will lead me to the men who hired them in France."

Daphne pressed a hand to her belly. "That's wonderful, Rafe. It's just what you wanted. Now we can go to France and find the other men and—"

Rafe's face turned to a mask of stone. "*We* aren't going anywhere, Daphne."

"But you'll need me. I speak Russian. You said yourself that Gabriel often speaks it to keep you from knowing what he's saying. I can help you."

Rafe shook his head. "It's too dangerous. I've already

put your life in danger twice. I won't risk it again. I'm taking the *True Love* and the crew and sailing for France without you."

Anger bubbled in Daphne's chest but she knew Rafe's mind was made up. He refused to admit he needed her. He refused to admit he needed anyone. There was no arguing with him at a time like this. This was it. He was going to leave her. It was over. She should have known it would end like this.

Rafe held out a hand. "Come on. I'm taking you home."

CHAPTER FORTY-ONE

Back in Julian's town house in Mayfair, Daphne sat on her bed turning the tiny replica of the *True Love* over and over in her hands. She traced the little mast with her fingertip, remembering how many knives she'd thrown near that towering piece of wood. She sighed. She'd been home for three days and it was raining, again.

She'd already told Delilah all the details she could in exchange for the girl's silence. She'd even included the harrowing bit. She hadn't told her *all* of the details, of course. She'd left out the part about Rafe nearly making love to her. It had been a feat, coming up with a believable story to tell Mother about why she had a large bruise across her cheek, but somehow she'd managed to convince her that she'd tripped down the stairs at Lucy Hunt's country house and Lucy—that dear—had made a show of profusely apologizing for the clumsiness of her servants who had obviously polished the wood on the stairs with far too much aplomb.

Julian, however, had taken a bit of convincing. The moment he'd seen the bluish-black bruise, he'd been prepared to storm from the house to kill someone. It had taken both Daphne and Cass a considerable amount of time to convince him to sit down and breathe. Of course, Daphne hadn't told him the truth of exactly how she'd got the bruise. No need to worry her brother further. The damage was already done. But she knew Julian suspected it had been more than an accident, as she'd informed him. Thankfully, once he realized she had no intention of telling him, he'd stopped asking questions. Apparently, a reputation for stubbornness was good for something.

Daphne stared out of the window into the dripping rain. The afternoon was so dull. Delilah had gone to take a nap. Mother had offered to play cards with her but Daphne had politely refused.

She wanted to practice throwing her knife. She found herself repeatedly touching her ankle to see if the knife was in her boot. She wasn't wearing a boot and she certainly wasn't carrying a knife. Not to mention her mother might have an apoplectic fit if she saw her daughter out in the gardens hurling knives at trees.

Daphne glanced down at her embroidered white day gown. Such a far cry from the shirt, breeches, and stockings she'd been wearing while pretending to be a cabin boy. She plucked at the top of her head where a useless ribbon sat holding up her bun. She missed her cap. She rubbed her silk stocking against her bedspread. Silk was certainly more luxurious than the wool stockings she'd worn as Grey. So why did she miss those, too?

Here she was. Back in her proper house, in her proper clothes, with her proper life. And it was all just too . . . boring. Why had she never noticed how exceedingly dull it was to live in a town house before? She meandered over to her writing desk and picked up her copy of *The Adventures of Miss Calliope Cauldwell*. She smiled to herself. Perhaps someday she would write a similar tale. If only Rafe had allowed her to go to France with him, the stubborn rogue.

A soft knock on the bedchamber door pulled Daphne from her thoughts. "Who is it?"

"It's Cass, dear," came her sister-in-law's sweet voice.

"And Lucy," added the duchess's bright one.

Daphne laid the book back down, swiveled, rushed over to the door, and opened it. "Come in. Come in." She ushered the two ladies into the room. They made their way over to the windows and sat in the two chairs that rested there.

"We came to check on you, dear," Cass explained, once she was settled. "How are you?"

Daphne resumed her seat on the bed and clutched the tiny ship in her fist. She sighed. "I'm . . . fine."

Lucy scrunched up her nose. "You don't sound fine."

Daphne put the back of her hand to her head as if checking for fever. "I honestly don't know what's wrong with me."

"I do," Lucy replied with a knowing smile and a twinkle in her two-different-colored eyes.

"You do? What is it?" Daphne sat forward on the bed and blinked expectantly at Lucy.

Lucy splayed her hands wide. "You're in love, dear. You're exhibiting the classic symptoms. Restlessness, fatigue, boredom. And I'd wager you've not spent so much as a moment without Captain Cavendish in your thoughts since you've got home, have you?"

Daphne's cheeks heated. She moved her hand down to

press on one of them. How had Lucy known? She glanced at the replica. Suddenly, she had the desire to hide it. "Well, I—"

"And that little ship in your hand speaks volumes," Lucy added with another nod.

Daphne's jaw dropped. "How did you see—"

Cass tapped her fingertips along the arms of the chair. "I must agree with Lucy, dear. I was madly in love for years with someone I couldn't have. I know the signs when I see them."

Daphne shook her head so vigorously her bun came loose. "I'm not madly in love with him. I'm not."

Lucy's smile was scandalous. She crossed her arms over her chest. "Are you, perhaps, just a little in love with him?"

Daphne set the replica on her bedside table. She stood and paced to the windows, standing in between the two chairs. "Very well," she conceded. "Perhaps. Just a little." Daphne whirled to face them and pressed her palms to both cheeks. "This is awful, isn't it?"

Cass and Lucy exchanged satisfied looks.

"Not awful at all, dear. It's wonderful." Cass reached up to squeeze Daphne's hand.

Daphne plopped down on the window seat and gave Cass her hand. "But it's not that easy. What about the blond doxy?"

Lucy cleared her throat. "Yes, about that. I hope you don't mind but Cass recounted that particular tale to me, and I have to say, I don't think it makes much sense."

Daphne's head snapped to face the duchess. "What do you mean?"

"I mean, why in the world would Captain Cavendish have been downstairs looking for *you* if he had a blond waiting for him in his bed? And why didn't he lock the door between the two rooms to keep you from finding her?"

Daphne's heart hammered in her throat. "But she was in his bed and—"

"And what?"

"You didn't actually *see* them touching, did you?" Lucy asked.

"No." Daphne's voice trailed off.

Cass winced and returned her hand to her own lap. "I have to say when I first heard it, it sounded quite condemning, but upon further reflection, I agree with Lucy. I can't say I'd believe that Captain Cavendish would take a woman to his bed with you in the room right next door, Daphne. It's beyond the pale even for a rogue."

Daphne shook her head. She didn't know what made any sense anymore but there was more than one reason she and Rafe couldn't be together. She said the only thing she could think of at the moment. "But Rafe's refused to allow me to go to France with him."

"Daphne, be reasonable," Cass replied. "That trip is far too dangerous for you. Captain Cavendish couldn't have asked Julian for such a favor. Even if he wanted to."

"Why not?" Daphne asked. But she already knew the answer and knew she was acting like a pouting child for asking.

"If it makes you feel any better, I can assure you Julian wouldn't have said yes," Cass added.

Daphne braced her palms on either side of her thighs on the cushion. She stared down at her slippers, dejected. "Has Rafe left yet? Do you know?"

Lucy's eyes twinkled. "Derek says he leaves for France in two days."

"Yes, and he's commissioned Jane to write a letter for

him. But I can't say any more than that. I'm sworn to secrecy," Cass added.

Daphne pressed her fingers to her eyes. "Why do I have this awful feeling that I'm never going to see him again?" She moved her hands down to her belly. "I feel sick."

Cass leaned over, put her hand on Daphne's forehead, and patted it softly. "You're in love, dear. We all feel as if we're going to be sick when we're in love."

"Oh, Cass, what am I to do?" Daphne asked, taking a deep breath.

"You can never go wrong if you're honest and follow your heart," Cass said, with a knowing smile. "Isn't that what you always told me, Lucy?"

Lucy pushed a bouncy black curl away from her forehead. "Yes, it is, but in this particular instance I believe more drastic action needs to be taken."

Daphne blinked and looked at Lucy. "Like what?"

"In this case, follow your heart means bring your gentleman up to scratch." Lucy punctuated the last word with a firm stamp on the floor.

A thrill shot through Daphne's chest. Did Lucy truly mean what she thought she meant? "Bring my gentleman up to scratch?"

Lucy gave her a resolute nod. "This is no time to be a shrinking violet. If you want Captain Cavendish, you're going to have to fight for him. You're the one who's told him you intend to marry a man from your list. He has no reason to believe you even want to see him again. Did you tell him you do?"

Daphne blinked. Panic rose like a rogue wave in her chest. "No. I didn't tell him. He was so adamant about not taking me to France with him. I thought it was clear that things were over between us."

Lucy folded her arms over her chest and shook her head. "But if you didn't tell him you wanted to see him again, why would he have any reason to think anything else?"

Daphne's stomach lurched. Her words from the other night came back to haunt her. He'd asked her what sort of men were on her list. "Titled, rich, handsome, loyal," she'd replied.

"So, it's safe to say I'm not on your list" had been his response.

She could kick herself now. Lucy was completely right. Why would Rafe think Daphne wanted anything more to do with him? All she'd ever asked of him was the annulment.

She turned frantically to Cass and searched her sister-in-law's face. "Cass, what do you think?"

Cass bit her lip and glanced away. "Of course I'd never tell you to do anything that would be unladylike or put you in danger."

"Please tell me, Cass," Daphne begged. "Truly. What do you think I should do?"

Cass met Daphne's gaze then. "I happen to remember a girl who tried to climb out of a window once and I do wonder where that girl is now."

Another thrill shot through Daphne's chest. Lucy was right and so was Cass. Despite the blond and the difference in Daphne's and Rafe's social standing and everything, Daphne couldn't let Rafe leave without at least trying to tell him that she loved him. She had to go to him.

She allowed a wide grin to spread across her face. "Where is he now?"

Lucy jumped up and clapped her hands. "That's the spirit! Be bold!"

CHAPTER FORTY-TWO

"Cavendish, I thought I might find you here."

Rafe looked up from his glass of brandy. He was sitting in a tavern, not by the docks, but still far enough outside of Mayfair that he hadn't expected to see Garrett Upton, the future Earl of Upbridge, striding toward him. Upton was dressed to the nines as usual. Black trousers, emerald-green waistcoat, expensively tailored black overcoat, and shining black top boots.

Rafe glanced down at his own rumpled attire. The same white shirt he'd been wearing for days, dark brown breeches, and scuffed boots. He'd never be as fine as the blue bloods. He glanced at the grim scene. A few barmaids, a few rough patrons. Dirty floor, chipped wooden chairs, mismatching glasses. His usual haunt, but certainly not a place for a swank like Upton. It was exactly where Rafe belonged, however. He fit right in here as if he were born to the place.

He squinted up at the future earl. "How did you know I was here, Upton?"

Upton pulled the chair over from the table next to him and straddled it. "Lucky guess, really. Claringdon told me you sometimes come here when you're not at Brooks's with him."

Rafe smiled a humorless smile. "Claringdon knows me too well." Rafe liked Claringdon. Claringdon was a duke now, it was true. But he hadn't been born to it. No, Claringdon had earned his title in the war. Claringdon was the type of man who made sense to Rafe. Though, he had to admit, he liked Upton as well. As the nephew of an earl, Upton had been born to the *ton,* but he was the only son of a second son, not meant for a title. It had been mere fate that had taken the life of his male cousin, Lucy Hunt's brother, in childhood. Upton stood to inherit an earldom one day but no, he hadn't been born for it. Upton had been a soldier, actually. He'd been shot in Spain. He'd nearly died. Rafe could respect a man like Upton. Hell, he did.

A barmaid brought a glass of brandy for Upton. He took it from her and tossed her a coin. Then he turned his attention back to Rafe. "I hear you're about to go back to France."

Rafe nodded. "I am."

Upton inclined his head and took a drink. "Not much work for a spy during times of peace. Is this your last mission?"

Rafe contemplated the amber liquid in his glass. "You know why I'm going."

Upton turned the glass around and around in his hand. "To find the men who killed Donald Swift?"

Rafe took a sip. "That's right."

Upton narrowed his eyes on Rafe. "You told me once I should take my own advice."

Rafe furrowed his brow. "I said that? When?"

Upton continued to turn the glass in his hand. "Last spring. When I told you how guilty I was over Harold Langford's death. You said you knew how I felt."

Rafe managed a half shrug. "I don't recall."

"I do." Upton's voice held an edge to it that hadn't been there before.

Rafe tipped back his head and took another drink. "And what was my brilliant advice?"

"I told you that you shouldn't blame yourself about Donald's death and you told me that perhaps I should take my own advice."

"I said that?" Rafe shook his head. "I'm an idiot."

"Funny. I thought it was quite wise." Upton finally took a sip of his own drink.

Rafe scrubbed his free hand through his hair. "I'm not wise. There's nothing wise about me."

Upton set down the glass and braced his forearms against the back of the chair. "Yes. I assure you, there is. I know you have your score to settle but I want you to remember something."

Rafe barely glanced up. "Yeah? What's that?"

"Don't allow guilt over Swifdon's death to haunt you."

Rafe gave the future earl a half-smile. "Ah, so you've come to return the favor, have you? Give me my own advice? Remind me of my wise words?"

Upton stood and bowed. "That's precisely why I've come. Well, that and another reason."

Rafe looked at him quizzically. "Which is?"

"I know when I see a man trying to drown his sorrows over a lady by drinking too much."

Rafe snorted. "You do, do you?"

"Yes, I do, and I thought I'd also give you a bit of advice I learned the hard way."

Rafe raised his brows and looked up at the man who stood next to him. "Which is?"

"Don't let the woman you love slip through your fingers because you're being too damned stubborn to admit you love her."

CHAPTER FORTY-THREE

Rafe was lying in his bunk in the captain's cabin of the *True Love,* tossing a coin in the air and catching it. He'd removed his boots and loosened his cravat. One knee was bent, the other leg straight. He stared unseeing at the wooden ceiling. Again and again he tossed the coin and caught it in the same hand. It was a reflex at this point. His mind was long gone, turning in circles exactly like the dropping coin. Tomorrow morning, he and the crew would set sail for France. The letters he'd secured from the Russian spies told him everything he needed to know about the location of the men he was after in France.

He should have been concentrating on the mission, but instead Upton's words were steadily haunting him. "Don't let the woman you love slip through your fingers." What did Upton know about it? *How* did Upton know about it? Was it that damn obvious that Rafe had feelings for Daphne? He tossed the coin again and caught it solidly in his palm. Damn it. He wasn't *allowing* Daphne to slip through his fingers. He'd never had her. She'd made it clear that not only did she not believe him about whoever the hell that blond woman had been, but she also had a list of a bunch of titled gentlemen from which she had already picked another husband. Rafe hadn't pressed her on naming the chap because he couldn't stand to know, if he was being honest. It would only cause that awful sick feeling in his middle to return. The same feeling he'd had when he'd met Edmund Fitzwell. Regardless, Daphne couldn't have been more clear that Rafe was not a suitable candidate for the position. Perhaps ironic, given that he currently *was* her husband, but that didn't matter. He'd give her her bloody annulment. He'd already sent a letter to his contact at the Home Office to get the thing started, quietly. And if his unsuitability wasn't enough, he'd nearly allowed her to be raped and killed on his watch. No. He was absolutely no good for Daphne Swift, regardless of how he might feel about her. He could offer her nothing but mediocrity and danger. He couldn't believe after what she'd been through at the hands of the Russians that she'd offered to go with him to France. But there was no possible way he'd risk her life again. No. The rest of this mission he had to complete. Alone.

He tossed the coin again. Upton's words still rankled. Besides, Rafe's situation wasn't exactly like Upton's. Upton had been wounded in Spain. His friend Harold Langford had taken a second bullet meant for Upton and lost his life. That had been Langford's choice. Rafe was a captain in His Majesty's army, sworn to protect Donald Swift with his own life. He'd failed. The two incidents were nothing alike.

Not only that but if Julian Swift found Rafe before the French did, he'd no doubt beat Rafe to a bloody pulp himself. Daphne had surely informed her brother of her near escape from the Russians. Rafe had promised to keep every hair on her head safe and she'd already had the makings of a large bruise on her face when he'd taken her home. Apparently, one of those filthy bastards had *struck* her. If he wasn't already dead, Rafe would have gone back and finished the job. He would make the rest of them pay, too.

Thump. Thump. Thump.

Rafe caught the coin and rose up on his elbow. Who was at the door? At this hour? It had to be after eleven. He consulted his timepiece. Yes, after eleven.

"Come in," he called, expecting to see Grim or Salty asking about some last-minute arrangements.

The door swung open and Grey was standing there, tight breeches, flowing white shirt, and adorable cap.

Rafe nearly rubbed his eyes. Was it an illusion? "Daphne, what are you doing here?"

She walked into the room and kicked shut the door with her booted foot. Her eyes never left his face. "I wanted to see you, Rafe."

Rafe leaped to his feet. "Does your brother know you're here?"

She shook her head. "Of course not. I came because I—"

He put up a hand to stop her. She didn't need to say it. "You needn't have come. Don't worry. I sent word to the Home Office. They're seeing to the paperwork for our annulment."

Daphne raised her chin. "I don't want an annulment. I want to consummate our marriage. Tonight."

CHAPTER FORTY-FOUR

Rafe's eyes nearly bugged from his skull. "You want to . . . pardon?" He cocked his head to the side. Surely he'd heard her incorrectly.

Daphne's small hand went to her throat and she began tugging at the cravat at her neck. "You heard me."

Rafe swallowed. Hard. Speaking of hard, everything in his body was going hard. Rock-hard. Including his cock. He stepped back and pushed against the wall behind him as if that could put more space between them. "I don't understand. I thought you wanted an annulment."

Daphne finished unraveling the cravat. She pulled it from around her neck with one sharp movement and tossed it in the corner. "At the moment all I want is to spend the night with you." Her voice was husky, hot. Her eyes were pools of liquid steel.

Rafe ran a hand through his hair. "How did you get here?"

"I have my ways. Does it matter?"

"Does Swifdon know you're here?"

"No." The one word shattered like a vase onto the floor.

Rafe couldn't drag his gaze away from her. She was mesmerizing him. He searched his brain for a coherent thought. "I thought you wanted a title. I thought—"

Daphne pulled off her cap, and shook out her long, blond hair. It fell in waves over her shoulders. Rafe gulped.

"You thought wrong. I want you," she said.

"Daphne, I—" His fingers raked through his hair again. *Think. Think.*

Daphne stalked toward him, her mouth quirked into a half-smile. "What's the matter, Captain Cavendish? Am I making you nervous? I never thought I'd live to see the day." Then she tugged at the buttons at her collar.

Rafe nearly leaped up the wall. "No. No. No. I can't. Julian will rip out my intestines. He'll finish what the French started. He'll . . ."

But Rafe's words trailed off as she pulled her shirt over her head. It followed the cravat into the corner. Rafe drew in a deep breath.

Her chest was wrapped in linen and she still wore her breeches. She shucked off her boots, one by one, and then began slowly unwinding the fabric from around her breasts.

"Don't do this," Rafe whispered. *Close your eyes, you fool.* But he couldn't, not with the sight in front of him, the linen slowly peeling away from her creamy skin.

"Too late," she said just as the linen fell away. She tossed the fabric into the pile with the rest and moved toward him. She stood merely a pace away from him.

Next, she began unhooking the fall of her breeches.

"You're going to get me killed," Rafe breathed. "Murdered."

She nipped at her pink lips with her white teeth. "I don't

want to kill you. I want to make love to you. We don't have to tell Julian anything."

Rafe moved then. No more acting like a quivering boy. He took one decisive step forward and grabbed her hands. Her breasts nearly skimmed his chest. He clenched his jaw. "Don't do this, Daphne."

Her eyes were pools of mist gazing into his. "Why not?" She let her mouth hang open and he was fixated on her tongue that darted out to wet her lips.

Good question. He poked out his cheek with his tongue and tried to think about anything other than his rock-hard member. "Because I can't resist you."

"Good." She pulled her hands away sharply and her breeches fell to her ankles. He swallowed again, knowing if he just looked down he would see her completely naked. Unholy torture.

"Rafe, you're the only man I've ever wanted. Take me to bed."

Oh God, she was naked. Completely nude. He forced himself to clench his eyes shut. Sweat beads popped along his brow. He had to be the reasonable one. Apparently, Daphne had lost all reason along with her clothing. "I'm leaving for France in the morning," he pleaded.

He felt her nearness, her warmth. Her hands were on his shoulders—she must have been on tiptoes—just before her soft voice whispered in his ear. "I'm not asking you to stay."

He licked his lips. She smelled so good. Like apples and roses and—

"Daphne, I . . . I want to, Lord knows I want to, but—"

"Then what's the matter?" Her hands tugged his cravat away and then her warm lips were at the base of his throat. *Jesus Christ.* Rafe's eyes remained tightly closed. If he opened them, if he saw her, saw what she was offering, there would no longer be a choice. No longer be a chance to do the right thing to send her away. "I could be killed. I might not come back," he offered.

Her whisper was hot in his ear and her fingers slid enticingly into the hair at the nape of his neck. "All the more reason to have this one night together. Besides, we're married, remember?" Her supple breasts pushed against his chest, all that separated them was the thin fabric of his shirt. Her nipples burned through it.

That was it. Rafe broke. He couldn't resist her touch. He opened his eyes and allowed his gaze to scan her body. She was perfection, all creamy white skin and glorious blond hair. Her breasts were delicate and round, her waist tiny, her legs, while not long, were perfectly proportioned with the rest of her. She was any man's dream. *His dream.* "I cannot make you any promises, Daphne," he breathed.

Her lips barely skimmed his, driving him mad. "I don't want promises. I just want one night with you."

CHAPTER FORTY-FIVE

Rafe's eyes closed again. A muscle ticked in his jaw. But as soon as he opened his eyes, Daphne knew she'd won. His eyes were bright and shining and he stepped back and gently pushed her to arm's length while his gaze devoured her body. "God, you're beautiful," he groaned.

She put a hand on one bare hip. "Does that mean yes?"

His hand rubbed across one of her shoulders. "I told you. I can't resist you." Rafe reached out, grabbed her fiercely, and pulled her into his arms. Then his mouth descended slowly, so slowly that Daphne wanted to cry. He was torturing her now. How quickly things changed. He kissed her, his mouth tangled with hers. Daphne strained on tiptoes to reach him, her arms threaded around his broad, muscled shoulders.

He lifted her then, under her knees, and gently laid her on the bed. She shuddered, the cool air finding all of the sensitive spots on her naked body. She thought she'd be embarrassed with Rafe looking at her so intensely without the benefit of the fuzzy head she'd had last time. She thought she'd be shy. But his blue gaze scanned every bit of her nakedness and all she felt was powerful, more powerful than she'd ever felt in her life. She sensed his leashed desire, knew he was holding himself back. But she didn't want him to. She wanted him to unleash himself completely . . . on her. She shuddered. She would just have to help him lose control.

He stood next to the bed, his eyes still raking over her. He unbuttoned his shirt and pulled it roughly over his head. His breeches and stockings quickly followed and were discarded in the corner. Daphne had a chance to look at him. His body was magnificent, so muscled and strong and perfect. The muscles in his abdomen stood out in sharp relief. A smattering of light hair covered his chest. His shoulders were so squared and strong. She ached to touch them again. He was a dream. A male dream. Her gaze dipped to his member. She'd only seen his but she was certain most such appendages weren't nearly as large as Rafe's. She hadn't had the chance to study it the night the Russians had interrupted them, but now she looked her fill. It was enormous. It jutted proudly from his thighs, strong and thick. She shuddered at the thought of it entering her. She remembered the unholy ache between her thighs the last time they'd been about to make love. She stared at his nakedness in fascination. Cass and Lucy had been kind enough to answer her questions, giving her an idea of what happened between men and women in bed. Of course, reality might be much different than the theories in her head, but all she could think about was how desperately she wanted to find out. *Now.*

"You have a bad bruise," he whispered, tracing the spot on her cheek where Billy had slapped her.

"It doesn't hurt anymore," she promised, turning her cheek away from Rafe's line of vision.

He clenched his jaw so tightly it popped. "I would rip that blighter limb from limb if—"

She pushed up on her knees and touched a finger to his lips. "Shh. It's over. Tonight is about us." She wrapped her arms around his neck and pulled him down on top of her.

He kissed her fiercely and wet warmth pooled between Daphne's thighs. She wanted him so much.

He lifted up on one hand and looked down at her, tracing the edge of her jaw with one finger. "Daphne, I hate to ask this, but I don't want you to have any regrets."

She searched his handsome face. "What is it, Rafe?"

"Nothing happened with that blond at the inn, but I want you to know—"

She wrapped her arms around his neck and pulled him back down to her. "I don't care about the blond. Lucy made me realize that it made no sense that you were coming to look for me if you had a woman in your bed."

"I swear I never saw her before you and I walked in. I think she—"

"I don't care, Rafe. I truly don't. That's in the past."

"But I swear I—"

"Shh. This time we won't be interrupted." She covered his mouth with hers and kissed him again with all the pent-up longing she felt for him.

Rafe groaned against her mouth. "I want you, Daphne."

"I want you, too."

"You're right. No one will interrupt us tonight. There's no need to rush." Rafe moved to his side and Daphne traced her fingertips along his muscled chest. She admired his wide shoulders and narrow hips. She moved her hand along his hip and dipped it behind him to rub along his backside. His eyes widened a little.

"I dreamed about touching you there for an age," she admitted.

Rafe kissed her again. "By all means, touch all you like."

She let her hand move up to his lower back and gasped when she felt the puckered skin. She leaned up and over and looked at the scars crisscrossing his back. Tears filled her eyes. "I'm so sorry, Rafe. I'm sorry they did that to you."

He pulled her hand away and kissed it. "It's nothing, Daphne. Your brother paid a far greater price."

"It's *not* nothing," she insisted, pushing up to her knees. She kissed the tops of his shoulders and ran her mouth down his back. She ran her fingertips along the scars. "You were so brave and strong to withstand this."

Rafe's breath caught in his throat against the lump that had unexpectedly formed there. He'd never felt such emotion from another person before. Never felt such caring. Certainly not when bedding a woman. But this was different. This was Daphne. He turned over, gathered her into his arms, and rolled atop her. His cock was nestled between the heat of her legs but he didn't want to scare her. He stayed there, unmoving, sucking at her bottom lip and nuzzling her neck until he felt the tightness leave her shoulders and the rest of her body.

"I'm shaking," she whispered.

"I am too a little," he said with the hint of a laugh.

She slapped lightly at his shoulder. "You are not."

"Feel this." He took her hand and placed it on his chest over his heart. The pounding there made Daphne's eyes widen.

"I'm excited," she whispered, "and a little frightened."

"Don't be frightened, my love. Don't ever be frightened with me." He slowly moved down to her breast and covered it with his mouth.

Daphne arched her back. "Oh, Rafe, yes."

His other hand came up to play with the nipple of her opposite breast and she arched even more, her back coming off the bed. "I never knew anything could feel this way," she whispered, pushing her fingers through his hair and holding his mouth to her breast.

He tried to move his mouth lower, but Daphne stopped him. "What is it, love?"

"I want to do it this time," she whispered, peeking up at him from beneath her impossibly long lashes.

At first, his brow furrowed, but then his eyes rounded when she began to shimmy down the front of him. "Daphne, how do you—" But his words were completely lost as soon as Daphne's small, pink, torturous mouth closed around his cock.

"Jesus Christ," he whispered fiercely through clenched teeth.

Her mouth moved up, then down, again and again, and Rafe clenched his fists into the bedsheets. He had no idea how or where she'd learned this since they'd last been together but at the moment he sure as hell didn't care.

As if she'd read his mind she momentarily pulled her mouth away from his tender flesh and said, "Lucy allowed me to borrow a pamphlet she'd read called *Secrets of a Wedding Night*. I learned quite a lot."

Rafe groaned. "It sounds like a wonderful pamphlet." He placed his hands under her arms and pulled her sharply up to kiss him. "But I can't take any more of that. Not now."

"Later then?" she asked with an impish smile on her face.

"Much later," he breathed into her fragrant hair.

He kissed down her neck and collarbone to her breasts again and plucked at her nipples with his thumb and forefinger, enjoying the gasp of delight it elicited from her.

She lowered her hand and closed it around him. "Two can play at that game," she said.

"I see," he murmured. "But I meant what I said. I can't take it. Not tonight. Not our first time." He pulled her hand up to his mouth and kissed it. He laid it near her head on the pillow, then he moved his hand back down and stroked between her legs. Daphne parted her thighs and one of his fingers slid deep within her. She moaned.

"Daphne," he whispered in her ear. "I can't wait. I must have you. Now."

"Yes," she breathed.

That was the only word Rafe needed to hear. He rolled over atop the gorgeous woman beneath him and braced his forearms on either side of her head. He kissed the tip of her delectable nose. "It will hurt but only for a moment."

Daphne nodded. She was certain Rafe knew *exactly* what he was doing. Perhaps that was the benefit to loving a rogue. But she couldn't be angry with him. She was so glad it was him. So glad it was him and not Lord Fitzwell or some bore. She nearly cried.

Rafe nudged her knees apart and Daphne held her breath. Rafe's thick hotness pushed at her most intimate space and it felt so good she nearly cried out.

He pushed into her, just a bit, then a bit farther. Her tight passageway expanded for him. "Yes," she breathed again against his neck.

Rafe pulled back once more and then pushed all the

way inside of her. Daphne cried out and clutched at his shoulders. The pain was quickly replaced by the wonderful fullness of him. He rocked against her and Daphne wrapped her arms more tightly around his neck, fiercely kissing his heated shoulder.

Sweat beaded on his forehead and Rafe pressed his mouth to hers, hard. He pulled out and pushed again, again. His groans filled the room. They filled Daphne's heart.

He reached down between the two of them and touched Daphne's most sensitive spot. He circled her there again and again. She became mindless, completely swept away into a sea of pure lust. No longer certain where she began and Rafe ended.

Spasms of pure pleasure overtook her, just before Rafe pumped into her one last time and groaned her name as he found his own release.

Moments later, Rafe rolled over and took her with him in his arms. Daphne wrapped an arm over his chest. She was breathing heavily. "That was . . . the only word that comes to mind is 'indescribable.'"

His shout of laughter cracked off the wooden beams on the ceiling. "Indescribably good, I hope."

"Absolutely," she said, rising up on one elbow to plop a kiss on his forehead. "Definitely indescribably good."

"That's good enough for me."

"I love you, Rafe," she whispered against his shoulder.

"Daphne, I—" He clamped his mouth shut and Daphne's heart tugged. She bit her lip against the sting of tears that touched the backs of her eyes.

"Get some sleep," he murmured into her hair.

CHAPTER FORTY-SIX

Dawn had not yet touched the sky when Daphne rolled over and blinked at her husband. Yes. He was her husband now. Officially. After what they'd done last night, he was most definitely her husband. And what a gorgeous husband he was. She smiled to herself and then hid her smile in the pillow.

She drifted off to sleep last night telling herself that while he might not have been able to tell her he loved her yet, he *had* to feel differently about her now. He just had to. She felt differently about him. Before last night she'd only been a little in love with him, but now, now, she was positively head over heels. That's why she'd told him as much. She stared at his features, softened in sleep. His perfect straight nose, his eyebrows that were a bit darker than his hair, the cleft in his chin. She lifted a finger to trace the outline of his cheekbone. He caught her hand in the air.

"I thought you were asleep," she whispered, laughing. "Your eyes aren't even open."

"I'm a spy," he whispered back. "My eyes are always open."

She snuggled closer to his side and wrapped her arms around him. "Make love to me again, Rafe."

He flipped over and covered her with his tight, muscular body. He kissed her long and deep; Daphne started to get warm and wet in all the right places.

He pulled his mouth away and Daphne knew a moment of regret.

"As much as I want to, my love, I must go see to my mission. We're shoving off at first light. I need to help you get to the rowboat and get back home safely."

Daphne's heart sank. She sat up and pulled the sheet over her breasts. "You . . . you're really leaving?"

He searched her face. "You knew I was leaving. I told you I'm going to France."

Daphne concentrated on breathing. "But that was before . . ."

"Oh, love." He pulled her fingers to his lips and kissed them. "I told you I couldn't make any promises. I meant it."

"I know. But I'd hoped—" She looked away wistfully and traced the outline of the bedspread with her fingertip. "Take me with you, Rafe."

Rafe had rolled over her and stood. He was already busily fastening his breeches. Daphne still couldn't help but admire his gorgeous chest.

Rafe shook his head. His eyes were quickly dimming. He was turning back into the spy with a mission, no longer the loving man she'd been with last night. "I can't," he said. "Your brother won't allow it. I won't allow it. You're not safe with me." He moved back over to where she sat up in the bed and rubbed his hands over her shoulders.

Daphne tried to ignore the little thrill that shot through her belly at his touch.

"Listen to me, Daphne. You're meant to be with a lord, a nobleman, a somebody. We both know that."

Searching his face this time, she desperately fought her tears. "You're a somebody, Rafe. You've always been a somebody to me."

Rafe let go of her, turned, and banged his fist against the wall. "No, Daphne. You're wrong. I'm not somebody. I'm not for you. You said it yourself, I'm not rich. I'm not titled."

She turned away so he couldn't see her dash the tears from her eyes. She bit the inside of her cheek so she wouldn't cry any more. "I never cared about that. I only ever wanted you." She climbed from the bed and began to frantically tug on her discarded clothing. When she finished, she turned back to face him, proud of herself for fighting back the tears that threatened to spill from her eyes and turn her into a complete ninny in his presence. How many times did this man have to reject her before she believed he didn't want her?

"I'm sorry, Daphne," he said softly. "I'll have one of the crew members escort you home and hurry back before we shove off."

"No!" she shouted, refusing to look at him. "I got here by myself. I can make it home alone as well. I'm not a child." She wrenched open the door, but his voice stopped her.

"Daphne." His voice was serious. "If I should die, and you find yourself with child . . ."

She swallowed. A baby? Rafe's baby? No, she wouldn't even allow herself to begin to hope. She held up a hand beside her head to stop him but she didn't turn to look at him. "Don't worry, Rafe. I can take care of myself and a baby should it come to that. Good-bye." She strode out the door and it slammed behind her.

CHAPTER FORTY-SEVEN

They weighed anchor at dawn but the wind was not favorable and their journey to the mouth of the Thames was slower than it should have been. Rafe spent the first half of the day reading his orders time and again. *Capture or kill the men responsible for the death of the Earl of Swifdon, Donald Swift.* He already knew the orders by heart but reading them repeatedly helped to keep his mind off Daphne.

Daphne. Damn it. He stood and paced in front of the writing desk in his cabin. Daphne. He wanted to think it had been a mistake to take her to bed last night, but no matter how hard he tried to tell himself that, he knew it was a lie. She'd come to him, wanted him, and he'd wanted her. They were married. If she were with child, she would be protected by his name. It might not be the best outcome and her reputation might suffer a bit for the lack of a wedding, but Julian would handle it and things would be all right for her. Rafe hoped there was no baby but only for her sake. Daphne was gorgeous, and intelligent, and courageous. Any man would be happy to take her to wife. She'd find her blue blood, one who wouldn't be too concerned about or perhaps even notice her lack of virginity. No. Her one night with him wouldn't ruin her. But it might well have ruined him. He loved her, damn it. He knew he did. He'd wanted to tell her last night when he was deep inside of her. But he couldn't destroy her life. And that's what he'd be doing if he made her hope there could be a future between them. No good would have come of it. It wouldn't have changed anything. He still had to risk his life for this mission and she had to go back to Mayfair and live the life she was born to. His declaration of love would have made her wish for things they couldn't have. It would have made her want to stay with him. Or made him not want to leave. It was better this way, having her hate him. She'd have a reason to find a suitable husband and forget about him.

Rafe rubbed his hand over his eyes. She'd said he was a somebody. *Her* somebody. But all he'd heard were the words from his father's mouth uttered repeatedly during his childhood. They'd echoed in Rafe's head. "You're a nobody. A nothing. You'll never make your fortune in this world." His father might not have been right, but he was close. Rafe wasn't a somebody the likes of which Lady Daphne Swift could stay with. She was naïve. She thought love was enough to make a successful marriage. But she was wrong. They lived in a society where an earl's daughter married to an army captain was something to be mocked, ridiculed. He refused to allow her to stand so much as a moment of censure by the people who made up her world.

He cursed and turned his attention back to his orders.

He must concentrate. He was so close to what he'd wanted for so long.

Two hours later, a knock at the door jolted Rafe from his study of the maps for their route. "Who is it?"

"It's me, Captain." Salty's voice traveled through the wood.

"Come in."

The door opened and Salty strode inside, a forbidding look on his face.

"What is it, Salty? It can't be that bad. We've finally made it to the Channel."

Salty rubbed his jaw. "There's something I need to tell you. And you're not going to like it."

Rafe narrowed his eyes on his crewmate. "I don't like the sound of your tone."

"It's Lady Daphne, er, Grey. He's stowed away."

Daphne knew the moment Rafe had discovered she was on the ship. A loud crack indicated that he'd slammed open his door, and the pounding of his boots on the steps leading up to the deck twisted her stomach into knots. This had seemed like a good idea when she'd been climbing down the ladder to the rowboat before dawn. She'd been sitting in the small boat, about to head back to shore, when pure anger had gripped her. She was tired of being told what to do by men. First her father, then Donald, then Julian, then Lord Fitzwell, and now Rafe. She was through with taking orders from them. And by God, she wasn't about to let the man she loved sail off and get killed by the same bastards who had killed her brother. She was going to help him whether he would admit that he loved her or not. Whether he would admit that he needed her help or not.

And she *could* help him in France. She *knew* it. That stubborn ass knew it, too. If only he'd admit it. He loved her, too. She knew that as well. She'd known it before last night, by his touch, his kisses. If she'd had any doubt, he'd banished it when he made love to her last night.

He'd called it *his* mission, but it was her mission, too. Her brother had been murdered, her true love had been tortured. It was her mission, too, and she would stay by Rafe's side and complete it. That was all there was to it.

She'd maneuvered the rowboat around to the far side of the sloop and climbed up using a bit of rope that Salty had left hanging off. Bless Salty. It was all she needed.

Once she'd made it up to the deck, the space had been thankfully empty. She sneaked past the mast, down to the kitchens, and hid herself in the cupboard. She'd meant to stay there as long as she could. The longer she remained hidden, the better chance she had to keep them from trying to turn around and take her back home, but an unfortunately timed sneeze had given her away and Cook had opened the cupboard and discovered her. At first she'd considered begging him not to tell Rafe, but she quickly discarded that notion. The ship's captain would have to be told about a stowaway. Cook had informed Salty and Salty had marched off to do his duty.

She was sitting in the kitchen with Cook, her belly a roiling mass of nerves, when Rafe came marching in.

"What in the hell are you thinking?" he shouted.

She winced. "Good to see you, too."

A muscle in his jaw ticked. "I'm serious, Daphne. This isn't a joke."

"I don't find it particularly humorous, either," she said.

Cook and Salty exchanged wide-eyed looks and quickly excused themselves.

"Answer me. What were you thinking?" Rafe insisted as soon as the two men had left.

Daphne calmly folded her hands together in front of her and rested them on the wooden table. She'd already decided how she would handle this. She would simply explain her rationale. "I can help you. In France. You need me."

"No. I don't. I need you to be safe. You've put yourself in far more danger than you realize."

Daphne swallowed. She remembered the moment Boris and Billy had come into her cell. The moment she'd been convinced she would be raped and killed. The terror she'd experienced when Billy had ripped open her breeches. The sickening feeling of the knife sinking into his chest and the tangy smell of his blood. The potential for that and worse lay in France. She was frightened, to be sure. But she was also a Swift and Swifts made their courage bigger than their fear. "I want to help you."

"Damn it, Daphne. I can't take you back now. You're risking the entire mission."

Her anger quickly resurfaced. She was capable, blast it. She might be a female but she could help. She stood and plunked both hands on her hips. "You once told me what you thought my problem was," she announced. "You said I was far too judgmental and far too coddled. You said my family softened every blow. Well, you might have been right about that. But who's being judgmental now? Assuming I can't love you because my blood is too blue. You're just as judgmental about my class as I ever was about your drinking. And as for being coddled, I think I've earned my place on this ship, sleeping in that cabin for days on end, pretending to be a member of the crew, interpreting Russian for you, being kidnapped, and knifing a man who attacked me."

Rafe put up a hand to stop her but Daphne wouldn't allow him to. "No, I'm not finished. You told me what my problem was but do you know what *your* problem is? You think you're the only person capable of doing anything. You reluctantly agreed to bring me with you to the ship because you're forced to admit you don't speak Russian. If you thought you could learn it in the span of a fortnight, I've no doubt you never would have arrived at my engagement party. But I'm not stupid. I know I'm not the only person in London who speaks Russian. You could have picked someone else. You wanted me!"

He tried to stop her again but she wouldn't have it. "You're far too used to relying only upon yourself and you refuse to admit that perhaps, just perhaps, from time to time, upon occasion, you may actually require a bit of help from another person!" Her chest heaved and her eyes flashed. She lifted her chin. "I am trained, Rafe. By the best. *You* trained me. I'm not putting the mission in danger and I'm not putting you in danger. I may be putting myself in danger, but that's a risk I'm willing to take. You needn't worry about me. I told you. I can handle myself. And I intend to."

Rafe paced away from her and scrubbed his hands through his hair. He turned his head to the side and shook it. She recognized the fear there. Fear for her safety. His voice was solemn. "I cannot keep you safe."

"You don't have to."

CHAPTER FORTY-EIGHT

They docked at Calais later that night after the wind picked up. They were pretending to be tradespeople who were merely in port to sell their goods. Rafe had spent the remainder of the journey poring through the letters in the bundle they had retrieved from Anton and Viktor. The men he wanted were in a small town just south of Calais. It was perhaps half a day's journey. Rafe would travel quickly with only Salty and Grim.

Rafe stood in the captain's cabin and tossed a few things in one small bag to take with him on the journey. A bit of food, some other provisions, one of the letters, two pistols and two knives. One of the knives was the one Daphne had used to kill that vermin near the docks. Rafe's throat tightened at the memory of Daphne fighting that giant. She'd kept her wits about her. She'd managed to stick him before he'd tackled her. She'd faced a man at least three times her size with determination and courage. Daphne was right. She could take care of herself. And she'd been magnificent telling him so.

Rafe had retrieved the knife from the man's body and brought it back to the ship. He hefted it into his hand and slid it into the pack. Then he surveyed the rest of its contents. They must travel light and be able to hide at a moment's notice.

"I'm coming with you."

Rafe turned his head. He had barely heard the door open and Daphne enter the cabin. She stood near the desk with her hands crossed over her middle.

"No. You're not," he answered simply, hefting the bag over his shoulder.

Daphne's feet were braced apart and she had a determined look in her eye. "Don't make me sneak behind and follow you, Rafe."

He swiveled around to face her and stared her down. "Don't make me tie you to the mast, Daphne."

She plunked her hands on her hips. "You should know by now that I'll do exactly as I please."

He tugged at the strap to the pack. "Why are you hellbent to get into danger? I cannot protect you. I already told you."

"And I already told you that I don't need your protection." Daphne's voice rose. "I've had to watch my two older brothers fight for their country while I've been forced to stay home and wring my hands and worry. I'm tired of wringing my hands. Donald taught me Russian for a reason. He thought it would be useful someday. And it has been. I'm going with you to avenge my brother's death and you're going to have to kill me to stop me."

Rafe clenched his jaw. He glanced toward the wall. "Damn it, Daphne."

"You're not going to kill me, are you?" She tapped her booted foot along the wooden planks.

He blew out a breath. "Of course I'm not going to kill you."

She inclined her head. "Then I'm coming with you."

They set out the next morning. Rafe had secured three mounts and was able to secure a fourth for Daphne's use. They intended to find the Frenchmen's camp, surround it, observe it, and then move in for the arrest. There were four of them or at least there had been. If Rafe, Salty, and Grim took them by surprise with pistols, they should be able to overcome and arrest all four.

The sun was beginning to set by the time their small group arrived at the little town north of Amiens. The journey had been uneventful and silent. Their orders were to arrest the Frenchmen but the villains might not agree to be taken alive. Rafe wished for the hundredth time that Daphne was safely back on the ship.

They halted about a half mile outside of the town, got off the horses, and took a drink from their canteens. Rafe shared his water with Daphne while images of their night together flew through his mind. He shook them away. There could be no distractions during this arrest. He must concentrate.

After they'd refreshed themselves, they remounted. "Their camp is on the outskirts of town on the east," Rafe said. "We'll find a place in the forest to stay until nightfall."

Another twenty minutes' journey found them deep in the forest on the eastern part of the town. Rafe chose a spot where they made their own camp.

Salty and Daphne tied three of the horses to nearby trees while Grim started a fire.

Rafe remained mounted. "I'm going out to their cabin to see what I can learn."

Grim and Salty nodded.

"Be careful," Daphne whispered.

Rafe nodded, too. He tossed his pack on the ground near the fire and left without a sound.

Daphne spent the next hour pacing around the campsite worrying about Rafe. He was alone out there with at least four men nearby who wanted him dead.

"Come sit," Salty finally said to her. "You'll exhaust yourself if you keep pacing."

Daphne made her way over to the campfire and took a seat on a pile of pine needles next to Salty and Grim. Both men remained quiet with determined looks on their faces. Daphne tried to mimic their determination. It would be ever so helpful to replace the fear and uncertainty that gnawed at her belly with steely resolve. And courage. Because ever since she'd delivered her I-can-do-this speech to Rafe, she'd been overcome with fear. Was this how brave men felt? It had to be. They had to have indecision and doubt and do what had to be done regardless. She'd resolved to see this through and she would. No matter how much she believed she might retch.

Grim had assumed Cook's duties. He hovered over the fire cooking a rabbit he'd shot with a bow and arrow earlier. Daphne clutched Rafe's canteen. The water was warm and tasted tinny, but she was grateful for it. No dainty cups of tea in situations like this. Grim handed her a bit of meat.

"Thank you," Daphne said, taking the food from him. She hadn't realized how starved she'd been until they'd stopped. None of them had eaten since gulping down some hard biscuits this morning. Taking a bit of the greasy meat, she scooted over and pressed her back against a nearby tree. She looked at the man who had transformed into Rafe's trusted second mate. Even though they were alone, she kept her voice low as Rafe had taught her to. "I suppose you're not to be Grim much longer after this mission is complete."

Grim rubbed the back of his neck. He, too, kept his voice low. "I'll still be Grim. It's what they call me. But I'll go back to being a general."

Daphne's eyes nearly bulged from her skull. She choked on the second bit of rabbit she'd put into her mouth. "You're a general?"

Grim laughed and tipped his hat. "General Mark Grimaldi, at your service."

Daphne turned to Salty. "Salty, don't tell me. You're an admiral."

Salty glanced over his shoulder and grinned. "No. Not quite. But I am a lieutenant. Lieutenant Richard Hartwell, at your service."

Grim handed Daphne more meat and she also ate it with her fingers. No extravagant place settings in the forest. "I thought you were going to say your last name had the word 'salt' in it."

"No, I just liked the name," Salty tossed over his shoulder.

Daphne watched the two men. "You're both dear to Captain Cavendish. I know he relies on you."

"And we on him," Salty replied.

Daphne glanced down at her lap. "I want you to know I will not be a burden here. I intend to help, not hurt."

Grim smiled at her. "If I didn't think that, my lady, I wouldn't have allowed you to come. Sometimes Cavendish needs more help than he'll admit."

Daphne returned his smile and spent the next few moments wondering if General Grimaldi had heard her speech earlier.

"And I've seen you throw a knife," Salty said with a laugh.

Rafe stepped through the nearby bushes just then. Daphne nearly gasped. She hadn't heard a sound. In fact, today she'd seen him as the cunning spy he was. The man had eyes like a hawk and reflexes like a cat. Had he heard what Grim had said? If so, he didn't give any indication. Did he think she would help him? No. Even after her convincing little speech, Rafe was certain she would be more trouble than help. She just wished she could convey to him that this is what she had to do.

Rafe took the canteen that Daphne silently offered him and sat on the far side of the fire. "According to the correspondence, the camp is a half mile in that direction." He pointed east.

"Did you find it?" Salty asked.

"I did," Rafe replied.

Both of the other men's faces relaxed a bit.

Daphne's gaze snapped to Rafe's face. "And are they there? The men we're looking for?"

Rafe took a swig of water. He nodded. "They're there. I saw them. All four of them. I could never forget their faces."

He had a haunted look in his eyes. It couldn't have been easy for him to have to confront the men who had tortured him.

Daphne blew out a deep breath. "Do you think they've been alerted to our arrival? They wouldn't have heard from Anton and Viktor since they were arrested."

Rafe rubbed a hand across his forehead. "That's not unusual for them. Their correspondence was no more than monthly and it's been less than a fortnight. But to be doubly sure, we asked Jane Upton to forge a letter to them indicating that they had found me and were bringing me back in one week's time."

Daphne's eyes rounded but she nodded. That was the letter Cass had mentioned. The clever Jane had spent months studying handwriting and knew how to disguise her own to look like someone else's.

"Besides," Rafe continued. "Our surveillance indicated that there were only the five others working together in London. Two are dead and Anton, Viktor, and the other are in gaol. There was no one else to alert them."

"Agreed," said Salty, more serious than Daphne had ever seen him. "They won't know we're here. We found Anton and Viktor's last letter before they were able to post it. They indicated they had everything under control. Mrs. Upton used that and added to it."

"The letters weren't in Russian, were they?" Daphne asked.

"No, surprisingly they were all written in French. But their contents were innocuous. To someone who didn't know what they were about, there would be nothing illicit to read if the letters were found."

Continuing to ignore her inner lady, Daphne finished her rabbit and wiped her hands on her breeches. "They won't have seen the smoke from our fire?"

"Perhaps," Grim said, handing a chunk of rabbit to Rafe, who took it eagerly. "But these woods are no strangers to travelers. It shouldn't be suspicious to them."

Daphne stood and dusted off her thighs. "Very well. What's the plan?"

Using his free hand, Rafe grabbed a stick and drew a

circle in the dirt near the fire. Daphne moved near him to watch. "They're in a cabin, here." He pointed to a smaller circle he made near the center of the larger one. "From what I could tell, there are only the four of them."

He drew a line on the far side of the smaller circle. "There is a tree line here. Daphne, this is where you'll stay." He glanced at the sky. "The sun has set. We'll go as soon as we finish eating."

"I want to go to the cabin with you," Daphne said. "If they say something in Russian, I can help."

"No. You'll be of more help to us outside. If the three of us are hurt or captured, we'll need you to ride like the devil's after you back to the ship and bring help."

Daphne knew Rafe had no intention of being captured. He was likely using the story as an excuse to keep her out of harm's way. But she supposed someone might need to stay back in case there was trouble. She would do her duty.

"Here." He handed her a pistol. "If anyone other than one of us comes near you, shoot them."

CHAPTER FORTY-NINE

Rafe led the way through the thick forest. Daphne was directly behind him, then Salty, then Grim. Rafe pushed branches out of the way and kicked at fallen tree limbs. They all remained silent, using hand signals and nods to communicate. The going was slow as Rafe breathed in the scent of the pine trees and summer flowers. God willing, Daphne would be safe if she remained at the edge of the forest once they arrived. He didn't have time to keep an eye on her and arrest these men. He needed to concentrate on the task at hand and worrying about her would keep him from it. He could only pray that she'd listen to him for once. Damn stubborn woman.

The walk wasn't long. They'd left their horses tied back at the campsite. It would make their group more nimble and much less conspicuous. As they trudged through the forest, Rafe's head turned at any little sound, any twig snap, any birdcall. He was on edge, because of the mission and more so because of Daphne's presence.

The smoke coming from the clearing stopped them. Rafe led them all to the edge of the tree line where they crouched down to watch the small house that sat nestled in the clearing.

"Between Calais and Paris," he said. "The perfect spot for traitors and thieves."

He crouched low and watched through the window. A fire inside the cabin illuminated the interior. One of the men stood in front of the window holding a mug and laughing. The Frenchmen appeared to be in the middle of a meal.

The laughing man turned and Rafe saw his face. He swallowed, hard.

Gabriel, they had called him. Rafe would never forget that name, or that face. It was the countenance of a man who had beaten and tortured him for months. The past came rushing toward him, kaleidoscoping time and making his vision tunnel.

Groans of pain rang in his ears. They were Donald's, not his own. Donald Swift. The man had given his life. He'd been honorable till the end. He hadn't given up a single secret. So they killed him. Then they focused their torture on Rafe. They knew he was the spy, the one who had the most information. They'd said Donald was nothing more than a useless aristocrat.

Rafe swallowed. Donald had been more than that. Much more. He was a brother, a son, and a friend. He had more nobility for what he'd endured than any title would ever be able to bestow.

Rafe narrowed his eyes on Gabriel through the window. These were the men who had stolen months of his life and killed the earl.

He was going to destroy them.

"On my count," Rafe whispered, without removing his gaze from the house.

Salty and Grim nodded.

"Daphne," Rafe warned in a voice that was low but commanding. "I needn't remind you how important it is to follow orders during a mission. Stay here."

"I will, Captain," Daphne promised. At least she wasn't going to argue with him at a time like this. Thank God.

"Three, two . . . one." The three men all moved but remained crouched as they emerged from the bushes. They each took a different position. Rafe went straight for the front door of the cabin. Salty went to the left and Grim to the right.

Daphne watched from the tree line lying belly-first on the ground with her heart lodged in her throat. Her jaw was clamped so tight it ached. Soon the men were only shadows in the darkness. She would stay where Rafe asked her. If something went terribly wrong inside, she might be of more use out here. But only moments had gone by before she severely regretted her decision. It was much worse watching and waiting and not knowing what was happening.

Time seemed to not only slow but to stop entirely. Her knees ached and so did her chest from unconsciously holding her breath. The chirping of the bugs in the brush nearby and the sound of a few birds overhead, coupled with the thud of her own swallows, were the only noises. The cabin was a dark smudge in the distance and her three friends had long ago blurred into the large shadow.

Daphne mentally counted to one hundred.

She did it again, closing her eyes and praying for their safe return.

Moments later, shots rang out and Daphne's heart

plummeted into her boots. She bit the back of her shaking hand, then leaned up on her elbows frantically searching the darkness. Smoke began to billow from the back of the cabin and flames were soon shooting out, too. The house was on fire and all she could see were shadows fleeing the burning building. But which were Rafe and his team and which were the spies? Had Rafe been shot? Was he dead? Wounded? Did he need her?

A group of men headed straight for her position. It had to be Rafe's team. How else would they know where she was? But until she knew for certain, she remained silent on her belly in the pine needles to remain out of sight.

"Did you hit him?" came a voice that was decidedly *not* one of Rafe's men.

It took her a moment to realize the voice was speaking in Russian but with a French accent. Odd but they must have been speaking in that language in case Rafe and the others could hear. They knew the Englishmen would speak fluent French.

"I'm not sure. I think so," came another voice. "I'm sure I hit one of them."

"Damn English. We should have killed that bastard when we had the chance," came a third voice.

They had all spoken in Russian. Daphne searched the darkness behind them. She didn't see any more shadows. Were Rafe and his men dying in the fire? She had to go search, to look for them. Help. But if she moved now, the Frenchmen would surely see her.

She glanced at the pistol that lay in the grass not an inch in front of her face. Blast. She couldn't shoot them. She was an awful shot, not to mention she only had one bullet. She shifted her leg and the knife moved against her ankle.

She allowed a smile to spread across her face. She'd taken a knife from the ship and placed it in her boot, but when she'd looked through Rafe's bag while he'd been out scouting, she'd replaced it with the one she preferred. The one she'd killed Billy with. She had a lot of experience with that knife. And she was glad for it now.

She clenched her fist, steeling her resolve. By God, one of these men had killed her brother and might have killed Rafe. She might be outnumbered. They might have pistols, too, but with the knife she could take at least one of them with her. She reached down into her boot and slowly drew the knife.

With the handle clutched in her shaky, clammy palm, she waited until the men had entered the tree line. She made out their shadows against the trees. One of them had a torch that must have been lit by a stick of wood in the cabin fire. There were four of them. Two on one side of her, two on the other. She said another brief prayer. It had been pure luck that they hadn't stepped on her.

As quietly as she could, she turned and watched as they began their retreat into the forest. She moved up and crouched on her knees. She must act quickly. The torch-bearer was the best target because she could see him most clearly. She waited for him to line up with a tree, to mark how quickly he was moving. Her breathing was rapid, shallow.

"For Donald," she whispered just before she expertly flipped her knife through the air.

The sound of the knife colliding with flesh was a dull thump and the man doubled over with a scream. He fell to the ground in a heap and the other three men came rushing back to lean over him.

"Are you all right, Michel?" someone asked in Russian.

Michel's voice was taut with pain. "I've been hit. They must be near. Run!"

"I wouldn't do that if I were you." Daphne barely recognized her own voice. She'd spoken in English and lowered her voice to sound like Grey again. She stood and made her way over the pine needles and fallen leaves toward the three men. The only pistol she had was trained on them, her hand shaking so badly she was thankful for the darkness.

The three men froze. They slowly turned to face her. The torch had fallen to the forest floor and caught a bit of brush on fire. The fire spread slowly but it was enough to illuminate the men's actions. She had the benefit of the cover of night, however, since she remained in the shadows in front of them. But how long would it be before they realized she was just one person? They most likely still had pistols, too.

"Put up your hands," she demanded in English.

"Oo ez et?" the ringleader asked in English. He squinted into the darkness.

"Hands up, first," she replied in as gruff a voice as she could muster.

All three of them complied and Daphne nearly sighed with relief.

She stepped forward a bit more but ensured that she remained hidden in shadows. The ringleader squinted at her still.

A whizzing noise sounded above her head as something flew over it. Daphne's eyes rounded. Her heartbeat shook in her chest. One of them had just thrown a knife at her. Its blade wiggled in the tree not three inches above her head. Her breathing sped.

"What are you doing?" one of the men asked, in Russian, speaking to whoever had thrown the knife.

"Apparently, he's short," another answered back in the same language. "That was our only knife."

Daphne closed her eyes and internally breathed a sigh of relief. That knife had come entirely too close.

"How many of you are there?" the ringleader asked, in French this time.

"Four," she answered with as much confidence as she could muster. "And we have pistols."

"I don't believe you," came his reply.

She moved forward far enough to allow the pistol to enter the ring of firelight so that they could see it. She prayed they would believe that the others were just in the shadows.

"He's lying," one of them said in French.

"I'm not lying," she answered back in the same language. "And I'm a crack shot."

"He is lying," one of them repeated, this time in Russian.

"I may be lying," Daphne answered in Russian, raising her chin, "but which one of you wants to take that chance?"

CHAPTER FIFTY

An owl hooted in the velvety black night sky. The stars were out but the little light they provided barely filtered through the dense foliage of the forest. The scent of evergreen and leaves lingered in Daphne's nose. She could barely hear over the sound of her own heartbeat. It throbbed in her ears, momentarily blocking out all other noise.

And then she heard them. Heavy footsteps thundering through the underbrush behind her. Thank heavens. She nearly sagged with relief. The sound surely heralded the return of her friends.

But how many and who?

What if only one of them had lived? What if Rafe was dead? What if the Frenchmen decided to call her bluff and run? Her breathing was fast and shallow. Her arm ached but she kept the heavy pistol trained on her enemies.

"Grey?" Rafe's voice rang out.

She nearly sobbed with relief. Rafe was alive.

"I'm here," she called.

Rafe's footsteps changed direction and he came running. By the time he arrived she realized Grim and Salty were both with him. *Thank heavens.*

"Are you hurt?" she called.

"Salty's been shot but he's all right."

Daphne took a deep breath. Her prayers had been answered. Thank God they were all alive. "I have something to show you."

The footsteps halted as all three of her friends ran into the clearing. Their faces were black with soot. They stopped short when they saw Daphne and the Frenchmen. The Frenchmen stood by the small fire, their hands in the air. Salty and Grim immediately pointed their own pistols at them.

Daphne could see Rafe's smile flash in the moonlight. "You caught them. All of them. You did it, Grey."

"Yes," she said with her own smile, tossing her head. "I did."

Rafe leveled his pistol on the men. His nostrils flared and his eyes took on a hard, icy sheen. "By order of the King of England, you are all under arrest for the Earl of Swifdon's murder."

CHAPTER FIFTY-ONE

Salty and Grim assumed the task of escorting the prisoners back to the ship. They would take the Frenchmen, three of the horses, and march all night. Daphne insisted on seeing to Salty's wound before they left. Fortunately, it wasn't deep. She'd already wetted their handkerchiefs so that all three of the men could wipe the soot from their faces.

While Rafe and Grim tied the prisoners' hands behind their backs, presumably in such a manner that they couldn't escape, Daphne commandeered the brandy that Grim had stashed in a canteen. She went over to where Salty sat under a tree and splashed the alcohol over Salty's wound.

Salty winced. "A damn shame, wasting brandy like that."

"I need to make certain it's clean," she answered, covering it gently with her handkerchief.

She patted his other shoulder. "When we get back to England, we'll have a doctor look at it but I expect it will be right as rain."

"Thank you, Lady Daphne," Salty replied quietly. "For everything."

After their two friends marched off with the horses and prisoners in tow, Rafe turned to Daphne. "We're going to the inn."

"What inn?"

Rafe helped Daphne mount the remaining horse. "The one in town."

"I didn't know there was one in town."

He swung up behind her and Daphne felt his hard, warm chest behind her back. She couldn't help her shudder.

"There is." Rafe maneuvered the horse to the left and they took off at a gallop. The rest of the journey was made in silence while Daphne desperately tried to guess at Rafe's mood. He'd seemed pleased by her capturing the Frenchmen but was he angry now, tired, merely glad it was over?

Within half an hour, they arrived at a little lopsided, whitewashed inn that stood in the center of the small town. It had two ruddy windows that revealed a large fireplace and several laughing patrons.

Rafe dismounted and reached up and put his hands around Daphne's waist. Again, she tried to ignore how good it felt.

"We'll sleep here tonight," he said. "And meet Salty and Grim back at the ship tomorrow."

"I don't need to stay at an inn. I can march, too. I'm quite capable—"

"I know what you're capable of," he interrupted. "Do you begrudge me a wedding night with my wife?"

Daphne couldn't help her smile that went ear to ear. She clamped shut her mouth and happily trotted beside him into the inn, where Rafe requested one room from the innkeeper. A thrill shot through her.

She smiled up at him almost shyly. "One room?"

"We're married, Daphne. It's official now."

She squeezed his hand and enjoyed the butterflies that flitted through her middle. "I know."

They ate dinner in the inn's main room but the meal was a blur to Daphne. All she could think about was what was going to happen after the meal. If Rafe wanted a wedding night, and admitted they were officially married, it meant that he loved her. It had to. Didn't it?

When he finished eating, Rafe tossed his napkin to the tabletop, then he stood next to her and offered his arm. Daphne took it with a small smile and allowed her *husband* to escort her upstairs to *their* room.

The door to their room shut behind them and Rafe locked it. He tossed his pack onto a nearby chair, then he stepped forward and nearly collapsed on the bed. "I can't believe it's over. I can't believe we finally got them." He sat up and let his head drop into his hands.

Daphne pulled off her cap and tossed it next to the pack. She scrubbed her hands through her hair. She quietly made her way over to sit on the bed next to him and placed a hand on his back. "It must have been difficult for you to see them again. To relive it."

Rafe blew out a breath. "I didn't have much time to relive it. I was thinking about Donald. What he went through. I . . ."

Daphne nodded. She motioned to a table where the innkeeper had already placed a bottle of wine. "Would you like a drink?"

Rafe turned to her, his eyes round. He took her hands. "I don't need a drink. All I need is you." He slid off the bed and knelt on the floor. He turned to face her and pulled her hands to his lips and kissed them. "My father used to tell me that I was good for nothing. That I'd never amount to anything."

Daphne vehemently shook her head. "No. Rafe."

"I've spent my entire life trying to prove myself, be good enough, stand on my own, never ask for help," Rafe continued. "It's not until I met you that I realized that's not always the best choice. You made me see that." He squeezed her hands. "Daphne, I can never make up for the loss of your brother but I want to spend the rest of my life trying. Nothing about our courtship or our marriage has been customary. I never formally asked you to marry me. I want to fix that now." He moved up to one knee. "I'm not a nobleman, and I'm not rich, but I love you with every bit of myself. You were right about me. I needed you today. And I'll need you tomorrow and the day after that and the day after that. I need you every day of my life because I can't live without you. Will you marry me, Lady Daphne Swift? Again?"

Tears stinging the backs of her eyes, Daphne fell to her knees next to him, rose up, and wrapped her arms around his neck. "Of course I'll marry you again, Captain Rafferty Cavendish. Of course I will."

He stood and picked her up and twirled her round and round. Then he kissed her deeply. "Will you come to bed with me?"

She glanced at the bed next to his leg. "We're nearly there."

He looked almost boyish, vulnerable, and Daphne loved him for it. "You know what I mean."

She smiled at him. "I don't even have to strip this time to convince you?"

"Not a chance."

"And you no longer think of me as a *sister*?" she taunted.

He shook his head. "Oh, love. I *never* thought of you as a sister. I only told you that because I decided it was better for my career and my longevity than having your brothers beat me to a pulp. There wouldn't have been enough left of me for the French if Donald had found out that I'd defied him."

Her mouth fell open. "You *never* thought of me as a sister? But you wouldn't even kiss me and you let me think—"

Rafe stopped her words by pulling her into his arms and kissing her again. "Seeing you in those breeches every day has been unholy torture."

A catlike grin curled across her lips. She wrinkled her nose slyly. "It was?"

He blinked at her from beneath his dark lashes. "Trust me. Unholy. Torture."

She pulled at her dusty cravat. "Want to see me undress again?"

He arched a brow. "By all means, but first, I've ordered a bath."

As if on cue, a knock sounded at the door. Rafe made his way over and opened it. Two servants marched in bearing a clawfoot tub. Soon after, bucket after bucket of hot water arrived, carried by serving maids. The maids glanced between Daphne and Rafe and gave Daphne tentative smiles. Daphne grinned back at them without shame.

After all of the servants left, the steaming bath remained in the center of the room. Rafe nodded toward Daphne. "You first," he insisted with a wicked grin. "Besides, after I get in, the water is sure to turn black. I have soot in places I don't even want to contemplate."

The servants had left a stick of soap and some linens

on a stool next to the tub. Daphne hadn't taken a proper bath in days. She was only too eager to slide into the steamy water. She ripped off her shirt and shimmied out of her breeches while Rafe groaned. Her boots and stockings were already long gone. She'd removed them while the servants were setting up the bath.

Completely nude and enjoying the way her husband's eyes devoured her by candlelight, she slipped into the hot water with a long sigh.

Rafe sat on the bed and watched her. "You're gorgeous, Mrs. Cavendish."

She somehow managed to put her hair into a bun atop her head, a few tendrils falling down around her shoulders. She turned her head and gave her husband a wide smile. "I like the sound of that: *Mrs. Cavendish.*"

Rafe put his hands to his cravat and began untying it. "Yes, well, you may be a widow, sooner than later, if Julian isn't in an understanding mood when we return."

"He will be," she said with a nod, pulling the soap from the stool and lathering her arms and neck.

"How can you be so sure?" Rafe's cravat came off in a quick tug and he unbuttoned his shirt. Daphne unabashedly watched him undress as she continued to lather herself, moving to her knees and legs.

"I'll just tell him it's what I want." She blushed beautifully. "Er, I mean, I'll explain to him that we're already married and we're grown adults, and . . . well, Julian is reasonable."

Rafe shook his head. "I can only hope he'll be reasonable about this."

She quirked a finger at him. "Come and help me with my bath, husband."

"With pleasure." Rafe stood and made his way over to sit on the stool next to her. He picked up the linens and laid them over his knee.

Daphne eyed his muscular chest and shoulders. She'd never get tired of looking at him. He gently took the soap from her hand and dipped it into the water next to her hip. "This is quite a sight," he murmured, staring down into the water.

"What is?" Daphne glanced down at herself to see her nipples barely skimming the water's surface. "Oh."

"The perfection of your body," he replied, not taking his gaze from her.

Daphne blushed. She sat forward while Rafe rubbed the soap between his hands and lathered her shoulders. Then she leaned back against the tub and closed her eyes as he turned his attention to her front. She moaned when he brushed against her nipples.

"I owe you an apology," he said softly.

She blinked one eye open. "An apology? You?"

"Yes, me. I told you that you wouldn't be of help if you came with us. You saved the mission."

Daphne closed her eye again and settled back against the tub. "Salty says sometimes you need people more than you admit."

"Salty's right," Rafe admitted.

He soaped her belly while Daphne clenched her muscles there and shamelessly wished his hand would dip lower.

"I need you," he whispered, leaning down and kissing her mouth gently.

"I need you, too."

Rafe dropped the soap in the water and stood. He unbuttoned the fall of his breeches and shucked off both boots and stockings. He leaned down to kiss Daphne again.

"You're magnificent," she said, wrapping her arms around his neck and pulling him into the water atop her.

Despite the small space, Rafe spent the next half hour both soaping and kissing his wife while she did the same to him. By the time the water began to cool, they were both entirely clean but Rafe had a raging cockstand.

He pulled Daphne from the tub and dried her hair and body with the linens. She did the same for him. When she reached his erection, she stopped. "Well, I—" Her blush was beautiful against her soft, creamy skin.

He traced her cheek with his thumb. "Come to bed with me. I need you. Now."

"Yes," she breathed.

He scooped her into his arms, carried her over to the bed, and laid her gently on top of the coverlet and then came down atop her and covered her with his nakedness. He kissed her deeply. Daphne's hands tangled in his hair and she arched against him. He smelled so good, like soap and male desire.

He grinned at her. "I want to kiss you everywhere."

"Please do." She giggled.

Rafe kissed her forehead, her cheek, her ear. Then he nuzzled at her neck. Daphne shuddered when he sucked at her collarbone. "You are gorgeous," he whispered in her ear. "Beyond perfect."

"No, you are gorgeous," she replied, tilting back her head to give him greater access to her throat.

His tongue traced down between her breasts and then he moved lower, catching a nipple between his teeth and tugging. Daphne's hands tangled in his hair. "Rafe," she breathed.

He nibbled at her, nipped her, bit her. She squirmed beneath him, wanting his hand between her legs. His mouth moved to her other breast and teased that nipple, too. Daphne arched her back.

She pushed her hands over his broad shoulders, reveling in their warmth and strength. Then she wrapped her hands through his hair and pulled his head up to hers. His mouth met hers in a fierce kiss. She moaned deep in her throat. His mouth moved to her chin, her neck again.

His hand found her breast. He teased her nipple between his thumb and forefinger. She arched her back again and moaned. "Oh, Rafe."

Then his hand moved lower and Daphne ceased to think. He found her core and he slid one hot finger inside of her. She nearly came off the bed. He drew his finger out and quickly found the little nub of pleasure between her legs. He circled the spot again and again. Daphne's head shifted fitfully from side to side. That amazing feeling built inside of her. The same one he'd made her feel on the ship the first time they'd made love. Intense, maddening, unique, new. And it was all because of Rafe's finger. It owned her. She clutched her arms around his neck.

"Let go, Daphne. Let go," he whispered in her ear. "I will catch you."

Daphne was mindless. Her hips moved of their own accord in time with the rhythm of Rafe's finger, and when her world exploded, she clung to his shoulders and whimpered.

Moments later, after the zings of pleasure had ceased rippling through her body, Daphne rolled over and pushed Rafe down to the mattress.

He eyed her warily. "What are you doing?"

"Something I meant to finish last time." She shimmied down his body, her mouth heading for his cock.

"No, Daphne, I—"

She smiled against his taut abdomen. "There's no use arguing with me. You know how stubborn I am."

Rafe considered it for a moment. The lady had a point. The moment her sweet lips touched him, he knew he had already lost the argument. "You feel so good," he whispered, his hands tangling in her lush hair.

She bent and allowed her lips to cover him entirely, then pulled herself back up and did it again and again. Rafe was mindless in seconds.

"It's too good. I—" He tried to pull her up by the shoulders but Daphne slid out of his reach, her mouth still on him.

"Please," he groaned.

She pulled her lips off him for a moment but squeezed him and Rafe groaned again. "Let me do this, Rafe. I want to see what happens if I don't stop."

Her lips were on him again, driving him mad, his hips moved against her mouth, matching her rhythm, his hand guiding the back of her head. *Sweet holy God.* His wife was a temptress.

She sucked him hard and Rafe growled. "Daphne, have a care, love. You're my wife. I can't spill my seed in your mouth."

He was still in her mouth when she grinned up at him. The only word he could use to describe her grin was devilish. She pulled her mouth away momentarily. "Why not? I told you. I like adventure."

Without pausing to argue with him more, Daphne took his cock in her mouth again. She sucked with perfect pressure and Rafe's eyes rolled back in his head. "God, Daphne, I—" She grabbed his balls and pressed the base of them in a spot that made his hips arch off the mattress. He was panting. "Jesus, Daphne, if you don't stop,

I'm going to—" She sucked him then, her mouth moving back and forth, and Rafe had no time to pull her away. Breathless and mindless, he released his seed deep into his wife's throat.

He looked up at her with eyes hazy with love, and lust, and surprise. She swallowed and wiped her hand against the back of her mouth and gave him a victorious grin.

Rafe struggled to catch his breath. He let his head drop back against the pillows. "I nev . . . I never felt anything li—like that before."

She lowered herself down to curl against him. "I find that difficult to believe."

"I'm entirely serious. What the hell was in the pamphlet you read?"

Daphne leaned against his chest and giggled. "It's a secret."

She traced her fingers along his chest, down his abdomen and lower. His erection was back. It had only been mere moments since his orgasm but Rafe was already hard for her again. He pulled her hand around him. "That was . . . amazing, but I want to make love to you, Daphne. Make you my wife."

She smiled against his shoulder. "You already have."

He kissed her hair. "This time I need to tell you how much I love you while I'm deep inside of you."

A thrill shot through Daphne's body. Rafe's hands found her breasts again and within just a few moments she was mindless with wanting him all over again. He knew just where to touch, what to suck, where to press. He had such power over her body—she closed her eyes—and it was delightful.

Rafe pushed her onto her back and rolled atop her. She welcomed his wonderful heavy weight. He pulled her hands up above her head and pinned them there. "Let me make you feel good again."

"Yes," she breathed.

Rafe kissed her lips, her neck, her collarbone. He skimmed his teeth along the plump edge of her breast and nipped at her nipples. She arched her back, the spot between her legs wet and wanting. His hair-roughened thigh nudged between her legs and pushed her knees apart. She welcomed it. He slid inside her with one sure, hot thrust. She gasped against his mouth.

Then her husband began to move. He slid in and out, his thrusts matching the beats of her heart. "I love you," he breathed, sweat beading on his brow. "I love you." Each thrust was another promise, another declaration. With her hands still pinned helplessly above her head, he moved his hips and his shaft pressed against a tender spot inside her that made Daphne cry out. Amazingly, she slid into another release, pressing her wrists against his hands and calling his name.

Rafe pumped into her one last deep time. He released her wrists and she wrapped her arms fiercely around his neck. "I love you, Daphne," he breathed, and she knew a moment of profound contentment holding her husband in her arms.

It was several minutes before Daphne floated back to reality from the haze in which the only thing that existed was her husband's body and the way he made her feel. Rafe was still hovering over her, pushing the tendrils of hair from her face and kissing her mouth in that sensuous way of his.

"Tell me something," she said.

"Anything, my love."

"Why did you pick Thomas Grey as my name?"

"So I could call you Grey, of course."

She blinked. "But why?"

"Because of your pretty eyes."

Daphne couldn't help her smile. "Is that so? I never suspected a thing."

"Of course you didn't." He kissed her forehead.

He moved to the side, taking her with him, and Daphne traced a finger along his muscular chest. "But it's not as if I'm perfect. It's as you said. I've always had my family fix everything for me. That won't happen again. From now on I intend to handle everything myself. Starting with telling Julian that we're married and we intend to remain that way. I can handle things myself."

Rafe rested his chin on the top of her head. "You proved that you can handle things yourself when you were abducted, when you stowed away on the boat, when you stood up to me and my stubborn refusal to see that I needed you, and finally when you held those men at gunpoint. Well done, Grey." He kissed the top of her head.

Daphne tipped her head back and smiled up at him. "I told them I'm a crack shot."

Rafe snorted. "I'm glad they didn't ask you to prove it."

"So am I. I'd already thrown the only knife I had. I'm glad you and Salty and Grim came soon after. I needed you, too."

He pressed a kiss to her temple. "We need each other, love. You've always been there for me when I've needed you. I learned that today."

"And that you cannot live the rest of your life with the guilt about Donald," Daphne added.

"That, too." He hugged her close. "I'm certain Upton will be pleased to hear that he was correct."

Daphne wrapped an arm around Rafe's shoulder. "I learned something today as well."

"What's that?"

"That being the opposite of tall isn't such a curse after all. I'll never complain about it again. Michel's knife sailed entirely over my head."

He squeezed her to him fiercely. "Thank God you're short. I don't know what I would have done if you'd been hurt."

"Yes, I suppose I must be grateful for it now. Even if it does make getting things down from the top of the wardrobe difficult."

Rafe's laughter filled the room. "You are adorable and I wouldn't want you any other way."

"Truly?"

"Truly." He pulled her into his arms and kissed her again. "I love you, Daphne Cavendish, my wife."

Daphne sighed and kissed him back. "And I love you, Rafe Cavendish, my husband."

CHAPTER FIFTY-TWO
One week later
The Earl of Swifdon's town house, Hanover Square

With Cass and Lucy's help, Daphne had managed to arrange another ball at her brother's town house. They'd planned it before she'd left to find Rafe on the sloop. Dressed in a bright pink gown with a matching topaz necklace glimmering at her throat, she stood at the top of the stairs waiting for Pengree to announce her to the crowd inside the ballroom just beyond the double doors. She pressed a gloved hand to her middle where her insides quaked with nerves.

"I feel as if I'm going to be sick," Daphne murmured.

"Well, you look gorgeous, dear," Cass said from beside her. Cass was wearing a light blue gown with white trim. "Don't worry about a thing."

Daphne smiled at her lovely sister-in-law.

"Oh, please tell me I may throw rose petals at your wedding, Cousin Daphne," Delilah said, spinning around in a circle beside her. The girl was wearing a bright yellow ribbon on the top of her head and a matching golden gown.

Her governess, one in a long string of ladies who became too exasperated with her antics to remain, had just given her notice. As a result, Delilah was quite unchaperoned this evening and she'd managed, as usual, to talk her aunt into allowing her to sneak down to the ballroom.

"I promise you may throw rose petals at our wedding ceremony," Daphne replied, smiling at the child.

"Not just any rose petals. Pink and white ones. Pink and white are the only sort of rose petals to throw at weddings. They are *trés* romantic," Delilah gushed.

Daphne shook her head. Now her twelve-year-old cousin was an expert at weddings? "Very well, pink and white," Daphne replied.

Cass laughed.

Rafe came sliding through the corridor, slightly out of breath. He stopped at Daphne's side and gave her a peck on the cheek. He wore impeccably tailored black evening clothes and a starchy white cravat that set off the bright blue of his eyes. Daphne's heart swelled. He was so handsome, her husband.

"I'm sorry I'm late," he breathed to Daphne, squeezing her hand as Pengree eyed the couple up and down.

"Bonsoir, Capitaine," Delilah said, giving him her most formal curtsy. "There shall be pink and white rose petals at your wedding ceremony."

Rafe's brow furrowed. He glanced at Daphne. "What's this?"

"Oh, ignore her. Did you talk to Julian?"

"Not yet but he agreed to meet with me in his study later."

"Well, he can't very well say no after we do this." Daphne nodded toward the doors in front of them where they could hear the crowd in the ballroom.

"Ready, my lady?" Pengree asked, tugging on the lapels of his livery.

"Ready!" Daphne replied with a gulp and a nod. She squeezed Rafe's hand.

Pengree opened the wide double doors, revealing the crowded ballroom. "Lady Daphne Swift," he intoned.

Daphne released Rafe's hand and took a tentative step forward. "If I could have your attention, please," she said in the loudest voice she could muster to the waiting crowd. She paused and glanced back at Rafe, who was hidden from the ballroom by the door she was clutching. "Oh, Rafe. I'm so nervous. What should I say?"

Rafe straightened his cravat and tugged at his cuff. "Say this, 'A fortnight ago . . .'"

Daphne turned her head back out to face the crowd and repeated his words. "A fortnight ago . . ."

"I cheated you out of an engagement ball at this very house by acting foolishly, which was very bad manners," Rafe continued.

Daphne repeated his words quickly. "I cheated you out of an engagement ball at this very house by acting fool-ishly, which was very bad manners."

"But I hope to make it up to you by going through with it now as originally planned," Rafe whispered.

"But I hope to make it up to you by going through with it now as originally planned," Daphne repeated, the smile on her face widening. She reached behind her to squeeze Rafe's hand.

"So, if you'll all just wait a moment," Rafe said.

"So if you'll all just wait a moment," Daphne repeated.

"I intend to announce my engagement to Captain Rafferty Cavendish."

"I intend to announce my engagement to Captain

Rafferty Cavendish." Daphne turned to him. "Oh, Rafe are you certain? Are you entirely certain? You're not just doing this because of the mission and the annulment and everything?"

"Not a chance, Grey." He winked at her.

Daphne turned to Cass. "Maid of honor?"

Cass's eyes were filled with tears. "I'd be delighted."

Daphne turned to Delilah. "Attendant?"

"Mais bien sûr," Delilah replied with another formal curtsy.

Daphne turned back to the crowded ballroom. "Yes. I'd like to formally announce my engagement to the most wonderful man in the world. Captain Rafferty Cavendish."

Later that evening, Daphne and Rafe sat on the settee in the middle of Julian's study holding hands. In addition to her pink gown, Daphne wore a sparkling ring on her third finger. She hadn't tugged at it in days.

Cass was curled into a chair near them drinking a cup of tea with a knowing smile on her face. Wearing his own formal black evening attire, Julian, however, had his hands folded behind his back and was pacing in front of his sister and her husband.

"Julian," Daphne began. "I promised Rafe that you'd be reasonable."

Julian hadn't said a word. That worried Daphne more than if he'd raised his voice. He continued his silent pacing.

A knock sounded at the door and Daphne turned her head to see who it was. Lucy and Derek Hunt, also wearing their formal attire from the ball, came striding through the door.

"Thank heavens," Daphne breathed.

Julian didn't acknowledge them.

"We came as soon as we received your note, Daphne," Lucy explained.

Cass raised a brow. "Called for reinforcements, did you?"

Daphne nodded so vehemently that one of her curls came loose from her coiffure and bobbed along her forehead.

Carefully stepping around the pacing earl, Lucy and Derek took seats in front of Julian's desk but not before they turned the chairs so they could be a part of the conversation.

"What have we missed?" Lucy asked, smoothing her hands over her green skirts as she settled into her chair.

"Nothing yet," Cass replied. "Just a lot of pacing. He seems to have been struck dumb."

Julian stopped his pacing directly in front of Rafe. The earl's hands remained folded behind his back and he braced his feet apart. Rafe's hand tensed in Daphne's.

"I have just one question for you," Julian said, eyeing Rafe down the length of his nose.

Rafe nodded and met his gaze. "Anything."

"You've professed your disdain of so-called blue bloods over the years. In light of that, how do you feel about being a part of this family?"

Rafe swallowed and stood, too. He was about a foot in front of the earl. "I would be honored to be a part of this family. If you'll have me." He bowed slightly at the waist.

"No more making light of blue bloods?" Julian asked, his face a mask of stone.

Rafe squared his shoulders. "Your brother gave his life

for our country. You nearly did as well. And your sister is one of the most steadfast patriots I've ever known. The Swift family may be noble, but you're also brave. I can only hope I make this family proud and don't bring disgrace upon it."

Daphne glanced around. All of the occupants of the study appeared to be holding their breath.

Julian turned abruptly on his heel and marched around to the front of his desk. He opened a drawer and pulled out a letter. He returned to the settee and handed it to Daphne. "You need to see this."

Her brow furrowed, Daphne took the piece of parchment from her brother's outstretched hand. "What is it?"

"A letter," Julian said. "From Donald."

Daphne's eyes widened. She gulped back a sob. "Donald?"

Julian nodded toward the paper. "Read it."

Daphne pulled it close with a shaking hand. "You must read it too, Rafe."

Rafe sat back down and read over her shoulder.

My dearest sister Daphne,

I asked Julian to give this to you after you and Cavendish had finally come to your senses and decided to remain married. I would never have allowed the marriage in the first place if I hadn't thought Cavendish the best man for you and you the best lady for him. It was obvious since I met him that you and he would suit. I know he'll make our family proud and you two will be happy together. Not to mention produce some fine-looking children.

Daphne blushed. Rafe grinned at her.

As I'm certain you've guessed, it wasn't entirely necessary for you and Cavendish to marry before you set off on the mission, but I suspected it would keep you two together long enough to realize that you were well matched. If you're reading this, you have discerned as much. Please know you have my blessing and I can only hope Julian agrees with me. I expect he will. He's wise, our brother. Best wishes for a happy life together, Daphne. With all my love to you and your new husband.

Yours,

Donald

Daphne's eyes brimmed with tears. She turned her face up to her brother. "Do you, Julian? Do you agree?"

Julian gave them a wide grin. "Wholeheartedly."

"And so do I," Cass added with a nod.

Rafe stood again and Julian held out his hand. Rafe shook it heartily. Both men were smiling.

"But how did you get this letter, Julian?" Daphne asked. "*When* did you get it?"

"Someone from the War Office sent it over," Julian explained. "Seems our brother had a premonition. I think he always knew he wouldn't return from France. He knew you both well enough to know you'd capture the men who killed him and he knew you two were meant to be together."

"I never realized how intelligent Donald was," Lucy said, dabbing at her eyes and handing a spare handkerchief to Daphne.

"He seems like he was both intelligent and kind," Derek added.

"He was both," Daphne said, wiping away her tears. "I loved him so much." She stood and hugged her brother.

Julian hugged her back. "So did I. So did I."

Rafe and Daphne sat down again while Cass took charge of the silence. "Well, now. Enough crying. This should be a happy occasion. Donald would want as much."

They all nodded.

"Agreed," Julian said. "We must plan how we'll go about making your marriage appear to have been planned all along. We'll have a wedding for appearance's sake."

"And Mother's sake," Daphne added.

"Precisely. We'll pretend as if the first marriage never happened," Julian said.

"I don't care what we do as long as we can tell everyone we're married." Daphne squeezed Rafe's hand.

Rafe kissed her atop the head. "Don't worry, darling, no one will ever pull us apart. Besides, we already—"

"Ah, ah, ah," Julian said, putting up a hand, palm first. "Please spare me."

Rafe gave him a devilish grin and so did Daphne. Cass giggled.

"I was only going to say that we already got permission from the War Office to use the *True Love* for our honeymoon. We're sailing off," Rafe said.

"To France?" Lucy asked.

Rafe shook his head. "No, not France. I don't care if I ever see that country again."

A muted gasp came from the other side of the door.

"Delilah," Daphne called. "You might as well come in. I know you're there."

A few seconds passed before the door opened and

Delilah came marching in. She was wearing her pink ballet costume and had a triumphant smile upon her face.

She took a seat on the settee next to Daphne and grinned at the married couple.

"Don't you look like the cat who ate the canary?" Daphne said, unable to repress her smile.

Delilah clasped her hands together near her cheek. "Oh, *j'adore* a happy ending and I just want to state for the record that I did it. I did it all!" She stood quickly and performed a pirouette.

Daphne's mouth fell open. She plunked her hands on her hips. "What did you do, you little urchin?"

Delilah curtsied to her, lifting the edges of her skirt daintily. "Why, I chased away that abominable Lord Fitzwell, of course, and ensured that you and Captain Cavendish were together. Though I'll admit Aunt Willie helped a bit, but I was *quite* instrumental."

"And ever so modest," Cass said with a laugh, taking a sip of her tea.

"Why should I be modest? I'm exceedingly proud of myself," Delilah replied, her nose in the air.

"As you should be," Rafe added with a laugh.

Delilah beamed at him. *"Merci beaucoup, Capitaine."*

Lucy's brows shot up. "I do believe I've discovered my own little disciple," Lucy said. She patted Delilah on the hand. "You're already quite good at plotting things, dear, and you're only twelve. Just imagine the trouble you could get up to when you're our age."

"It boggles the mind to consider," Daphne said.

Derek stood. "I was waiting till all was settled before I mentioned this, but I had an interesting audience with Wellington and the Prince Regent earlier today."

Daphne's eyes went wide. "What did they say?"

Derek bowed and spread his hand out in front of Rafe. "Meet the newest viscount of the realm, my lady."

Rafe shot Daphne a sly look and grinned. "It's true."

Daphne clapped her hands. "Oh, Rafe. You're a viscount now? Why didn't you tell me?"

Rafe shrugged. "Apparently, torture and heroics will get you a viscountcy these days. And I didn't say anything because I wanted your brother to accept me as your husband without a viscountcy. The same way you did, my love."

"Ha. Now you'll *have* to accept us blue bloods, Cavendish," Julian said with a laugh, clapping his new brother-in-law on the shoulder.

"The official reason for the title was for bringing justice to the Earl of Swifdon's killers," Derek said. "And there are lands and monies that come with it."

"I insisted upon being a spy viscount of course," Rafe replied. "At least, I intend to help whenever I can, but I think I'll stick to English soil from now on. I may be expected to spend my time at gentlemen's clubs, but I'll feel useful if I'm able to help here in London."

"What did the Prince Regent say about that?" Daphne asked.

"He said he thought it was perfect because he could use a member of the aristocracy who is a spy and whose wife just happens to speak Russian," Rafe replied.

"I quite agree with him. We are a fine combination," Daphne said with a laugh, clutching her husband's hand to her side.

Rafe turned to her, his face solemn. "I explained to the prince that *you* were the real hero, Daphne. He said as you're already a lady and married to me, that shall suffice. Though he does agree you should be rewarded with a medal for your bravery."

Daphne leaned over and kissed him on the cheek. "I don't want a medal or a viscountcy. All I ever wanted was you."

Delilah sighed dramatically. "Ah, *amour.*"

"But it's you who should be knighted," Rafe insisted to Daphne.

"I am already a lady. And now you are a lord."

"Oh, I'm a lord now, am I? Not a rogue?" Rafe grinned at her.

Daphne patted his shoulder. "You'll always be a rogue, my love. My *irresistible* rogue."

The butler entered the room and cleared his throat. "There's someone here to see you, Captain," Pengree said, directing his gaze toward Rafe.

"Someone came *here* to see *me*?" Rafe pointed at himself.

"Yes," Pengree replied. "I must say, he's quite—well, he's . . ."

"Who is it, Pengree? Did this visitor give a name?" Julian asked.

"A Mr. Daffin Oakleaf, my lord."

Daphne looked at Rafe. "Who is Daffin Oakleaf?" But Rafe's face was turning a mottled shade of red she'd never seen before. He was angry.

"Show him in, Pengree," Julian replied.

They all waited a few minutes for Pengree to return with the guest. When the man walked into the room, Daphne gasped. Cass clapped a hand over her mouth. Lucy's eyebrows shot up straight. Claringdon blinked. And Julian looked twice.

Rafe's face was a mask of stone.

The man looked exactly like Rafe.

"There are *two* of you!" Delilah exclaimed, her eyes wide as saucers. She looked as if she might faint.

Claringdon was next to speak. "Either the government has learned how to duplicate people or I'd say we're about to meet your twin, Captain."

The man bowed. "Daffin Oakleaf, at your service."

"We both know that's *not* your name," Rafe said through clenched teeth.

"Of course it's not. But I can hardly go by Cade Cavendish any longer," the man replied, and Daphne noticed that he had the same cleft in his chin as Rafe did. She kept glancing back and forth between them. The only way she could tell the difference was that Daffin, or Cade, or whatever his name was, had much longer hair. "Rafe, this is your brother?" she asked.

"Yes," came Rafe's monotone reply. "My twin brother."

"That's right," Cade said. "I must say, I'm thrilled that you're claiming me. Though I suppose with our looks, you don't have much choice, do you?"

Rafe narrowed his eyes at the man. "I thought you were dead. That is, until that blond climbed into my bed unexpectedly last spring."

"Yes, sorry about that," Cade replied. "Amanda told me you were not particularly excited to see her. She sends her apologies. She did think she'd found me. Not knowing I was a twin of course."

Daphne's mouth fell open. She gaped at Cade. "That was *your* blond?"

"One of them," Cade replied with a grin even more devilish than his brother's.

Daphne turned to Rafe. "Why didn't you tell me you had a twin?"

Rafe shook his head. "It's such a long story. I don't know where I would even begin. As I said, I believed he was dead."

Cade marched over to the sofa, plopped down, and put his boots on the table, crossing his feet at the ankles. Then he folded his hands behind his head and leaned back, comfortable as you please. "Why don't you start at the beginning, dear brother? We have all the time in the world. For the time being, I'm back."

AUTHOR'S NOTE

Dear Reader,

I hope you've enjoyed reading Daphne and Rafe's story. From the moment they stepped onto the pages of the other novels in the Playful Brides series, I knew these two were destined to be together.

As many of you may know, obtaining a divorce or an annulment during the Regency period in England was not only extremely rare, it was exceedingly difficult. Because I loosely based this story on one of my favorite plays (and movies!) of all time, Philip Barry's *The Philadelphia Story,* I took the liberty of beginning the story with Daphne and Rafe already married and in search of an annulment. In reality, the Prince Regent did not have the authority to dissolve a marriage or even to expedite an annulment. An annulment would have had to have been based on either impotency, insanity, or a close familial relationship between the bride and groom. While it's not probable that this story would have taken place in quite this fashion,

I always say that I'm a storyteller, not a historian, and as a storyteller, I'm more concerned with the what-ifs than the why-nots. I so enjoy taking a bit of license in order to bring you the most amusing romplike what-if my imagination can conjure.

As always, thank you so much for reading my stories. You are the reason I spend my time writing.

Valerie Bowman

Thank you for reading *The Irresistible Rogue*.
I hope you enjoyed Daphne and Rafe's story.
I adored writing about these two adventure-loving characters!

I'd love to keep in touch.

- Visit my website for information about upcoming books, excerpts, and to sign up for my email newsletter: www .ValerieBowmanBooks.com.
- Join me on Facebook: http://Facebook.com/ ValerieBowmanAuthor.
- Follow me on Twitter at @ValerieGBowman, https:// twitter.com/ValerieGBowman.
- Reviews help other readers find books. I appreciate all reviews whether positive or negative. Thank you so much for considering it!

Coming soon...

Look for the next novel in this irresistible series by
Valerie Bowman

The Untamed Earl

Coming in May 2016 from St. Martin's Paperbacks

"Sexy, satisfying romance."—*Kirkus Reviews*